THE

STAND-IN

by

DAVID N ROBINSON

CROSETS PUBLISHING

ISBN 978-1-8380055-2-8

Cover designed by BespokeBookCovers.com

Published by Crosets Publishing

To one or two special friends.

You know who you are . . .

Prologue

Nine months ago, The Black Sea

'Tell me, father, when you and the Russian President play chess, who usually wins?'

It was a fair question. For a moment, Oleg Usmanov wondered if his normally silent teenage son, Viktor, was attempting to distract him.

'Actually, our approaches are different,' Usmanov said, one hand hovering over a white bishop. When he and his oldest friend had been students together, the pair had played a lot of chess. Nowadays, there simply wasn't the time or opportunity.

'I win, more often than not. Not always. Whilst I'm trying to think multiple moves ahead, he is usually more of a tactician. A determined opportunist. I might win more games, but he has this knack of pouncing on a moment's weakness and surprising his opponents.' He moved the bishop diagonally across the board and took an unprotected rook. 'Like this. Check,' he said with an ironic smile.

Viktor groaned.

'I never saw that. Damn!'

1

Taller and more powerfully built than the man now occupying the highest office in the Kremlin, Usmanov was a man who enjoyed exercising his influence from the wings. He was happy to leave the limelight and footlights for others. A chess player by choice and, as only his good friend the President was ever brave enough to joke, a spy solely out of necessity, Usmanov usually wore a fretful look of intense concentration: the worried frown; the prominent nose; and angular jaw over which he maintained a close-cut, salt-and-pepper apology for a beard. A distinctive rather than handsome man, Usmanov was mostly bald, except for small tufts of grey-black hair over his ears. Viktor dryly referred to it as his father's Lenin look, although Usmanov's substantial frame together with his broad, muscular shoulders quickly dispelled further comparison with the much leaner Russian revolutionary.

They were sitting at a small table close to the beach at Amasra. This was a popular Turkish holiday destination on the Black Sea coast, roughly equidistant from Ankara and Istanbul. The mid-afternoon sun was beating down harshly, the restaurant's large parasol offering welcome protection. This was an increasingly rare moment for Usmanov and his son. A chance to spend time together and relax. More and more, the day job had an unerring knack of getting in the way. Given who was ultimately pulling the strings, perhaps it was hardly surprising.

'I'm going to lose this game.' In the same way as his father, and indeed his grandfather before him, Viktor hated not winning.

Usmanov put a restraining hand on his son's arm.

'Wait. Study the board carefully. There is a way, but it requires courage.'

'I hate these plastic chess pieces. None of yours back home are ever plastic.'

It was true. Usmanov was a fanatical collector of old and rare chessmen. Some were ivory, a few were metal, but the majority had been meticulously carved out of hardwoods. They were kept in various display cases, both in the house in Istanbul and back in his apartment in Moscow.

'It's an important part of learning to play chess, adapting to different boards and different pieces. These are not too bad.' He picked up a captured black knight, turning it over in his hand and studying the detail with a professional eye. 'Not exactly an Oleg Raikis masterpiece.' He was referring to the famous Russian sculptor whose chess collections were amongst the world's most revered. 'These work fine for the beach. Let me show you something.'

Viktor was growing up to be a fine young man. Although he had his mother's eyes, in all other aspects the sixteen-year-old was fast becoming the image of his father. He boasted a similarly broad physique and had plenty of youthful muscle tone.

'Study your queen. See how you've surrounded her with so much protection.' Usmanov touched several pieces with a finger. 'This rook here, this bishop and these two pawns: they are all focusing their energies on defensive, not attacking, play. This second rook,' – he pointed to a lone castle sitting next to the black king on the baseline – 'is now the king's only protection. Yes, there are two pawns in front, but the king is vulnerable. What you need is a different strategy. Let me switch to playing black and I'll show you what I mean.'

He swivelled the board around, looked at his son and smiled.

'My move, I think?'

Viktor nodded, watching as his father moved his queen diagonally to take a pawn directly in front of Viktor's white king.

'Check.'

Viktor stared in amazement. Not believing his luck, he grinned broadly. Quick as a flash, he took black's queen with his king.

'Didn't you see that? You've just lost your queen. White is about to wipe the board.'

'You think so?'

'Sure.'

Usmanov deftly moved a knight to another weak attacking position. Viktor pounced for a second time, this time using his bishop to take his father's knight.

'Not so clever now, Papa. That's two major pieces you've lost in two goes. I don't get this wonderfully different strategy you were mentioning.' He beamed at his father who, to Viktor's irritation, sat with an annoying grin on his face. 'What's so funny?' Viktor snapped after yet more silence. 'Black is about to lose. I told you it was hopeless.'

They remained like this for some time. Viktor tried to be defiant, but a nagging doubt was creeping around the edges.

'Can you see it yet?'

'That you're about to lose big time, you mean?'

'One of the best attacking strategies is sacrifice. Used sparingly, it can be devastating.'

The young man scowled. Deep furrows were forming on his forehead.

'I don't get it,' he snapped, testily.

'I needed to entice your king forward and get your bishop out of the way. To do that, I chose to trick you. I sacrificed two of my best pieces. You, sadly, took the bait.'

'But without your queen, you're in a terrible position.'

'That's what I wanted you to believe,' said Usmanov, picking up the rook that had been protecting the queen and moving it in front of the now-exposed white king. 'However, whilst you were distracted by my sacrifice, I have become free to deliver this simple, killer move. White is powerless to stop me. Checkmate.'

Viktor stared in disbelief.

'How in heaven's name did you do that?'

'I tricked you. I made you look elsewhere. In your zeal to take my queen, you made yourself vulnerable.' He ruffled his son's hair and smiled at the bewildered look on his face. 'Remember this lesson. Sacrifice. It's one of the very best chess moves, one that can turn the tables of advantage faster than almost anything.'

*

Usmanov was sitting in the back of his Mercedes limousine, being driven to Ankara to catch the late flight to Nicosia. He was musing over the chess game with Viktor, recalling the boldness of sacrifice as part of a winning strategy. A germ of an idea was forming. Could there be an opportunity to use sacrifice as part of a plan to sow deceit and mistrust in the West? It was an intriguing idea. Perhaps he should make time to discuss it with his oldest friend. If anyone might be able to help Usmanov make such an idea work, it would be him.

PRESENT DAY

Chapter 1

London

Passengers arriving from Paris began emerging from the secure area at St. Pancras station. The automatic doors swung open as people came through in waves. Calum Ross, watching and waiting, spotted a young man in a mustard-yellow sweatshirt casting occasional glances in his direction. He hadn't noticed him before. Another, a beefcake chauffeur-type with a thick neck, his bulging muscles constrained by a tight-fitting suit, was close by. He kept refusing to look in Ross's direction. There was no sign of the bomber-jacketed woman he'd spotted earlier. The one with dark, curly hair and sporting a cavernous black bag. Ross stepped to one side as a cleaner came by, sweeping odds and ends of rubbish with a dustpan and brush as she went.

Suddenly, there she was, dragging a small, roll-on bag in her wake. Handbag tucked under an arm and wearing sunglasses. Ross would have recognised her flowing brown hair anywhere. She glanced around at the bank of faces in front of her, appearing not to notice Ross at first. Instead, she turned to the right in the direction of the taxi rank. Which was when he saw the small, black rucksack on her back – the same light, waterproof variety that was instantly familiar. Ross raised an arm and called out her name.

'Calum!' she exclaimed and offered her hand. Which, in a very British way, he took in his, pumping furiously, their agreed meet-and-greet protocol in full flow. 'Nice cardigan,' she whispered, his hand still in hers, her brown eyes wide and full of anticipation.

'I wondered if you'd notice. Sorry about the nerdy anorak as well, but it's been raining. Let me take something,' he said, offloading the rucksack onto his shoulder. 'This way.' He pointed ahead of him. 'This is new,' he said, raising the rucksack a little. 'Where did you get this?'

Natalia turned her head towards him, her face showing surprise.

'Why, from you! It arrived with your note, in my hotel room in Paris yesterday.'

'Really?' Ross said, his voice incredulous. 'We can discuss that later. Right this moment, we need to get a move on. Otherwise we'll have to queue for a taxi.' They set off together, Ross aware once again of the woman in the leather bomber jacket. She was suddenly in their wake. He saw her reflection in a shop window as they began walking through the concourse. 'I was going to order an Uber, but the bank blocked my card,' he continued, lengthening his stride.

'Do we have to walk so fast?' Natalia was struggling to keep up.

'Unfortunately, we've got company,' he replied quietly, not letting up the pace. 'Don't look around but there are at least two following us.'

'You have the chess set?'

'Of course,' he said, feeling the lump in his anorak pocket as he walked.

'Guard it with your life.'

Up ahead, a lone man in a cloth cap and quilted jacket was standing outside a sandwich shop. He was pretending to stare at his phone. Ross caught him sneaking an occasional glance in their direction. Bomber Jacket was still behind them. Yellow Sweatshirt had also magically appeared from nowhere, a few steps ahead of

Bomber Jacket but on the other side. Probably others were lurking in the wings, most likely the beefcake chauffeur one of them. It dawned on Ross that what the man had said all those months ago had been right. It hadn't been necessary to go to spy school after all. He knew instinctively when he was in danger. He also knew what he was going to do about it.

'Pull over there to the left. Wait by the wall.' He nodded towards an exit that led to a side street running parallel with the station. Ross came to a sudden halt, Natalia passing in front of him as he sidestepped to the left. He let the rucksack slide to the floor. The youth in the mustard-yellow sweatshirt never saw that move coming. He was past Ross before he realised what had happened, his startled reaction giving away any semblance of cover. The woman in the bomber jacket was different. She was more skilled, almost managing to conceal the four-inch steel blade in her hand. Almost, but not quite. As she drew parallel with Ross, he grabbed her wrist, twisting her arm rapidly into an armlock, the knife flying and falling to the floor. Ross kicked it to one side and pinned the woman down, twisting hard. The man in the yellow shirt shouted 'Police!' but Ross ignored him, instead applying further pressure to the woman's shoulder and elbow.

Which was when Beefcake made his appearance. A silenced 9mm handgun was in his right hand. The man in the cloth cap and padded jacket was simultaneously calling for reinforcements. Ross waited his moment as Beefcake got closer, the distance less than five metres and closing.

The man made two mistakes. The first was to use a single-handed pistol grip. The second was to aim his gun, not at Ross but at Natalia. The first mistake presented Ross with an opportunity to deflect the handgun, the second a small window to do something about it. He let go of Bomber Jacket's arm. With his hands raised in a mock 'hands-up' gesture, he advanced swiftly and lunged, grabbing the gun hand and whipping it across Beefcake's body, twisting his opponent's wrist hard. Simultaneously, he head-butted the man in the nose, using forward momentum from the attack to aim a right knee hard into Beefcake's testicles. Ross tried to wrestle the gun free, but his opponent was strong. The two men fell to the floor, the gun sandwiched between their bodies. Ross tugged hard, but the weapon refused to move. Suddenly, there was a muffled explosion. Heat seared Ross's thigh before Beefcake's body went limp, the gun now free in Ross's hand.

'He's got a gun!' came a cry from a distressed passer-by as Ross stood up. Pandemonium was starting to spread like wildfire throughout the station. Yellow Sweatshirt and Cloth Cap turned towards Ross. Both recoiled when they saw the gun. Which was how the woman in the bomber jacket managed to get away with it. With Ross's back momentarily turned, she got to her feet. Scooping the knife off the floor, she ran out the door to the left, past a frightened Natalia who had retreated into a corner to keep out of trouble. Not far enough, as it happened. The stabbing blade still penetrated her abdomen almost to the hilt before her attacker fled the station. Natalia let out a bloodcurdling scream.

'I've been stabbed, help! Do something, please! God, Calum, I'm bleeding,' she said, her hands covered in blood.

'Somebody call an ambulance!' Ross yelled to anyone who was listening. The young policeman placed a finger in one ear, shouting loudly into a concealed microphone. The man in the cloth cap and quilted jacket, now less than thirty metres away, gave no reaction. Instead, he kept advancing slowly.

'Put the gun down, sir.' Ross looked to the side and saw another man from earlier. A chauffeur type who'd been holding a piece of card with a random name written on it. Not Beefcake, but someone else. The card abandoned, he was now holding a gun, pointing directly at Ross. This time, the man was using a double-handed grip.

'Call an ambulance. Help save this woman.'

'One should be here any minute. Now, put the gun down.' There was a steely determination in the voice.

'Calum, are you . . . can you hear me?'

'I'm here,' he said, turning his attention back to Natalia, squatting down beside her. 'An ambulance is on its way. Hang in there, you'll be fine, I promise.' He squeezed her hand, hearing the loud, alternating pitch of a fast-approaching siren. The stroboscopic blue light was already bouncing off the concourse walls as it pulled up outside.

'Don't let Oleg's people . . . get you . . . run . . . get away . . . find the . . .' Her voice was faint as two paramedics ran to her side, both kneeling to check vital signs and to inspect the knife wound. There was little that Ross could do for the moment.

'I repeat: Put. The. Gun. Down!' The man with the gun was inching nearer, his weapon hovering in Ross's direction.

Ross stood and looked at the surrounding scene. One man with a gun pointing directly at him. Plus at least one undercover police officer next to him. A third, a rough type in a cloth cap, also closing in on his position. Fast-approaching footsteps of yet another could be heard pounding through the concourse. Coming to assist. Multiple sirens too, some increasingly close.

Time to decide.

Given the last twenty-four hours, life was becoming complicated. Very, very complicated. There was now a dead body with Ross's fingerprints on the weapon that killed him. Hanging around in police custody, answering endless questions wasn't attractive. His chances of being allowed bail this time looked slim. Even Natalia had told him to run.

The man with the handgun would have been on a risk assessment course. He was unlikely to shoot in the still-crowded, but rapidly thinning concourse: the chances of a ricochet were too high.

The open doorway, however, was behind him. A few feet away. It was tempting.

Without losing eye contact with the man with the gun, he carefully lowered his weapon to the floor. Inch by inch, until it was finally resting on the ground. He glanced briefly at Natalia. The paramedics were busy getting lines up and doing what they could to stem the blood flow.

Which was the moment Ross shouted, 'Look out!', pointing to something behind the gunman's back.

The precise moment he bolted for the open door.

Chapter 2

Moscow

Usmanov's plan to steal money from the Russian Foreign Intelligence Service had been relatively straightforward. What was always going to be problematic was keeping this treachery hidden from Russian officialdom. One investigator in particular was likely to be on Usmanov's heels: a man by the name of Nicolai Kozlov. To say that there was little love lost between the two, enmity that went back years, would be an understatement.

Usmanov's father, Ivan, had been a KGB officer. He and his wife had just the one child, Oleg, born at the time when Nikita Khrushchev was slowly winning the internal struggle to become First Secretary of the Soviet Communist Party. A chess fanatic and ardent proponent of the 'long game' in the world of espionage, Ivan Usmanov had proven to be a shrewd operational planner. Someone adept at manipulating agent networks to sow disinformation. Spotters working for the upper echelons of the KGB were quick to harness Ivan Usmanov's talents. They encouraged him to craft carefully conceived stories in attempts to misinform the West about the operational prowess of the wider Soviet Bloc. These were the original snippets of fake news, arguably way ahead of their time. Usmanov's star was in the ascendancy and his rapid promotion was leaving several contemporaries feeling bruised in his wake. Then, at the height of the Cold War, Usmanov's networks were exposed by a leak of information to the British. Overnight, Usmanov became damaged goods. Despite the long, inevitable internal enquiry, the traitor was never identified. Privately, Usmanov had his suspicions about who had been to blame: one particularly embittered junior colleague who seemed jealous of Usmanov's meteoric rise through the ranks. A man constantly trying to put Usmanov down on any occasion. A resentful young Russian by the name of Anatoly Kozlov.

Losing an agent network took its toll on Ivan Usmanov. Struggling to clear his name, unable to cope with the humiliation and with his career put on hold, Oleg's father found himself in a dark place. When the official enquiry could find no formal evidence of any mole inside the KGB, Ivan Usmanov decided to take matters into his own hands. He confronted Kozlov in his Moscow apartment late one evening after work. At the end of what neighbours afterwards described as a long and heated argument, several gunshots were heard. Usmanov was later seen driving away from the neighbourhood in a hurry. Days later, the battered old Skoda with Usmanov's slumped body behind the wheel was discovered in dense birch forests to the south of the capital. The cause of death had been a single, self-inflicted gunshot wound fired from Usmanov's service revolver.

Shaken by the loss of his much-loved parent, the eighteen-year-old Oleg Usmanov vowed to continue the journey his father had begun. After studying law at Leningrad State University, he and one of his closest school friends, a man ultimately destined for the highest office in the Kremlin, both joined the KGB on the same day. As fate would have it, exactly one year later, Anatoly Kozlov's son, Nicolai, made an almost identical career move.

It was Usmanov's career that initially accelerated than either of the other two, a fact that might have continued had not his close friend decided in 1991 to resign from the KGB and focus his energies on political ambitions. Kozlov, meanwhile, was showing signs of being a tenacious investigator. Oleg Usmanov and Nicolai Kozlov disliked each other from the outset. With echoes of his father's resentment bearing through, Kozlov frequently tried to point the finger of blame for several operational failures on Usmanov. None of these early attempts to discredit Usmanov succeeded, however. Usmanov showed himself to be a shrewd operator: able to keep his nose clean, adept at running agent networks, and skilled at devising modern-day equivalent strategies to those created by his father. When Usmanov's oldest friend eventually succeeded in his ambition to become President of the Russian Federation, it was always only ever going to be beneficial to Usmanov's career – and salt in an already open wound for Kozlov.

With the KGB disbanded, its two successor organisations were living proof that the historic whole was not always as big as the sum of its two successor parts. The SVR, responsible for foreign intelligence, and the FSB, for domestic intelligence, were both substantial organisations in their own right. Doubtless, in part, aided by his friend secretly monitoring his career, Usmanov rose rapidly through the ranks of the SVR. Most recently, he had been appointed as Second Secretary of the Russian Federation's diplomatic mission to Turkey. In reality, Usmanov was Head of Station in what was fast becoming the hottest seat in terms of SVR foreign *rezidentura*: responsible for a strategically vital network of agents and informants in those countries in the Balkans and across the Middle East to Afghanistan that shared a common border with Russia. The problem countries. The locations where the Russian President needed an experienced operator. Someone who could be trusted. Which was why Oleg Usmanov had been the perfect choice. Based, in theory, at the Russian Embassy in the Turkish capital, Ankara, but in practice living out of a suitcase, Usmanov preferred to spend most of his time when in Turkey not in Ankara but in Istanbul. He used the Consulate there as his working base. Istanbul was also where Viktor, his son, was at school, and where his wife, Natalia, preferred to work.

Kozlov's career, meanwhile, had initially taken him in a different direction. After the breakup of the KGB, he first became an investigator within the domestic security service, the FSB, where his investigative skills came to the attention of the then Head of the Comptroller's office of the Russian Federation, Sergei Borodin. Borodin wanted Kozlov to come and work with him, to assist in the fight against corruption within the highest levels of the Russian government and its agencies. Within six months of Kozlov's arrival, Borodin was unexpectedly promoted to become the Russian President's Chief of Staff. This left a vacancy in the comptroller's office. In the absence of other suitable candidates, they appointed Kozlov as Borodin's interim successor.

Kozlov proved an unpopular leader. He was not someone who relished or invited teamwork. He was also quick to make enemies, but it never seemed to faze him: he was a man driven to achieve results, regardless of the personal consequences. By the time Sergei Borodin had completed his five-year tour of duty in the Kremlin and was chosen, by the Russian President, to be the next director of the Russian Foreign Intelligence Service, Borodin asked Kozlov to come and join him back in the SVR. He need a Special Investigator – someone who could be Borodin's personal trouble-shooter. Kozlov accepted. Within the SVR, there was not a small amount of disquiet at the appointment. Throughout the rest of Moscow officialdom, there was a collective sigh of relief.

*

Nicolai Kozlov was staring at the computer screen with a frown. He was looking at an operational cash expenditure report that covered the SVR's overseas *rezidentura*. Funding of overseas intelligence operations was generally a black art. Money typically funnelled its way in and out of various bank accounts, conduits and cut-outs before reaching its intended destination. Keeping track of costs was almost impossible. In Kozlov's experience, however, there was one proxy indicator that was useful to keep an eye on: the amount of physical cash being spent. Hard currency, usually provided to agents directly through an embassy or consulate's banking section. Because of sanctions, cash was at a premium. All overseas residences were under strict instructions to pare back expenses. Most seemed, on the face of it, to be achieving this. One location – it just so happened to be Oleg Usmanov's residency in Istanbul – had spent a staggering 68 per cent more than plan, and some 80 per cent more than the previous year. Having dug a little deeper, Kozlov had learned that on one occasion five months earlier, Usmanov had requested a special cash drawdown of two hundred thousand dollars in cash. This was an unprecedented amount, certainly enough to warrant further investigation. The fact that it was Oleg Usmanov who was in the spotlight made it much more poignant.

One reason Kozlov had been happy to accept Borodin's offer to come back to the SVR was because it provided him both access and opportunity to keep an eye on Oleg Usmanov. Indeed, he had made a start on that objective only a few days ago. Sergei Borodin had summoned him to his office and instructed him to find a way to curtail Usmanov's wife's reckless philandering. She was currently conducting a none too private affair with a British school teacher. Curtail be damned! Kozlov had swiftly commissioned certain non-attributable operatives to take care of the wretched woman permanently. In his mind, it was the opening salvo in a broader, Kozlov-inspired campaign to bring about the downfall of one Oleg Usmanov, once and for all.

The sudden increase in Usmanov's cash expenditure was puzzling. Why was the President's oldest friend suddenly on a spending spree? And where was it all going? His investigative instincts sensing something out of the ordinary, he reached for the phone on his desk and lifted the receiver.

'Irina, get me Oleg Usmanov on the line. I need to speak to him urgently.' While waiting for the call to connect, he navigated his computer web browser to the BBC news channel. The lead story was a report about an emerging terrorist incident at one of London's mainline stations. Seconds later, his reading was interrupted by the phone on his desk ringing loudly.

'Yes!' he said sharply.

'Oleg Usmanov on the line for you.'

Irina would never know it, but her boss was actually beaming broadly as he took the call.

THE DAY BEFORE

Chapter 3

London

First, he noticed the man. Then he noticed the rucksack. Only later did he appreciate their significance. By then it was too late.

That morning, school-perfect loafers and chinos had been cast aside for trainers and jeans. The razor and iron had also been dispensed with, along with the trusted linen jacket. Instead, the much-loved, rather middle-aged-looking cardigan was being taken for yet another outing. The resultant, somewhat unkempt image of Calum Ross – a man seemingly at ease with both life and himself – was fairly accurate: once more back in England after six months in Turkey; his bank balance finally in funds after a long and protracted fallow period; no ties such as a wife, children or mortgage to distract him; and, most important of all, the scent of illicit romance still lingering.

He was waiting for a train at Oxford Street station, heading to a sports shop south of the river in search of a support strap for a recent knee injury. Four grimy-faced construction workers stood in a huddle. They were at the end of their shift, joshing loudly, dressed in orange overalls adorned with strips of high-vis luminescent material. Their strident tones were causing occasional heads to turn. Two Japanese women standing nearby were studiously ignoring them, instead peering intensely at a map of the Underground system, pointing and gesticulating, a pair of matching pink suitcases covered with stickers resting on the platform beside them. To one side, a scruffily-dressed man was scrolling his way through something on a mobile device. Perched on metal seats affixed to the station wall, three women, their faces and heads covered by burqas, were hunched in conversation.

The Victoria line was running like clockwork. The previous train had recently clattered out of the station, its red tail lights disappearing into the tunnel as Ross took up his position on the platform. A brief period of silence ensued before the familiar, low-level rumble of another train could be heard. It began as a muted hiss, distant wheels in contact with metal rails. Then came the subtle change in airflow, turbulence gently buffeting everyone waiting at the station. As the crescendo of sound and energy built to a climax, a jarring rattle of approaching carriages passing over points echoed loudly. Moments later, the train burst angrily out of the tunnel and braked rapidly to a halt.

Ross was standing close to where a pair of double doors slid open. Moving to one side to let departing passengers get off, he entered the train along with the Japanese tourists and the man with the phone. The construction workers and burqa-clad women had chosen another carriage. With no shortage of seats, Ross chose one in the middle. The man with the phone sat opposite. Both positions afforded a clear view of the carriage in both directions. Only as they were taking their seats did Ross notice the rucksack. Previously slung out of view over a shoulder, it was now centre-stage, resting on the floor in the small space between himself and the man opposite. A warbling sound rang out, followed swiftly by the synchronised noise of the automatic doors slamming closed. Seconds later, the train was on its way, accelerating quickly as it entered the tunnel.

The man with the rucksack had olive skin and dark features. Caucasian, certainly. Possibly Slavic, definitely not of British origin. Aged mid to late thirties and slightly overweight, he was sporting several days' stubble growth and wore faded jeans and a grubby navy-blue sweater vest frayed at the cuffs. His footwear was no better: cheap trainers with heels worn down on one side and with parts of the sole separating from the uppers. Ross, his mind half-filled with thoughts about a woman called Natalia, found his eyes drawn to the rucksack. It looked new, a lightweight waterproof variety that wouldn't hold a great deal. Enough for a folded raincoat and a few books, or maybe a packed lunch – not a lot more. It was black, with shoulder and chest straps the same colour. Useful for a short hike. Not particularly heavy and with enough space for the bare essentials only. The bag's newness contrasted with the owner's otherwise dishevelled appearance. Its size and shape made it look more like a bag a woman would choose. It seemed out of place, an accessory that didn't belong.

Ross glanced at the man's face and noticed something he'd missed. The eyes. They were roaming the carriage, scanning left and right. Tiny beads of perspiration had appeared on the man's forehead and upper lip. Ross looked back at the rucksack. It wasn't empty, that much was obvious. However, it wasn't crammed full either. No wires were visible, which was a good sign. As was the fact that the man wasn't holding on to it. It lowered the probability of a hidden wired detonator being secreted in a palm.

Another man, who had been standing at the far end of the carriage, chose that particular moment, midway between stations, to sit down. Ross, senses heightened, glanced up at the sudden movement. He watched as the man navigated his way precariously around the two pink suitcases belonging to the Japanese women and slumped into a vacant seat. Into the seat immediately next to the man with the rucksack. Directly opposite Ross. On the right-hand side of the first man. Or left, from Ross's point of view across the narrow divide.

Which was fine, except for two tiny details. Firstly, this man also had a rucksack. As the rolling motion of the train caused him to fall heavily into his seat, he too had slipped his off his shoulder and placed it on the floor of the train. In front of his left leg. Crammed up close and personal with the first rucksack. Which was now directly in front of the other man's right leg. Meaning that the two rucksacks were touching.

The other was slightly more problematic. The nature of the second rucksack itself. Like its neighbour, it was black. With shoulder and chest straps the same colour. It, too, looked brand new. A lightweight waterproof variety that wasn't going to be holding a great deal. Full, but not crammed to busting.

The two rucksacks were identical.

The second man, in his early thirties, had thick, black hair slicked across his head in comb-over. Under a New York Yankees half-zipper fleece, he wore a white shirt and black jeans, the shirt hanging loose outside his trousers. He also had trainers – however, they were a newer make and model than those worn by his neighbour. On the face of it, an ordinary passenger, carrying a small rucksack which just happened to be identical to its neighbour. Coincidences happened, Ross knew: he simply wasn't a big believer in them.

A recorded voice announced that the next stop, Green Park, was approaching. The train was already braking, the carriage juddering as its wheels passed noisily over points and junctions in the rails below.

Both men looked up from their mobile phones as if some obscure signal or message had passed between them. Each glanced briefly at Ross before looking away. The moment the train entered the station, the man wearing the Yankees fleece sprang to his feet. He waited for the train to slow, arching his back in a stretch before picking up his rucksack and making his way to the double door exit to Ross's right.

Which might also have been fine, except for another highly significant detail. A fact that many – arguably most – would not have noticed. Something ordinarily lost in the blink of an eye. A magician's trick, carried out when everyone was meant to be looking elsewhere.

The man had picked up the wrong rucksack.

Ross checked to make sure, but there was no doubt. The doors, by this stage, were open, the man amongst the first to leave the train, in a hurry to be elsewhere. Ross looked at the other passenger who, to give him credit, was having suspicions about what might have happened. Flustered, he undid one of the side pockets, hurriedly checking inside.

'Shit!' he cried to no one in particular. 'That man's run off with my rucksack.' The accent sounded Eastern European. He looked directly at Ross. 'You've got to help,' he pleaded, by this stage on his feet and about to race for the door. 'It's got my passport, credit cards, money – everything! Please help! I have to stop him.' He elbowed his way past other passengers and hurried off the train, breaking into a clumsy run as he took off in pursuit.

This might have been the end of the matter, but for one more – this time vital – detail. In his haste to reunite himself with his belongings, he'd left the other rucksack behind. The one that technically belonged to the second man. On the floor of the carriage. Immediately in front of where Ross was sitting.

The driver's voice came over the intercom, urging passengers to move further down inside the carriages. It was then that Ross realised he had a decision to make. The unscripted moment where instinct, rather than rational thought or pre-agreed lines, takes over. When basic survival training, whether taught or self-learned, kicks in. With a momentary flash of trepidation, he grabbed hold of the rucksack, jumped to his feet and jostled past people towards the exit to his right. He had just stepped down onto the platform, rucksack slung on one shoulder, when the warbling sound rang out and the train doors slid closed behind him.

He looked for signs of where the other two might have headed, but saw nothing that gave any clues. Instead, he ran along the platform in search of the exit. A short distance away was the entrance to a bank of escalators leading up to the main ticket hall below ground level. He hurried to the nearest escalator and sprinted upwards, taking the steps two at a time, scanning the crowds in front for signs of the other two. His recently injured right knee began complaining under the sudden stress and exertion of the steep – and rapid – ascent. A few weeks earlier, he had twisted the knee during a run around the back streets of Istanbul. Physiotherapy was, in theory, meant to be ongoing. In practice, thinking he might be fit enough, he'd skipped a few sessions. As he raced up the stairs and felt the muscles and ligaments complaining, he was regretting having cut short his rehab.

Reaching the concourse at the top, he paused to catch his breath, scanning the crowds of departing and arriving passengers – but to no avail. He jogged to a nearby down escalator, still drawing a blank as he turned around and headed in yet another direction and stopped, now confused, sweat showing on his brow. Too late he noticed the police dog by his feet, suddenly intent on following him around. Which is when he looked up to see three members of the British Transport Police approaching rapidly, the same moment the dog began to bark.

'Heh, have you seen two men, both in a hurry?' Ross called out, panting. The three uniformed officers looked at each other briefly, still advancing towards Ross. 'One was wearing a New York Yankees fleece, mid-thirties. The other a white Caucasian, slightly older? They left this rucksack on a Victoria line train.' He lifted the offending bag off his shoulder to show them.

The police dog, a small black-and-white spaniel, kept barking, its nose probing the air close to the bottom of the rucksack. One officer, the dog handler, moved to stand behind Ross. A second policeman stepped forward to stand immediately in front of Ross.

'I need you to place your bag on the ground please sir.' He was a large, muscular man about the same height as Ross. The dog handler took hold of the rucksack and placed it on the floor to one side. He raised a finger at the spaniel who was now sitting, obediently, beside the bag, tail wagging.

'What's inside?' The policeman's face was now up close to Ross's, both men sizing each other up.

'I've no idea,' Ross answered without blinking. 'As I said before. A man left it on a Victoria line train a short while ago. I don't enjoy seeing unaccompanied luggage left on trains. It makes me nervous. So, I picked it up. Then I bumped into you.'

'Why don't we take a look then?'

'Go ahead,' Ross responded. 'It's not mine, as I told you.'

The policeman squatted down and opened the rucksack a little. After some tentative probing, he stood up and turned to face Ross. Reaching behind his back with one hand, he spoke in a confident and well-practised manner.

'I am placing you under arrest on suspicion of being in possession of a substantial quantity of narcotics.' As the man continued to inform Ross of his rights, a pair of handcuffs appeared in his hand. Ross was no longer going from A to B. He was being diverted to Point C. Point C would be nothing but hassle and bureaucracy. He was led by the arm, past the ticket barrier and up a small flight of stairs to street level. Waiting at the curb close to the exit was a white, unmarked police car. One of the arresting officers opened the rear door and shoved Ross inside. Another climbed into the seat beside him.

Only after the car had begun pulling away did Ross see them. On the opposite side of the street. Two men whose body language spoke a thousand words. Chatting to each other, sharing a joke: hardly strangers in any way, shape or form. One, a man in a New York Yankees fleece, had a rucksack over one shoulder. It was black, with shoulder and chest straps the same colour. His companion, a slightly older, scruffy-looking Caucasian, was ambling beside him. They were chatting like friends. In that brief instant, Ross knew. He had been set up.

Chapter 4

London

West End Central police station was situated on Savile Row, a
street more typically associated with the bespoke tailoring of suits
and clothing for men. The building was a nondescript, six-storey
edifice clad in Portland Stone. However, there was also a back
entrance on Old Burlington Street and it was here that the police
driver took Ross.

Once inside, his handcuffs removed and all pockets emptied of
possessions, they led him to a holding cell in what the burly
officer-in-charge dryly referred to as the custody suite. The cell
was small, basic but functional, the air stale and slightly rancid.
Intermingled odours from previous occupants were present but
difficult to discern. There was an overriding smell of liberally
applied disinfectant. The walls were a creamy, off-white colour
with many chips and scuffs in the paintwork.

They left Ross on his own to stew for forty-five minutes until
the same officer returned and escorted him to an interview room.
The first thing he saw was the offending black rucksack sitting on
a small table. Two police officers that Ross had not seen before,
one male and the other female, entered the room shortly after.
They were accompanied by one of the arrest team from Green Park

tube station. The latter stood silently at the edge of the room whilst the other two took control of proceedings.

'Name?' the female officer asked. She spoke with a slight Scottish accent, a soft burr rather than anything harsh. Ross spotted the name 'McIlvoy' on her identity badge. It had swung briefly to face the front as she had sat down. Now it was back around the other way, a Metropolitan Police crest and logo on the rear all that was visible. She fixed Ross with an uncompromising gaze. These weren't uniformed officers, which meant they were part of CID. Dressed in navy, a simple jacket over a top and trousers the same colour, McIlvoy looked harassed.

'Calum Ross.'

The room was windowless, the concrete walls covered with a plaster skim and several layers of the same yellowing paint, chipped and battered. McIlvoy's male colleague was silently taking notes, filling in blank spaces on various police forms contained within a manila file. He never spoke a word, filling in the intervals by chewing on the plastic cap of his cheap ballpoint pen. His name badge was hidden within the recesses of a crumpled, single-breasted grey suit jacket. The jacket, at least one size too big, had been buttoned up when he'd walked into the room. It was still buttoned up, even now he was seated.

'Is this your rucksack?'

'No.'

'Mind if we look inside?'

'Go ahead. It is not my rucksack.'

Donning a pair of disposable plastic gloves, the woman called McIlvoy picked up the black bag and upended it on the table. Two items landed unceremoniously in front of all three. First, a clear plastic bag containing a white powder. Smaller than a bag of flour, it looked possibly like some kind of narcotic. If true, it was likely to be bad news for any person caught in possession. Worse was to come. Landing with a heavy thud shortly behind the first bag came another. It, too, was clear, this one containing a small brick-shaped item. It was more like a bar of soap wrapped in greaseproof paper.

The wrapper was the giveaway. The block itself would be inert, a lot like Plasticine. Easy to shape and mould by hand, it could even be safely cut with a knife. When combined with a detonator, however, it would be lethal. A terrorist's weapon of choice.

Both police officers looked at each other briefly, eyebrows raised.

'This looks to me like cocaine.' There was a gleam in her eyes as she held up the small bag of white powder. A probable conviction was on the cards and the adrenaline was pumping. This was suddenly her case to win. She held the bag near her nose. More of a theatrical gesture than anything definitive. Seconds later, her eyes never having once left Ross's, she put it down gently. 'That's a class A drug, for the avoidance of doubt.' She picked the bag up once more and placed it in the palm of one hand, trying to guess its weight. 'Probably less than a kilo. In which case, it'd be a category two offence. For possession, you'd be looking at a minimum five to seven years custodial. This, however,' she said, holding up the other bag, 'is likely to make matters a whole lot more complicated. If this is what I think it is, then you're in deep shit. This could bring an additional minimum of anything from three to twelve years custodial, arguably more. All because of one small, insignificant-looking rucksack. Anything you want to say?'

Ross swept his hair off his forehead and looked at her thoughtfully. As if considering a chess move.

'Do I need a lawyer?'

'It's not for us to advise. Given the likely charges, it's probably advisable.'

'Then please find me one. Until then, I shall exercise my right to remain silent.'

*

They led Ross back to his cell in the custody suite to wait for the duty solicitor to arrive. The only item of furniture was a concrete slab, on top of which was a thin, blue plastic mattress and an apology for a pillow. He lay down and closed his eyes, his mind wrestling with an array of emotions: frustration; anger; bewilderment; and, not least, disappointment. What was so ironic was that, until that day, everything had been going so well, at least as far as the last six months were concerned. After a lifetime of career fuck-ups, being given the chance, in his early forties, to serve his country once again, using life skills that were innate or had been honed and refined over the years, had been liberating, if a trifle confusing. He'd had a lot of ground to make up, that was for sure, which only heightened his sense of disappointment at finding himself set up that morning. He'd never seen it coming, that was what was so maddening.

As an adopted child of only mildly interested parents, he'd experienced school as a catalogue of wasted opportunities: if he hadn't proven to be such a strong middle-distance runner, Ross would have dropped out altogether. Then, as the spooky recruiter had reminded him a few months earlier, there had been the failed drug test. That had been the low point. With few friends, a bruised ego, and spirits flagging, he had quit university and joined the military, as much out of desperation as any real career plan. It proved to be a lifeline. To his surprise, he found that he was good at soldiering, even passing the selection boards for those Special units that those in the higher echelons seemed to think he might excel in. Which had been all fine and positive for a few years until the Iranian Guard ambushed his small four-man unit on a secret reconnaissance mission deep within the Karkas mountains, close to the Iranian nuclear site at Natanz. Ross, wounded, had evaded capture. His three colleagues hadn't been so lucky. Alone, out of radio contact, and with only his training to fall back on, he had lived off the land in the deserted mountain region for several weeks to allow his body time enough to recover. Eventually, when he was fit enough to make his way, undercover, to the British Embassy in Teheran, strings were hastily pulled, connections made and an escape plan devised that allowed Ross, finally, to head home to face inevitable questions at the hands of army medics and shrinks. Assessed as burnt out and physically in poor health, he had undergone a period of rehabilitation and then quietly left the army, taking up a new career as a teacher. Nothing permanent: mostly supply teaching, standing in for others when there was a vacancy. Like his relationships with women. Except until recently, when he'd met a Russian woman called Natalia and had fallen madly and deeply.

*

Back at her desk, waiting for the duty solicitor to arrive, DCI Lauren McIlvoy was also wrestling with her emotions. No sooner had the old wound finally healed, something like this would happen and she'd be back, exposed and vulnerable, having to face her demons once again. Demon in the singular, to be accurate. One particularly unpleasant man by the name of Brendan North.

The precise details surrounding North's arrival and departure in McIlvoy's life had become blurred as time had passed. On balance, this was probably a good thing. The less the memory of their brief relationship was front of mind, the better. Despite her thirty-seven years, eighteen of which having been spent painstakingly inching her way up the male-dominated police promotion ladder, she was still single and emotionally unattached. Both factors she blamed, in no small measure, on North. She had been carrying the emotional scars for the last twelve years.

North had been on the equivalent of what today would be called the Met's Fast Track programme when they'd first met. Heading for the top, as he told her only the second time they'd gone out together. It was typical of his self-assured arrogance. Unlike McIlvoy, North had been to university. It gave him a swagger that initially she'd thought amusing, if not charming. They'd dated for a while, and she'd moved in with him shortly afterwards. They'd bumped along, more or less happily. Until the night of his thirtieth birthday. The moment she'd finally found herself up close and personal with the real Brendan North. Not the one she thought she'd been living with. This was a different person. One whose sexual depravities had scared the living daylights out of her.

Traumatised and unable to face going into work for a period, McIlvoy had vowed to avoid all future contact with North. He, on the other hand, seemed emboldened by the whole grisly episode. He would call her at work, taunt her with his sexual innuendos, all part of a pattern that showed his perverted, controlling nature. Then, out of the blue, a miracle. North applied for a transfer to the domestic Security Service, MI5, and was accepted. Overnight, the demon in McIlvoy's life vanished. No further contact.

Until one day, recently, she learnt that North had been reassigned as one of the Met's senior MI5 liaison officers. The go-to man for McIlvoy and others to speak to whenever a case or circumstance required liaison. In particular, terrorism cases. These were normally the purview of SO15, a specialist unit within the Met, but the rulebook required anything with a possible terrorist dimension had to be brought to the attention of MI5. Liaison. It was the bane of a hard-working policeman or woman's life. Especially if it meant having to deal with someone like Brendan North.

So, when Calum Ross, no previous convictions, found himself arrested by members of the British Transport Police for possession of a block of plastic explosive, they expected her to go by the book. The book required DCI McIlvoy to liaise with MI5. Which explained why she was struggling. Once more, she would have to pick up the phone and talk to Brendan North.

Old wounds were about to be reopened.

Chapter 5

London

Ross's interrogation had resumed after three hours of delay, this time in the presence of the duty solicitor. Jonathan Richards was an overworked, overweight, middle-aged man. He arrived at Savile Row police station looking harassed, tired and distinctly grey, having rushed from a previous client meeting. In a suit that hadn't had a press in a long while and with a tie that was fraying at the edges.

After a snatched conversation with McIlvoy, he'd been shown the report the arresting officer had made and briefly skimmed it. Next, he'd spent time with Ross in his holding cell in the custody suite, giving a long lecture about what was likely to happen and what he thought Ross, the defendant, should and shouldn't say. Once he was satisfied that he had fulfilled his duty to brief his client, together they had been escorted by a uniformed police constable back to the interview room. McIlvoy and her silent male colleague in the oversized suit jacket were already waiting, the policeman from the arrest team no longer present. Richards positioned himself in a chair alongside Ross, facing McIlvoy. The other policeman sat to one side.

'Mother's maiden name?'

Ross's mind was wandering. He guessed McIlvoy's age to be mid to late thirties. Short, jet-black hair that she wore long over the ears, blue eyes and an angular jawline. She was pleasing on the eye, though not his type, nor was he interested. Probably single. She had that edge that comes with an education courtesy of the School of Hard Knocks. He should know – Ross was an alumnus himself.

'I was adopted. I never knew my mother,' Ross replied with a sigh. McIlvoy's note-taking colleague was frowning. There didn't appear to be a space on his form for an answer like that.

'How about your adopted mother's maiden name?'

'Kerslake.'

'Place and date of birth?'

'My adopted mother or me?'

McIlvoy had looked up, eyes momentarily flaring. Her weary expression had "smart-ass" written all over.

'You, for starters.'

'My adoption papers state that I was a home birth. Address unknown. Somewhere near Birmingham. I believe my date of birth to be July fifteenth, 1977. Plus or minus.'

'Believe? Either you know or you don't.' McIlvoy glanced fleetingly at her male colleague. Both raised their eyebrows. The smart-ass label was now confirmed.

'I was an unwanted child. Abandoned. All I can tell you is what it says on my birth certificate.'

'Do you have your passport with you?' She looked up at Ross, pen in hand, and swept a stray strand of jet-black hair behind an ear. It was a practised manoeuvre, a gesture he'd noticed earlier. Different from the way he tried to control his unruly locks, but that's what tickled him. She was getting impatient. Good, so was he.

'No.'

At which point, Richards made his only significant contribution to the meeting.

'His passport details will surely be in the system?' McIlvoy looked sideways at Richards with an icy stare.

'Currently employed?' she continued, hardly missing a beat.

'No.'

'When were you last employed?'

He contemplated his answer before replying.

'Until about three days ago.'

'Doing what?'

'I've been working in Istanbul these last six months. At the British School, on a short-term teaching contract.' She was checking something within one of the files as he spoke. Ross noticed a frown forming on her face. 'It was a maternity cover,' he explained further. 'Teaching maths and athletics. Also chess.' These revelations caused McIlvoy to stop and look up. She stared at Ross in silent contemplation. Whether she'd been impressed or simply didn't believe him, it was unclear. However, something had struck a chord. They were still a long way from Point C.

The process trudged on.

'So, tell me,' she said a while later. 'Why, exactly, did you feel obliged to pick up the rucksack?'

'Out of a sense of duty, I suppose. Stray bags on planes and trains are usually problems.'

'In what way?'

'Well, if I hadn't picked up the bag, the only other option would have been to pull the emergency cord and get everybody off the train.'

'Which is arguably what you should have done, wouldn't you agree?'

'No, actually, I don't.'

'What about the risk to yourself?'

'Life's full of risk. The man appealed to me for help. More than most, I reckoned I probably stood a fair chance of catching up with them.'

'More than most?'

'I'm an athletics teacher. Part of the time. I train as a triathlete. I'm pretty fit. Well, I was, until I twisted my knee recently in a Hash.'

She leaned back in her chair, arms folded.

'What's a Hash?'

'A form of running club. Hare and Hounds type of thing. Some call them drinking clubs with a running problem. It's very social. You should try it, it's fun. This one was in Istanbul. In and around the old city.'

'I believe you.' She uncrossed her arms and shook her head. For the first time, there was a hint of a smile.

'Okay, I get that there was this bag at your feet. I also get that this stranger is panicked and asks for your help. I further get that you might be public-spirited enough to want to get a stray bag off a busy train. What I don't get is why you didn't feel any apprehension. What if it had contained a bomb? What if people on the platform or escalator had been killed as a result? Not to mention yourself. You didn't worry about these sorts of things?'

'Sure, after the event. A bit. At the time, no. For me, it was a split second, three-way decision. Do nothing; pull the alarm; or help the guy and get the bag off the train. There was no time to open the rucksack casually, take a peek inside and make sure everything was safe. It was a 'do this, this or that' decision. Like playing speed chess. Have you ever played?'

She stared at him again, this time shaking her head in a more pronounced manner.

'Well, you should. You've got five minutes, start to finish. It's a great game. Teaches you a lot about making decisions in life.'

'I'm not sure most people would have done what you did.'

'You can't say that unless you were there. I disagree with you. All I did was make a rapid assessment, choosing one particular path and then committing to it.'

'You speak – and appear to act – like someone who plans and analyses a lot. As if calculating this move and that is part of your day job. Have you ever served in the military?'

Ross didn't reply, instead swivelling his body towards his lawyer. 'I suppose these questions are all relevant?'

'I think, Calum,' Richards whispered confidentially, 'that unless you feel there's a reason not to say something, it's best to answer them.'

It took yet more time, but eventually they had enough information for a full statement to be produced. Under the watchful gaze of Richards, various revisions were made to the first draft. Finally, the statement was ready for Ross to sign. At which point McIlvoy, with due prompting from Richards and with what Ross considered to be feigned reluctance, agreed that the detainee could be released, no formal charges at this stage, pending further police enquiries. They'd taken his prints, a copy of his driving licence, details of just about every electronic means of getting hold of him from his mobile number to his email address, and then he'd been handed over to a different custody officer to get his possessions back.

Meaning that it wasn't until after ten in the evening before Ross finally emerged from the police station's back entrance on Old Burlington Street. He stood on the pavement and breathed in the London air. It wasn't clean, that was for sure. However, it didn't smell rancid, which was a plus. Nor were there any lingering odours of disinfectant either. For those reasons alone, it was a joy to be outside.

Chapter 6

London

As Ross approached his front door, a single light on a sensor blinked on. He fumbled for his keys. Then the hairs on the nape of his neck started to rise.

The door was slightly ajar.

There was no sign of forced entry. However, the door was definitely open. He entered the hallway stealthily, standing rock-still on the threadbare carpet. He could see nothing in the darkness, his ears straining for extraneous sounds. Unable to hear anything, he paused still further, sniffing the air. Nothing. No strange noises, no unfamiliar lingering odours. Increasingly convinced that the apartment was empty, Ross quietly closed the front door and turned on the hall lights. Again, he waited. If anything was likely to flush out a random burglar, it would be the lights coming on. Finally satisfied that he was indeed alone, he tiptoed across to the partially open living room door, reached inside with one hand and flipped the light switch, simultaneously pushing the door wide open.

Which was when he saw the chaos.

Someone had ransacked the room. Every item of furniture, every one of his belongings, even the pictures on the walls: they had all been upended. In the bedroom, it was the same story. Even the kitchen had been thoroughly trashed, the contents of cupboards and drawers lying strewn everywhere.

About to call the police, he stopped himself. After all he'd been through that afternoon, there seemed little point in contacting anybody at such a late hour. There wasn't much an overstretched police force was going to want to do about a routine burglary late at night. No lives had been lost. Everything would wait until morning.

Heading back to his bedroom, Ross knelt down to check something. It was a section of skirting close to where his bedhead had been. A small piece of wooden boarding which, when removed, revealed an opening to a cavity beneath the floorboards. It was where Ross had hidden the few valuables he had in his possession: his passport, a tablet computer, and a sizeable amount of spare cash that he hadn't wanted to carry around with him. The good news was that the wooden skirting didn't appear disturbed. That assessment soon changed as he prized the piece of wood away and felt inside. The space under the floor was empty. Ross peered into the void to make sure. All of his possessions had been cleaned out.

Why? Why would a random burglar, someone intent on trashing the place, have been so meticulous as to check the skirting – and then replace the wooden board so carefully? Was this the reason for the stunt on the train earlier – to keep Ross in custody for enough time to allow someone else to do all this, knowing that his apartment would be unoccupied? Was a bit of money, his passport and a tablet computer worth all the hassle? Angry and violated by the intrusion, he felt an impulse to get away from the place. He'd find somewhere to spend the night. Even if it meant paying, he didn't want to sleep here, not amongst all the debris.

On the point of leaving, he remembered one last place he hadn't checked: a small coat cupboard off the hallway. It was mainly a storage space, somewhere for cleaning equipment, suitcases and the like. He opened the door, turned on the light and, for the second time that night, stopped in his tracks.

On the floor, where the vacuum would normally sit, were several rucksacks. Maybe five, all in a disorderly heap. As if discarded in a hurry.

They were all the same, the by now familiar lightweight waterproof variety that wouldn't hold a great deal. Black, with shoulder and chest straps the same colour. All brand new.

Identical to the ones on the train earlier.

One by one, he searched them – side pockets, inner compartments, everything. All were empty. Someone had gone to a lot of trouble. It felt scary. Spooky, almost. Akin to being stalked. His first impression on the Tube that morning was that he'd chanced upon someone who'd simply made an honest mistake. Then he'd seen the two men together and realised he'd been set up. Now this. This went a whole lot further. It proved, as if he needed any proof, that he was being carefully and deliberately targeted. The questions from earlier were still the same. Who was doing this – and why? Could Natalia's husband really be the one pulling all the strings?

With a final search around the apartment, he doused the lights, on an impulse stopping to examine the front door itself. It seemed, from the light in the stairwell, to be undamaged, suggesting that someone had opened it with a key. Or someone had picked the lock. Either way, it was in good enough shape that Ross could secure the door with his key before leaving. There was a hotel near Camden Lock, about two miles away. He'd get a room and call the police in the morning.

Plenty of buses plied Kentish Town Road at night. In next to no time, he was walking through the lobby of a sterile-looking chain hotel overlooking the Grand Union Canal.

'Can I help?' the night receptionist said, greeting him with a weary smile. She was on her own, the lobby area deserted. Ross noticed she'd been playing solitaire on her computer.

'Do you have any rooms? I don't have a reservation, I'm sorry.'

'I'm sure we can find you something. Is it for the one night?' She had an interesting accent, possibly Scandinavian. The solitaire screen vanished as she began typing on her keyboard.

'For the moment, yes,' Ross said. 'I might want to extend a few days. I won't know until the morning. Is that likely to be a problem?' Natalia was arriving the next day. They might both be grateful for a comfortable – and discreet – bolthole, especially given the state of his apartment.

'We have a large group leaving in the morning,' she said, peering at the screen. 'At the moment, we're showing plenty of availability. Check again after breakfast if you're interested. Now,' she said, looking up at him with a smile, 'we have a springtime promotional rate that includes breakfast.' Taking his card, she swiped it through a reader and then stared at the screen. Frowning, she typed again, using the mouse to click on various items. Then, after rubbing the card's magnetic strip against her sleeve, she passed the card through the reader one more time.

'I'm sorry,' she said at length, frowning as she handed the card back to Ross. 'Your card's been declined. Do you have another? Or cash would work. Whatever you prefer.'

Ross delved into a trouser pocket and removed a small billfold. He peeled off several twenty-pound notes and handed them over.

'I'm sorry about that,' she said, checking that he'd given her the right amount of money. 'Sometimes these machines have a mind of their own. Anyway, here's your room key. The elevator bank is over there.' She passed him a folded piece of card containing his room key. 'Do you need any help with your luggage?'

THE BACKSTORY

Chapter 7

Seven months ago, a nondescript rented office near London

'We believe, Calum, you might be perfect.'

'Might?'

The lighter flared, the man inhaling deeply on his newly lit cigarette.

'Nothing's certain,' he pronounced, smoke swirling.

'Great.'

'People either have what it takes or they don't. We think you have it in spades.'

'A burnt-out soldier, trying to make ends meet by doing the odd bit of teaching? How does that work?'

'It works fine. In fact, in your case, it works bloody brilliantly. All we do is conceal some bits and embellish others. When the lights go up, you'll be on stage, cast in the lead role. A stand-in teacher. Question is, will you be able to cope? Acting a double life, I mean.'

'Are you kidding? For the money you're offering, with no success fee, what's not to like?'

'It's never only about the money.'

'It helps. Trust me, when you're as skint as I've been recently, it helps.'

'Money's not why we do stuff. Not people like you and me.' He ground his cigarette into the saucer, immediately reaching for the packet.

'Have you ever hit rock bottom?'

'Sure. Plenty of times.'

'Then you'll understand why I'm willing to consider this.'

'You've got to want this with a passion, Calum. For it to succeed, I mean.'

'It would help if I knew exactly who you guys were.'

'People like you. Decent, professional people who enjoy working hard behind the scenes to get things done.' The cheap lighter flared once more.

'Which side are you on?'

He waved a hand dismissively, his head shaking slightly.

'Before that?'

'Similar to you, my soldiering career was in units with the word "Special" stamped everywhere.'

'And now?'

'I've become a bit spooky.'

'Bloody brilliant! Land of Hope and Glory, I presume?'

'Of course, bloody Land of Hope and Glory. Just nothing mainstream.'

'What the fuck does that mean?'

'It means we don't exist.'

'Why?'

'Too much politics. Too many bureaucrats. Plus, way, way too many lawyers.'

'How do I know that you are who you say you are?'

'You don't. You have to trust your instincts. Feel proud to have been talent-spotted. Rekindle your latent passion to serve. Remember, we only go after the very best of the best.'

'So, what's this all about?'

'There's a highly delicate situation that needs addressing.' He drew deeply on his cigarette, exhaling slowly as he continued watching the other man.

'Why me?'

'Because, Calum, we believe you're the man uniquely able to get this thing resolved. Once and for all.'

*

'What makes you think she'll be interested?' The cigarette packet was by this stage, two-thirds empty.

'We watch and we listen. What she tells her friends. Occasionally her colleagues. We know how she's feeling. About life, about love. Most important of all . . .' He checked to ensure he had his companion's full attention. 'About fidelity.'

'How the hell do you know that?'

The man shrugged, saying nothing. Ross noticed that his index finger on his left hand was missing, the stub ending immediately above the knuckle.

'I may not be her type.'

'That's a risk we're prepared to take.'

'What exactly are we trying to achieve?'

'We want her secrets, Calum. More accurately, we want her husband's secrets.'

'And he is who, exactly?'

'A powerful man with many, many secrets.'

There was yet more painful silence, the air thick with smoke and unspoken emptiness.

'Listen, Calum. The moment she arrives in the UK, secrets galore stuffed in her knickers, that'll be when it's time for us to re-emerge from the shadows and offer the pair of you protection. That's a cast-iron commitment, by the way. However, we have our suspicions that others may try to beat us to that particular offer.'

'Really? Why?'

'Because, when you screw the wife of a famous Russian spy, and when his wife steals his secrets, do you really think the rest of the spy world will sit back and let it pass by unnoticed?'

*

'Listen up, Calum. Somewhere along the journey, contact is likely to be made. From people in an official capacity. Not people like you and me, playing in the shadows. People trying to persuade you to do their bidding. From that moment, life will get complicated. Friend or foe, we're not yet entirely sure. Think of it as a nibble on the line.'

'How will I know?'

'You'll know. You may not know who it is, but you'll know.' The man grimaced. The cigarettes had been abandoned. Now he was chewing nicotine gum. 'It might be the French, it could be the Germans; possibly the Israelis; or even the Americans. We suspect first to the bait will be the Brits.'

'Hang on. That's us, isn't it?'

'You're forgetting. We don't exist. Not officially. Nor unofficially. We're off the books. This is a freelance Calum Ross production, remember.'

'I'm confused.'

'Don't be. When MI5 or MI6 or MI-whoever come along, the very fact that they're there is good news. Remember: they report to the angels. We report directly to God.'

'Who are we again?'

'The righteous, Calum. Whatever happens to you on this journey, whatever mess and complications that arise, ultimately it'll be us watching your back, ready to absolve all sins and misdemeanours.'

'Do I get that in writing?'

'Nope.'

'I didn't think so. How do I contact you in a crisis?'

'You don't.'

'What about sending me to spy school?'

'Special Forces warriors don't need spy school. We only go as instructors. What the fuck do you want to learn at spy school?'

'You tell me.'

'Fuck all. You and I are better than that. We learnt things in the military that spies only dream of.'

'If I can't contact you, how do I let you know when I've been approached by someone?'

'You don't. Remember, we'll be watching, the whole time. What we want to discover is who else is interested. We think it will be revealing.'

'Why?'

'Because when someone has something to hide, you discover they go to extraordinary lengths to cover their tracks.'

'And this is going to happen?'

'It'll happen. You need to be prepared. Play along, but hard to get. When a fish nibbles the bait, let the line out a bit. A tussle or two is to be expected. Don't be overeager. If MI5 or 6 make contact, make them wait like anyone else. They must know nothing of our private arrangement. That is for God himself. For sure, if one team notices, others will be equally aware. Just keep the woman safe. Whatever you do, it's imperative that you don't screw that objective up.'

'And if I do?'

'Then it won't matter how many "Special" units you may have been part of. You'll be on your own and in the very deepest of shit.'

Chapter 8

Four months ago, Aleppo and London

The story of Usmanov's venture into money laundering began with an overnight express train from Istanbul to Adana in the south-eastern corner of Turkey. The train across Turkey was one of Usmanov's favoured methods of getting to and from the troubled areas of the Middle East. It was a comfortable journey and less conspicuous than flying. It enabled him to be met by a car and trusted driver before being sneaked quietly over the border into Syria, diplomatic credentials easing his passage with the Syrian border guards. From Adana, it was a six-hour journey by road to the historic city of Aleppo, still devastated by the ravages of Syria's endless war and reduced in places to rubble and ruin. A few hotels were still operating in the city. On this trip, Usmanov checked into a former western-branded luxury hotel that was looking distinctly tired and jaded.

Usmanov's normal *modus operandi* was to bring with him copious amounts of cash stashed in an overnight bag, usually US dollars, the currency of choice for greasing palms and paying off agents and informers. On this particular trip, however, Usmanov had more money with him than usual. In fact, he had surprised his Consulate's banking section a week earlier by asking for two hundred thousand dollars in cash in one hundred-dollar bills.

Eyebrows had been raised, but no questions had been asked. With Usmanov, they never dared, banking section staff understanding something of Usmanov's official role at the Consulate and knowing better than to challenge someone who was a close friend of the Russian President. Whilst the cash had indeed been delivered, a note of the request had been passed up the chain of command to superiors in Moscow. Checks and balances: that was the way the Russian system always worked.

*

'Tell me, what have you got?' Usmanov and his guest were sitting in a quiet corner of the lounge bar. It was the final meeting of the trip and, for the Russian agent, the most important so far. The two men were drinking tea, Usmanov's guest a scruffily dressed man in black jeans and a tattered leather jacket. Despite his downbeat appearance, the Syrian was animated.

'You will find this unbelievable. Discovered in Idlib, during the recent fighting. A villa, belonging to an old, wealthy Syrian family, was recently hit by a bomb and the property looted.' He gingerly removed a small leather sachet with a draw-string closure from an inner jacket pocket. Loosening the strings, he tipped a tissue-wrapped object into the palm of one hand. Carefully, he unwrapped it until the small item was exposed. Both men stared at the piece in silence. 'It's 10th century. Carved ivory, it appears to be identical to a chess piece that sold at auction for a huge amount about five years ago.'

'Remind me again?'

'A supposed masterpiece of Syrian carving, thought to have been made for an Egyptian monarch. The single chess piece sold at auction in London for almost three hundred thousand dollars.'

'And this, you think, is the matching queen?'

'It is unquestionably authentic. Radiocarbon dating has verified its age.'

'Who did the analysis?'

'A scientist friend of mine. Someone I use regularly at the University of Damascus.'

'How much do you want for it?'

'I believe three hundred and fifty thousand dollars would be a fair price.'

Which was when the negotiation began in earnest. They took more tea; they ate sweet pastries; and after a pleasant but prolonged period of bartering, the two men shook hands at a price of two hundred and twenty thousand dollars. Usmanov passed over a briefcase containing two hundred thousand dollars and withdrew two further ten thousand-dollar bundles from his overnight bag. In return, he received the chess piece, once more wrapped in tissue and placed back inside its tiny leather pouch.

*

Three weeks later, Usmanov was to be found dining with a reclusive German by the name of Alexander Timmerman. There were eating in the latter's spacious London residence, waited on by Timmerman's personal butler. The four-storey town house was located right next to Onslow Gardens in Kensington. The property was more a museum than a private residence, the multi-billionaire former businessman being an avid collector and investor in all forms of art and artefact. Deep underground the property, in a space where other London-based billionaires might have built swimming pools and garaging for rare and expensive cars, Timmerman had one of the largest private art collections in the world. Spread over three floors below ground were gallery upon gallery of some of the world's finest pieces. Many would never see the light of day again since their provenance was not what the auction houses liked to call assured. To an investor such as Timmerman, that particular detail was of little consequence.

Like Usmanov, the German had known the current Russian President for many years. When Usmanov had expressed an interest a few years earlier in investing in chess pieces, his friend had introduced him to the German. The two men got on and Usmanov purchased a rare Cybis porcelain chess set from Timmerman. It remained, to this day, one of Usmanov's most cherished investments.

'You mentioned that you have something special for me to consider, Oleg,' the German said as they shared the last of the 1963 port from a crystal decanter. 'May I see it?'

Usmanov put down his wineglass and removed the leather draw-string pouch from his jacket pocket. He watched as the German unwrapped the tissue paper from the chess piece, using his linen table napkin to pick up the carved ivory figurine and examine it.

'Well, well, well,' he said eventually. 'This is exceptional. You know who bought the matching king a few years ago at auction, don't you?' The gleam in his eyes as he spoke confirmed to the Russian everything he already knew.

'Is the other piece here?' Usmanov asked.

Without saying another word, the German got up from the table and beckoned for Usmanov to follow. They walked to a staircase in one corner of the room and descended two floors. Passing through two locked doors, they arrived in the middle of a vast gallery, motion sensors activating a sophisticated lighting system. On several walls were glass cabinets containing artefacts and sculptures of different shapes and sizes. Timmerman walked to one corner and peered into a waist-high cabinet that exclusively contained old chess pieces.

'There it is,' he said pointing, laying Usmanov's ivory queen on the glass immediately above and to one side of an almost identical piece in Timmerman's collection below.

'Amazing. They do, indeed, look identical,' Usmanov conceded.

'Do you know how rare what you have brought today is?'

'I wouldn't be here otherwise. I presume you'd like to make me an offer?'

'Has it been radiocarbon tested?'

'Yes. At the University of Damascus. It's 10th century.'

'I bought the king at auction for three hundred thousand pounds.'

'That was five years ago.'

'True. So, here's my offer. Assuming that you're prepared to leave this with me so I can conduct my own tests then, on the assumption that it really is as old as you claim it to be, I will offer to pay four hundred thousand pounds. Would that be fair?'

Usmanov tried to keep his emotions in check.

'Alexander, if you are happy to pay that price, we have ourselves a deal.'

'Excellent. How would you like to be paid?'

'I've a new Swiss bank account where you can wire the money.'

'Perfect. Then I suggest we head back upstairs. If you can then let me have the account details, I will do the rest. Assuming everything is as we believe it to be, you will have your money within three days.'

Chapter 9

Four months ago, Istanbul

Even before Natalia appeared on the scene, Calum Ross had fallen in love with Istanbul: its history; its cultural heritage; the food; and especially the people. This was a place at the crossroads of Europe and Asia, the intersection made more complicated, more exciting, more beautiful by the narrow isthmus of water that separated the two continents, a dividing line that ran straight through the city's centre and thus became its beating heart. This vibrancy, this mishmash: it was intoxicating.

The school Ross was assigned to was no exception. Everyone – the staff, parents and pupils alike – was universally polite and welcoming. Ross's school-provided accommodation on the campus, a few kilometres to the north of Taksim Square, was basic yet functional. A small rectangular living space with a pull-down single bed and a simple bathroom and kitchenette to one side. It was clean; he wasn't sharing with other people; and it was provided free of charge. His contract required him to cover for a maths teacher on maternity leave: in reality, they expected him to perform several extracurricular activities such as athletics, swimming and tennis coaching; and, out of school hours, running the school's chess club. He had thrown himself into these with passion, energy and good humour. Attributes, Natalia had whispered intimately that first time they'd been together, nestled uncomfortably close on his narrow bed, she found profoundly attractive in a man.

'Just to be abundantly clear, Calum,' the headmaster, Gerald Granger, had said the first day Ross had presented himself for duty at the school, 'there are certain red lines you need to be aware of.' Granger was sitting behind an antique desk piled with papers when Ross was shown into his large study. After a perfunctory handshake and an exchange of pleasantries, Ross found himself ushered into a vacant chair in front of the desk, leaving Granger to resume his command-and-control position behind the paperwork. A British expatriate out of the old school, Granger favoured a three-piece suit, a silver pocket watch on a chain, a crisply ironed cotton shirt and an institutional tie bearing crested motifs. Plus, naturally, proper shoes: black leather brogues, suitably buffed to a parade ground shine.

In the way that inferior clothing can make the British feel instantly inadequate, Ross had felt scruffy in his crumpled linen jacket, chinos and open-necked shirt. Perhaps, he reflected as he'd taken his seat, that had been the point? Granger then gave a well-rehearsed soliloquy for the next fifteen minutes, a performance that Ross had little choice but to endure. He covered the school, its ethos, its enviable reputation, and the pride that resulted from its academic and teaching achievements. The oration was delivered affably, softly but with a firm authority, a headmasterly tone doubtless honed over the years to good effect.

Granger had listed his red lines as if reading from the statutes. 'Teachers may not consume alcohol whilst on school premises. The same applies for drugs. As you might expect, we have a zero-tolerance policy on these matters. Finally,' he had said with emphasis, 'whilst intimate relations between members of the teaching staff are actively discouraged, intimate relations between members of the teaching staff and any parent are totally forbidden. They always have been, are now, and evermore shall be, offences that give rise to instant dismissal. Do I make myself clear?'

Ross had nodded obediently.

'One more thing, Calum, before you go. Your grace and favour accommodation here on campus. It's small for a reason. If you feel the need to entertain guests whilst you are with us, kindly do so someplace else, away from the school premises. Certain teachers in the past have abused this rule and caused themselves, and the school, embarrassment. We set high standards here. Please do your best to maintain them. Now, if you'll excuse me, I must get on.' Without a pause for questions, he had dived back behind his paperwork and Ross was dismissed.

*

It took about six weeks before Ross's life became truly complicated. Before then, during what Granger described to one mother at a parents' evening as Ross's 'settling-in period', his appearance in and around the school was something of a novelty. Who was this stand-in teacher from England? What was he like? Was he married – if so, why hadn't he brought his wife with him? If they were curious about his background, they were only in admiration of his physique. Not bad for someone supposedly in his early forties, they would mutter, this useful piece of age-related gossip being something that the headmaster had supposedly let slip whilst watching a school soccer match a few weeks earlier.

On the day in question, school was drawing to a close and parents were gathering. Ross was wearing the well-worn cardigan, this oddly eccentric wardrobe item, as ever, worn with the bottom three buttons undone. One might have been considered normal; two, some might have thought stylish; three hinted at laziness. Unruly, dark hair rounded off the image: long at the back, scraggy at the front, swept to one side with a flick of the fingers. Often whilst fretting about a complex maths equation in front of a class. Or mulling, as he was that afternoon, over his next moves during school chess club. He never saw her arrive. Nor did he know how long she had been there. Full of his characteristic energy, hair flying, he was busy bounding between four chessboards on separate tables, moving a pawn here, a bishop there. Looking his slightly dishevelled best. One of his pupils was Viktor, a sixteen-year-old Russian with a natural talent for the game. Natalia was his mother.

As the game ended, Viktor, defeated – but only narrowly – looked up and saw his mother watching from afar. She smiled, but Viktor simply shook his head, the burden of defeat still heavy. She had scowled, pursing her lips in gentle mockery, and Ross had, deliberately and consciously, caught this exchange out of the corner of an eye. He had turned his head to look at her. It was the same moment that she turned and look directly at him. Which was when she paused, raised an eyebrow in that special way of hers, and smiled.

In that fleeting instant, both knew. Red lines were about to be crossed.

Chapter 10

Four months ago, Istanbul

'Hi,' she said, sweeping a stray lock of curly brown hair to one side. 'I'm Viktor's mother. Natalia.'

Their eyes locked, hers wide and sparkly. Ross, cheeks flushing, quickly looked away, flicking his own hair to one side as if mirroring her opening moves.

'Calum. Calum Ross.' They shook hands, Ross feeling long, soft fingers embracing his own. 'I'm the new teacher.'

'I know. Viktor told me. Are you liking Istanbul?'

'Yes,' he answered truthfully, delivering his lines with well-rehearsed ease. 'I'm slowly getting to know people.'

She nodded, then turned. 'Viktor, get your things. I shall be waiting.'

Natalia's son grunted and walked away slowly.

'No one likes to lose,' Ross said.

'You are good. Viktor tells me these things, and I see for myself. So much,' – she gave a little shimmy, her arms slightly raised at the elbows as she swayed her body from side to side – 'energy! Four games at once and you are winning!' They both laughed. 'You must teach me. I am no good. For a Russian, this is not appropriate.'

'I'd be happy to.' More big smiles.

'Viktor tells me you are also tennis coach. Is that correct?'

'I'm okay,' he said, his cheeks reddening once more. 'I've been doing the odd bit of coaching.'

'Then you must coach me, I absolutely insist.'

'I'd be happy to,' he said, with a chuckle, more a release of nervous energy than outright laughter.

'Then I shall make arrangements. I would like this very much.'

'Me too.'

'Where are you staying?'

'Here on campus. I have a tiny apartment out the back, in the block behind the staff common room. It's nothing grand but, hey. It's free and there's no commute. I'm not complaining.'

Viktor was back once more, a heavy school bag slung over a shoulder.

'Ready?' she asked, but got no reply.

'You did well, Viktor,' Ross said. 'I think next time you might even beat me.'

'I hope so,' came the stony-faced reply.

'Calum, I enjoyed very much meeting you,' she said, again shaking his hand, this time holding him for a second or two longer than he expected.

'Me too. I hope we might meet again soon. Let me know about the tennis, if you're interested. Whenever is convenient.'

'I will make it my business, I promise.'

*

The next day was a Saturday. Ross had been out for a long run and was taking a shower in his apartment. The campus was quiet, and he'd been planning to go to a film that afternoon. All during the run, he'd been replaying over and over his conversation the previous afternoon. Natalia had surprised him. He could feel the hunger in her, remembering her sexuality as she'd performed that little body wiggle. Now that he'd met her for real, he was excited about what might happen next. Perhaps the recruiter had been right: maybe he could be a good match for her. He dried his hair and wrapped the towel around his waist, wandering through to the kitchenette to make coffee. Which was when he heard the gentle tapping on his door. He checked the knot on his towel and gingerly opened the door.

'Natalia.' She was standing, sheepishly, he thought, on the small landing outside the entrance.

'Calum, I surprised you, I am sorry. Is this convenient?'

'Sure. Of course. I'm delighted to see you. I was making coffee. Come in.' Ross checked the corridor to make certain no one was watching and, once she had stepped inside, closed the door behind her. Immediately he noticed her fragrance. It was soft with gentle musky tones: apricots and honey with a hint of spice.

'Perhaps this is a bad moment. Forgive me.'

'Don't apologise. I've just been for a run.'

'I should have rung. I did not have your number, I apologise.'

'That's okay. Please excuse the state of the place – it's a tip.'

She placed a warm, soft hand on his bare shoulder.

'I hadn't noticed.'

'I ought to get dressed.'

'Really?'

Which was when she leant forward and kissed him, a full, on-the-lips embrace that lasted several seconds.

'I had thought you might teach me chess,' she whispered, one hand wrapped around his neck, the other hand creeping its way down his spine. 'But now I am sensing that we might have other plans.' She released the knot on his towel and let it slide to the floor.

Chapter 11

Four months ago, Istanbul

The panoramic backdrop from the suite's floor-to-ceiling windows was constantly changing. Movement was supplied by a steady stream of passenger ferries, tankers and cargo vessels plying the Golden Horn. Mood music was courtesy of the weather, the 180-degree view from their corner suite revealing thunderous cloud formations swirling in perpetual motion. Colour was lent by random acts of nature's own making, momentary bursts of sunshine transforming the winter gloom into vibrant displays of colour: minarets and low-rise buildings became shaded in yellows, greys and browns; gardens and trees took on lush, verdant hues; and, most dominant of all, the waters of the Bosphorus transformed from dull ink-black into a rich, azure blue.

Conscious of the limitations of Ross's apartment, the two lovers had upgraded the location of their red-line-crossing second rendezvous to a corner suite overlooking the Bosphorus. The Swiss-owned hotel had a tennis club. Natalia was already a member. She was, she had whispered in the aftermath of their first cramped but passionate encounter, definitely in need of tennis coaching. Ross, supply teacher to all and any but tennis coach by private appointment only, confirmed that he'd be happy to oblige. Later, she'd given a fleeting synopsis of this fiction to her husband,

Oleg. He was back in Moscow, and she casually informed him by phone that Viktor's chess teacher was offering ex-curricula tennis coaching at the weekends. To give both parties credit, that first Saturday morning they had played some tennis. Briefly. Until a late-January storm engulfed them in a deluge, compelling them to hasten indoors. Where, as a journalist with many connections, Natalia had twisted a few arms and found herself in possession of a certain room key. One of Granger's red lines thus avoided. Perhaps, though, not the most important one. Not that either of them cared.

'Have you had many lovers?' It was a question typical of her Russian directness. They were entwined on the bed, the large double-duvet, previously cast aside, temporarily back in favour.

'You wouldn't believe me if I told you.'

'Are you married?' She was drawing imaginary patterns on his chest with an index finger.

'It's a long story.' Ross's fingers were slowly weaving their way in and out of Natalia's long, chestnut hair.

'We have time.'

He leant over to kiss her, but she turned away, playfully.

'Answer my question.'

Ross began kissing her fingers, one by one. Slowly, carefully, he placed more kisses on her wrist, then up her arms to her shoulders. Finally, he kissed the soft skin of her neck, just beneath the chin. She let out a soft moan.

'You were saying?'

'About Mrs. Calum,' she purred, but by then they had become distracted.

'I was married once,' he announced sometime later. 'We met at university. Loughborough, in the middle of rural English nowhere. A great place to study, if you're into athletics.'

'So?'

Ross exhaled loudly. He lay on his back on the bed and stared at the ceiling. Time to remember his lines.

'Married at twenty-one, separated at twenty-three, divorced one year later.'

'With what reason?' Tiny dimples appeared on her cheeks as she smiled.

'Me, mainly. I screwed up. More accurately, I screwed around. Plus, just when I was making a name for myself on the track, I failed a drugs test. I'd reached the national squad. Sandra, my then-wife, had been selected as well. The Sydney Olympics of 2000 were less than a year away, and I blew it. Team GB banned me for four years. I still believe it was unfair. I'd been prescribed nasal drops and they contained steroids. I hadn't a clue. I should have declared I was taking them, but I didn't: it was my own stupid mistake. I lost the appeal. It finished my athletics career and ended my marriage. Sandra went to Sydney and won Bronze. I stayed home, drank too much, and quit athletics. Life's a bitch.'

There. No stage prompts required.

'Life can be complicated, certainly.'

'Perhaps. I was angry for a long time. Bitter. Resentful, even. I lost focus and began drifting all over the place.'

'You have children?'

'No. Parenthood doesn't combine too well with being a triathlete.'

'A triathlete? Impressive.'

'Sandra was from the start. I only took it up after we split, when I'd fallen from grace. I was a middle-distance runner originally. She was a good all-rounder. Still is, to be fair. Her career progressed well, especially without me. Anyway, enough about me. What about you?'

'What about me?'

He sensed a coldness. Instinctively, he nestled his own body closer under the duvet.

'A bit of the Natalia Life Story would be good. Who exactly is this beautiful woman in the bed next to me? What about her husband? Does he treat her nicely? Those would be good places to start.'

The dimples on her cheeks disappeared, her face set cold: furrowed frown lines appeared on her forehead.

'Natalia Borisenko is successful journalist working for Rossiyskaya Gazeta,' she began. Coldly and clinically at first, then with more confidence. 'In Istanbul, Natalia is foreign correspondent. She is married to Oleg Usmanov, ordinarily a man of only mild importance in Russian Embassy here in Turkey. Do not be deceived. My husband is powerful and dangerous man, with powerful and dangerous friends. As the wife of such powerful man, and mother of his child, I have no option but at all times to be happy and completely faithful. Do we understand each other?'

'Possibly. Why?'

'Because it is necessary to have this understanding, assuming we are to continue with this, how should I say? With this kind of tennis coaching.' She gave a watery smile. 'Regardless of how badly he treats me in private, in public, I can only ever be the faithful and happy wife of Oleg Usmanov. This is what is expected.'

'Except that you and I are currently sharing a bed.'

She smiled more fully this time.

'Yes. It is deliciously complicated, don't you think? This way, I do not embarrass Oleg. Yet this way, I can also both improve my tennis and screw the infamous former British athlete known as Calum Ross.'

As with Granger and his red lines, with Natalia, there were ground rules. She explained these later when they were preparing to leave.

'Do not contact me. Not by phone or by email. Trust me, Oleg or his people will be listening. Sometimes, I may call. You will not know the number. Please, never return my call.'

'But I want us to meet again. Like this. Like we have today. How can this be possible if I can't call?'

'I want this as much as you. Perhaps more. However, my husband is jealous and dangerous man. It is necessary to be cautious. We must pretend we do not know each other. If you see me at school, do not talk unless I speak first. Viktor is intelligent. He will see our romance if we let him. He is his father's son. In matters of the heart he will confide in his father, I know these things.'

'So, I have to wait until you call me, is that how it's going to work?' There was a hint of sadness to his voice.

'There's a WhatsApp group I use with journalists. We don't know each other, but we share information, some we use, some we ignore. Join this group. Use a different name. We can use a simple code.'

'What sort of code?'

'One I use when necessary to be careful. Journalists like football. So, you and I can send messages about football games. Any day we mention is always one day ahead. If we want to meet Sunday, my message will mention a game on Monday. If not convenient, you respond with 'cancel' in your message. See, it is simple. We meet here, at tennis club: always at the same time, always on practice courts and in tennis clothes. It is better that way. Trust me, with Oleg, it is better that way.'

'How do I contact you?'

'You don't. Never directly. Send a WhatsApp. Ask if anyone can get tickets to the next Besiktas game here in Istanbul. I will then call. On the phone, we never, ever, use names. You don't call me Natalia. I never call you Calum.'

'We will be like spies.'

'Be careful what you wish for, Calum.'

Chapter 12

Three months ago, Switzerland

Usmanov's growing bald patch meant he was seldom without a hat of some description. For his six-monthly visit to the Swiss mountains in the canton of Vaud, he favoured a black, woollen variety designed specifically for harsh, Alpine winters. Although the ski season was more than halfway through, Usmanov knew from experience that a visit to Villars in March could bring unpredictable weather. Not that he had either the time or inclination to ski himself.

The journey was invariably a testament to Swiss efficiency. At Geneva airport, his diplomatic passport enabled him to be waved through the formalities. With his only luggage a shoulder bag that never went in the hold, he was typically in the Arrivals concourse within minutes of landing. From there, he would stride out of the secure area, past waiting family members, ski representatives and drivers milling around expectantly, and make his way to the airport railway station a short distance away. Precisely one hour and twenty minutes later, the train having meandered around the north side of Lake Geneva, past small vineyards set on steep slopes leading down to the lake, he would arrive at Aigle station in the canton of Vaud where his next mode of transport would be waiting – a rack-and-pinion, metre-gauge mountain railway. Within five minutes of transferring from one to another, it, too, would be on the move, more sedately and gently than its mainline cousin, navigating firstly the streets and traffic of Aigle, past close-packed houses with their neat but tiny gardens, alongside a few small vineyards before the final, short climb to the mountain resort of Villars.

Usmanov liked to plan these trips to arrive late morning on a Saturday, allowing plenty of time, once the train had reached the terminus in the centre of Villars, to find a taxi for the short ride to the Michelin-starred restaurant above the village at the far end of town. A short drive, also, from the international boarding school from where his lunch guest would also be taking a taxi. The Collège Alpin Beau Soleil was one of the most prestigious, and certainly one of the most expensive, private boarding schools in the world. Its alpine location, combined with the eye-watering fees, allowed its privileged pupils the chance to engage in activities – not simply skiing – that most children their age could only dream of. Madeleine Simpson had been headmistress for over ten years and had a fearsome reputation. Even Usmanov, a man reputed to be able to strike fear into the hearts of men simply by means of a frown, was wary of her.

That particular Saturday, a heavy overnight fall of snow already cleared and the sun shining brightly, Usmanov stepped from the train and went in search of a taxi. The driver, if he was unenthusiastic about the prospect of such a short fare, didn't show it. Less than ten minutes later, Usmanov was entering the hotel, pleased to learn that his guest had arrived moments earlier and was seated at their table. Usmanov removed his hat and checked that his jacket and lambswool sweater weren't rumpled by the journey, before proceeding to join her in the dining room.

'I shall miss these lunches,' Simpson said sometime later, raising her glass of *vin mousseux* in a toast. Usmanov clinked his with hers and nodded. As ever, her appearance that day was immaculate.

'As will I,' Usmanov added with a hint of regret. Even though Simpson was undeniably an elegant and refined woman, despite Usmanov's repeated efforts to be charming, she had remained a closed book as far as his attempts to forge a closer relationship were concerned.

Over the course of nine previous meetings, they had established something of a routine. They would choose the smaller of two lunchtime tasting menus, always sampling the recommended wines to match each course. Slowly and deliberately, they would discuss the school and its achievements, talk appreciatively about the generous benefaction that Usmanov had bestowed on the school by virtue of several large, anonymous donations, only eventually circling around to the welfare of the young man in question: his achievements, his issues, her assessment of his potential, and the options for the young man, once he'd left. Usmanov had, somewhat uncharacteristically, got into the habit on these occasions of taking notes, knowing that he would be expected to give a detailed verbal report at a later stage, not trusting his memory to remember all the salient facts that his friend would demand. For this, he used a small, pocket-sized notebook covered in soft, black leather, a cherished present from his late father.

'There is one issue that I believe you should be aware of,' Simpson said towards the end, once the waiter had cleared the cheese plates. She dabbed the edge of her mouth with the folded corner of a table napkin before continuing. Usmanov raised an eyebrow and tilted his head, draining the last mouthful of Humagne Rouge from his wineglass.

'At Collège Alpin Beau Soleil, we pride ourselves in running a successful, mixed boarding school. All of our young adults, men or women, are equal members of our educational community. We deliberately do not have mixed boarding houses. However, there are plenty of opportunities for the young to develop confidence in themselves.' She looked at him over her wineglass, both hands holding the fine crystal as she chose her words. 'Their sexual orientation, in particular.' She shuffled in her chair, adjusting her position awkwardly.

'I see,' Usmanov said once she had finished a short while later, tugging at his goatee beard whilst scribbling furiously in his notebook. 'I don't suppose that there's any room for ambiguity?'

'None. There was . . .' She looked at the table as if searching for sudden inspiration. 'An *incident,* shall we say, recently, when there was no ambiguity. We've dealt with it, we've moved on, but to answer your question, the answer is a categoric no.'

It was only some time later, whilst Usmanov was staring fixedly at Lake Geneva from his train seat, that the anxiety caused by Madeleine Simpson's unexpected disclosure gradually began to subside. This plot twist that Simpson had unexpectedly revealed might turn out to his advantage. Perhaps it might even strengthen the whole *maskirovka*?

He picked up his mobile device and began scrolling through his unread messages. There was nothing of any consequence until he reached a mail from Sergei Borodin. He felt his stomach muscles tighten as he read the message.

Nicolai Kozlov was once again working for Yasenevo. Borodin had appointed him his special investigator!

On every level, this was bad news. For Usmanov personally and for the deception that was now underway. Kozlov would find every opportunity to probe and investigate Usmanov, of that he was in no doubt. With stolen SVR funds sitting in Usmanov's private Swiss bank account, he had to hope that he could keep Kozlov at bay for long enough to avoid the operation going pear-shaped.

For the first time in a long time, Usmanov felt vulnerable. The stakes had been now been raised. If he was found guilty of treachery and deceit by his oldest foe, then it wouldn't matter how many friends he had in high places, he would be a dead man, of that he was in no doubt.

He checked his watch. He would make his connection at Lausanne with time to spare. Perhaps it was just as well he had planned to make a little diversion to visit the Gnomes of Zurich after all?

Chapter 13

Two months ago, Istanbul

The weather was mild, the wind for once calm. Ross, dressed in his tennis-coach whites with a blue zippered fleece on top, checked his watch. Natalia was five minutes late. He removed an overstuffed tennis bag from his shoulder and laid it on the ground next to a large bucket of practice balls. Tennis was their cover, Ross happy to act his part to the hilt.

He waited for another ten minutes. Then, just as he was about to write her off as a no-show, there she was. Waving an arm enthusiastically as she half-ran, half-walked in his direction, a bulky racket bag in one hand and a bottle of water in the other. Even with her hair tied at the back, the red hues and copper undertones shone through.

'Calum, I am sorry,' she said, shuffling the tennis bag under her left arm and extending a hand in greeting. 'There were complications.'

'It's no problem. I'm glad you made it. Is everything all right?'

Natalia unzipped her jacket and quickly began stretching leg muscles. 'Fine,' she said loudly. Then, in a much lower voice. 'Today we must play tennis. One of Oleg's men has followed me. I tried to lose him. However, he is there, in the corner – no, don't look, pretend we are having a lesson.'

'Okay,' Ross said, choosing a racket from his bag before rolling several balls down to one end of the court. 'You take that end,' he said, pointing to where the balls had come to rest, 'and let's warm up.'

A while later, he stopped. 'Try changing your grip,' he called out. Natalia made a few attempts to get this right, but not to Ross's satisfaction. 'Let me show you.' He came to the net and she followed suit. Holding her racket hand, he gently twisted the handle. 'Like this, not,' he continued, twisting it back a little, 'like that. Show me.'

She demonstrated the revised technique, he both nodding and frowning in equal measure, all the while speaking in a stage whisper.

'Does your husband suspect something?'

'I think not,' she muttered. 'He suspects everyone. This is one of his games. God, I need to escape, Calum. The way he treats me is no longer tolerable.'

'Go back to the baseline.' Ross's voice was loud once again. 'I'll send a few easy balls your way to practise. Here we go.'

A while later, it was time, he announced, to practise her serve. He came down her end with the bucket of balls and stood alongside her.

'I want to take you to bed, Calum. I'm sorry about this,' she whispered when he was in earshot.

'Practice working on throwing the ball higher. Look, let me show you.' He stood behind her with his body pressed against hers, taking her left hand in his, his right holding the racket hand. 'Try to throw the ball up a few times and I will guide your other arm.' Then, softly. 'Run away with me, Natalia. Come with me back to England. I want to protect you, to love you. I don't want us to be apart any longer.' Losing concentration whilst Ross was whispering in her ear, she sent tennis balls all over the court.

'Forget the serve,' Ross said loudly. 'Practise throwing the ball up. See how high you can get it.'

'I cannot simply escape my husband,' she grunted, attempting to practise what Ross had coached her. 'It is not possible. He will kill me. It's the way he works.'

'That's better. Try repeating that. Good, and again. Very good. Now combine that with bringing your racket hand up and behind your head before hitting the ball. Let me show you how.'

As Ross demonstrated his serve technique, he spoke with urgency.

'There has to be a way to control your husband. To stop him making your life such a misery. Is he ever unfaithful?'

'Of course he's unfaithful. A man like Oleg has many mistresses. I know these things.'

'You have a go,' he said loudly, stepping back before speaking in hushed tones once more. 'Then the man will have secrets. Find them. Secrets that can be used against him. Secrets that will ensure he keeps away from you forever.'

Chapter 14

Two weeks ago, Moscow

Oleg Usmanov received his summons in the usual manner. It arrived having bypassed the formal Russian diplomatic channels. It had also circumvented the Russian foreign intelligence services' protocols. That last part had been easy: his old friend had once been a senior KGB officer. A man who knew a lot of the tricks. Especially of the type that agents needed to deploy to avoid official scrutiny.

The summons came in two parts. Both unconventional. Both easy to decode and reassemble. The first was simple. An email sent to Usmanov by an international courier company. It informed him that a package was going to be delivered to his home address the next day, between 14.30 and 15.30. It required Usmanov to press a button confirming that the package delivery time and date were acceptable. Which he duly did. The second part required Usmanov to visit a certain poetry page on Facebook and search for a particular post. Then, scanning the poem attached to the post, he took the first letter from each alternate line to create the message. Hiding in plain sight, his father used to call it. He smiled when he saw the location. The Four Seasons hotel, Moscow. He checked his watch. He would catch the Aeroflot flight just after midnight out of Istanbul. It would give him roughly four hours of sleep on the plane. It had the bonus of getting him to Sheremetyevo early in the morning. Before the morning peak of Moscow's traffic madness.

No sooner had he placed his bulky, six-foot frame into his assigned business class seat than his eyes closed and he was instantly asleep. Out of habit, he wedged his head between the edge of the seat and the window to save his neck from jarring. He came to the surface briefly after takeoff, reclining his seat as far as it went, before falling back into deeper slumber. Thereafter, he remembered nothing more until twenty minutes before landing. This time a flight attendant was leaning over him. Blonde, with her hair coiled in a bun and with a pretty smile, she was pressing the buttons on the panel beside him to revert his seat into an upright position. Her face looked vaguely familiar. He smiled thinly and she asked if there was anything he wanted before landing. He declined and drifted back to sleep again. He woke for the final time as the plane's rear wheels hit the runway. Safely on the ground and taxiing to the assigned gate, Usmanov switched on his mobile phone. There was an email from the courier company. Reconfirming delivery that afternoon between 14.30 and 15.30.

By the time his driver pulled up outside his Moscow apartment, it was after six in the morning. Time for a shower and a little self-indulgence. He had invited Elena, a young researcher from SVR's headquarters in Yasenevo, to join him for a working breakfast. She was researching a piece about the refugee crisis. In particular, its continued impact both in the Balkans and across the wider European Union. It was fertile ground for SVR planners, keen to sow seeds of division and mistrust. Which ostensibly was why Usmanov had asked Elena to meet him in person during this fleeting return visit to Moscow. The pair had something of a history of working together. Usually, in very close proximity, as it happened.

Elena left the apartment shortly before noon, the majority of her debriefing having taken place between the sheets of Usmanov's king-sized bed. It was just gone one-thirty when Usmanov, freshly showered and wearing one of his better suits and a light tan overcoat, stepped out of his front door.

The driver dropped his distinctive-looking passenger at the Ritz-Carlton hotel, Usmanov telling him he would call later when his business was concluded. He strode confidently into the hotel, through the security checkpoint. Once safely in the lobby, he stopped and turned casually, checking that his driver had indeed departed. Satisfied that he was now on his own, he moved down a side corridor, out of sight of the lobby area. He deftly removed his overcoat, reversed it so that the navy-blue inner lining was on the outside, and from a side pocket took a matching blue cloth cap which he placed on his head. Moments later, a much less distinctive Oleg Usmanov emerged from the hotel's side entrance. It was a sunny spring day, a slight chill still in the air as he began the short walk to the Four Seasons hotel, less than five minutes away. Up ahead, painted in the same claret red as the Kremlin walls, the façade and twin spires of the State Historical Museum stood guard over Manezhnaya Square. To the right, marked by the circular turret positioned at the corner of the Kremlin wall, lay the entrance to Red Square. He crossed the busy road, weaving in front of police barricades that marked the start of the pedestrian-only area ahead. The entrance to the hotel was on the left.

The sandstone-coloured hotel complex, originally built in the time of Stalin's rule in 1935, was actually a modern reproduction. The historic Hotel Moskva was demolished in 2004, replaced with, in many respects, a carbon copy but with modern features that included plumbing that worked, underground parking and the very latest technology. Usmanov removed his cloth cap before entering the hotel, passing through another security checkpoint to be greeted by one of the hotel managers who recognised him immediately. He, in turn, escorted Usmanov to a bank of elevators to one side of the lobby area that would take him directly to the seventh floor. Upon arrival on the VIP floor, the manager led him to a room with the label 'Pozharsky Royal Suite' above its door. The manager pressed the discreetly-placed doorbell, which chimed faintly before, seconds later, the door opened and Usmanov was ushered inside.

He was greeted by two athletic-looking, muscle-clad men of indeterminate age: ex-military or, more likely, specialist close-protection officers. Once the door was closed, Usmanov was subjected to a thorough body search, rough hands leaving no parts untouched. Collars and cuffs were checked for hidden needles and weapons whilst the contents of all pockets were placed on a table by the door and examined in minute detail. As for his phone, this was placed in a lead-lined box, the lid being sealed tightly closed. Finally, handheld scanning devices were used to check for hidden electrical or metallic devices, particular care being taken to examine Usmanov's shoes. Determining him to be clean, the two men stood back whilst Usmanov adjusted his clothing. He was then beckoned by one of them to follow him into the room itself.

The suite was enormous, the size of several two-bedroom apartments that most Muscovites lived in, all joined together. Over and above the elegant soft furnishings, the luxurious carpets and exquisite wall hangings, the most impressive thing was the view. From several large windows – including from a small private terrace – were views over the Kremlin, Red Square and, to the left, the multicoloured onion domes of St Basil's Cathedral.

'Oleg Ivanovich!' called a familiar voice from behind him a few moments later. The President of the Russian Federation advanced into the room, smiling as he embraced his old friend. They gave each other a protracted hug before the President pulled away, still holding Usmanov's arms. 'Why, look at you! You look more like Vladimir Ilyich every day.' The two men laughed. Despite their years of friendship, dating back to their school days, Usmanov couldn't help but be intimidated by the power and office that his friend now held.

'That's what my son says,' Usmanov retorted. 'You, however, look better than ever.' They separated and the President gestured Usmanov towards one of the sofa chairs set around a low, wooden coffee table. They were alone, the hired muscle having retreated, closing the door silently behind them as they left.

'Tea?' Usmanov's oldest friend asked, pouring a cup from a pot brewing on the side.

'Thank you,' Usmanov said, accepting the offered drink. 'So, my friend, how are you?'

'Fit and well, thank you. How are the family?'

'They are doing fine. Viktor is playing chess with promise. I don't see them as much as I would like. Too much travelling. Family life is not uncomplicated, as I'm sure you appreciate.'

'There are always distractions.' The Russian President clasped his friend on the shoulder as he placed his teacup on the table and sat down. Usmanov took this as his cue to sit. The two men looked at each other, eyebrows raised, both smiling.

'Do you know how rare this is? To escape from over there.' He nodded at the window giving on to the Kremlin. 'There, I am always under constant supervision. To spend an hour like this, without fear of interruption, somewhere totally private: it is very satisfactory.'

'I suppose you came by car?'

'No. When they rebuilt the Moskva hotel, they created an underground garage. One or two of the old Kremlin tunnels thought to have been permanently sealed or forgotten about are, very unofficially, back in operation.'

'How very convenient.'

'Precisely. Exceptionally convenient. Especially when there are delicate matters to be discussed. In particular of a private nature, when one doesn't need various officials listening in.'

'Like today.'

'Indeed. Tell me, what news. About the young man I mean?'

'Well, mostly good.'

Usmanov then proceeded to paint a deceptively lifelike portrayal in various hues, in the manner of a skilful forger, the picture in most aspects appearing as close to the original artwork as possible. He described academic and sporting achievements that were all true to the fact, but danced around one subject with extreme care and finesse.

'Any girlfriends you are aware of?'

'Apparently none.'

Usmanov could feel his heart pounding, sweat seeping down the back of his neck. He had rehearsed these and similar lines over and over, consulting the notes he had made from his most recent conversation with Madeleine Simpson from within the pages of his leather-bound black notebook. The consequences if he got this particular bit wrong would be ruinous.

'Is the legend intact? No strangers starting to poke their noses where they shouldn't be?'

'Nothing to concern us so far. There are no links for anyone to pick up. Either back to you or to DESTINY. We have worked hard to cover all traces. That said, I did spot Yoshi Nathan at Geneva airport as I was leaving the other day.'

'Please tell me they, of all people, haven't picked up the scent?'

'I think we're safe. It was a random sighting. Geneva's a busy place for spies.'

'DESTINY's not been asking awkward questions? About her son, I mean.'

'Not that I've been made aware. As you know, she's not my agent. I'm not even supposed to know who she is.'

'It's for your protection. What you don't know, you can't tell others about. I admire and respect DESTINY enormously. There's an excellent chance she'll make it to the very top. That would be an amazing bonus.'

'Unbelievable.'

'There's enough money?'

'Everything is taken care of,' Usmanov said, the knot in his stomach beginning finally to relax. 'The money is untraceable but yes. The money is the least of our worries.'

'Very good,' the President replied, winking at his friend, a moment's secret shared. He drew forward suddenly, forearms on knees.

'You remind me. On a different subject, a word to the wise,' he said with some gravity. 'The woman you have been spending time with here. Elena, I think her name is. She may be good between the sheets, but there is concern at the Lubyanka that she might have allegiances with the DGSE. I'd be very wary. From one old friend to another.' He tapped the side of his nose with a forefinger.

Usmanov, if he looked surprised, didn't show it.

'Duly noted. Is someone taking care of matters, or do I need to close the file? Permanently, that is?'

'I don't think anything dramatic is called for. Yet. The French have been trying to infiltrate our networks for years. We can't allow them to use you to steal our secrets. Now, my friend, we must say our goodbyes. Are you heading back to Turkey tonight?'

'There's a flight at five-forty this evening. Assuming, as ever, that I beat the traffic.'

'Which airport?'

'Sheremetyevo.'

The President looked at his watch.

'I'll have one of my drivers plus an escort at the front of the hotel in ten minutes. You'll make your flight with time to spare. View it as a perk of having a friend in high office. Give my love to Natalia,' he said, and the two men exchanged a hug. 'How is she, by the way?' He was walking to the door as he spoke.

'To be honest, a bit distracted.' The President turned one final time to look at this friend.

'By another man?'

Usmanov nodded.

'A British teacher.'

'Having an occasional Elena is one thing. Good or bad, they can be discarded or dealt with. However, when someone with as many secrets as you have has a spouse playing away from home – well, alarm bells start to ring.'

'I know. It's a problem I'm about to deal with.'

With that, the door opened in front of him and the two close-protection officers escorted the President of the Russian Federation out of the room.

Chapter 15

Ten days ago, Istanbul

'Elope with me.'

'I can't. I told you many times before. It's too complicated.'

'You can. I will protect you, I promise.'

Without responding, she kissed him. First on the end of his nose. It was a feather-light peck. Then again on the lips, with the same lightness of touch. They were lying naked, side by side, facing each other. It was only a few days before Ross was due to finish his contract.

'I love your passion, Calum Ross. I love you wanting to look after me.' She touched him gently with the tip of her finger as she spoke, tracing imaginary lines on his face. 'Why not stay here? Come and live in Istanbul.'

Ross laughed. For a man on a mission, the one thing he hadn't bargained on was falling in love.

'You and I can't keep living a secret life out of a hotel room. You need to get away from Istanbul. Away from that bully of a husband.' The last time the two lovers had met two weeks ago, Natalia had arrived with a bruised face and blackened eye from where Oleg had hit her. 'Come to England with me. Or anywhere. We can start a new life together. It would be amazing.'

'You do not understand Oleg. If I elope, I told you, he will kill me. It is that simple. Russian men are vindictive. My husband will not tolerate such behaviour. On that matter, I know I am right.' She looked at him, her eyes searching his. 'He will also kill you, Calum. Of that, I, also, have no doubt.'

'Bring Viktor with you. Your husband won't do anything foolish to you if it risked harming his son, surely?'

She rolled onto her stomach, chin on her elbows, looking no longer at him but out the window, her eyes red and puffy.

'That would not work. Viktor is nearly seventeen and his father's son. If Viktor came with us, they would kill me and steal him back. I do not believe he would come with his mother.'

'Then leave without him. I will protect you.'

She rolled back to face him, tears rolling freely down her cheeks.

'What does your husband really do?' he asked later. 'You say he is well-connected. In what way, exactly?'

He was lying on his back, staring at the ceiling. She was on her side, resting her head on Ross's shoulder: his arm wrapped around her, both nestled under the duvet, eye contact intermittent. Moments of confession, as he liked to think of them.

'Oleg Usmanov is Russian spy,' Natalia said after a long pause. 'An important spy, working for Russian government. He keeps many secrets. Especially from me,' she said, with genuine venom. 'He pretends to work at Embassy, but that is, as you say in English, pure bullshit.' She pronounced this as "bull-sheet". 'Oleg is also unusual. He is old friend of our Russian President. They were at school together. My husband sometimes does special favours for his friend. He thinks I do not know about this, but he is a fool and forgets that I am journalist.'

'Wow!' Ross said, barely keeping the surprise from his voice. 'You kept that particular plot twist until the end.'

'It was not relevant.'

Ross stroked her shoulder with one hand, staring at the ceiling in thought.

'Yet it could be,' he said in time.

This caused them both to make eye contact.

'How?'

'A spy such as your husband, especially one as important and powerful as you say, will have secrets. By definition, it's his job.'

'You sound like a spy, Calum Ross.'

'I'll be anything I need if it encourages you to elope.'

She stared at the ceiling, biting her bottom lip, her eyes still. Then she turned her head towards him.

'I remember what you said that time a few weeks ago when we played proper tennis, not bedroom tennis.' She smiled thinly. 'Blackmailing Oleg Usmanov would be highly problematic. He would not appreciate such treatment. Respect, yes: like, no. Especially if it came from me.'

'Then think of a way around it. There has to be a way.'

They dressed in silence, once more back into their tennis gear. Ross stared at the view across the Bosphorus towards Asia.

'I shall miss Istanbul. This hotel, its special meaning, our time together.' Once more, there was a hint of sadness in his tone.

'I am thinking. There is special place in our house, here in Istanbul. Oleg's private space. In the wall, behind a big picture, he has this safe. It is not unusual. But there is also second safe. One that Oleg thinks is so secret he believes not even I know about. It is for his most private papers.' She caught him staring at her in bewilderment and laughed for the first time in a while. 'Don't look at me like this! I am journalist! I always find the truth about things. Especially about men.'

'Can you open the safe?'

'No. His secretary at the Consulate is only person he trusts. When he is away, she visits the house to deal with private papers. Especially any needing to bypass Embassy scrutiny.'

'Are there a lot like that?'

'She is coming tomorrow. Oleg is in the Balkans. Well, that is what he tells me, what do I know? He could be anywhere.'

'But he won't be at home.'

'Not unless his plans change.'

'She is authorised to open this safe?'

'Probably. She will know how it it is possible. The Russian way is to have back-up procedures. She is my husband's.'

'Are you sure?'

'Positive. I have made it my business to have leverage over this woman. She has a secret lover. A French man. They meet often, when my husband is away. I have photographic evidence.'

'Wow!'

'I keep telling you, Calum. I am journalist, I know these things about people, it is my business.'

'Okay, so you convince her to open the safe. Will you be able to look inside without your husband knowing?'

'That might be problematic. Oleg Usmanov can be highly devious. He will lay traps I do not know about. Hopefully, I find something. Treasure, even. If so, it won't matter if he knows it was me. By then, he'll have too much to lose.'

Chapter 16

A week ago, Washington

Hidden amongst the leafy suburbs of Fairfax County, Virginia, on the south side of the Potomac River, lay the sprawling complex of the George Bush Center for Intelligence. In the community of Langley, this was the headquarters of the US's Central Intelligence Agency, fifteen minutes by car across the river from the White House. From the air, this sprawling complex looked more like a giant car park set amongst the trees than the global hub of American covert espionage activities. Closed to the public, its inner core accessible through multiple layers of ever-increasing scrutiny, the maze of grey corridors with lockable doors appeared to be a hive of inactivity. Nowhere more so than on the fifth floor, the inner sanctum where the Directorate and their deputies had their offices.

Deputy Director of Operations, Nancy Turley was sitting in one corner of her anonymous-looking office with Herb Okumura, Europe, Middle-East & Africa section head in Turley's Operations group and a veteran field agent of over twenty-five years. They had just finished listening to a crystal-clear recording beamed by encrypted laser link from the US Embassy in Moscow via a National Security Agency listening station in Finland, the onward transmission verified and designated 'DDO eyes/ ears only'.

'Fucking incredible, Nancy!' Okumura, head in hands, was still staring fixedly at the speaker on the table. 'Unbelievable.'

'Beyond our wildest dreams, eh?'

Seven years earlier, shortly before the Toronto-based Four Seasons hotel group opened its doors in Moscow on the site of the former Moskva hotel, it had been Okumura who had proposed secreting state-of-the-art listening devices throughout the building, which, by that stage, was nearing the end of a ten-year reconstruction programme. The idea was to use highly sophisticated wireless routers, technically part of the hotel's Wi-Fi system, to permit passive eavesdropping to be undertaken without fear of detection from signal scanners. The technical boffins in Langley's research labs were confident that this could be achieved and Okumura was given responsibility for overseeing implantation. It proved to be an immediate success, the NSA enthusiastically monitoring and disseminating conversations as and when they were deemed of interest.

'You don't think it was a spoof?' Turley continued.

'No way! I know both these people's voices. I know the way they talk, even to each other. That was the A-team, make no mistake.'

'Should we at least do a voice analysis?'

'Sure, Nancy, but not right this minute.'

'Your take on this?'

'We've had tabs on Usmanov on and off for years. He runs a tight and loyal ship in a part of the world that is amongst the world's leakiest and most deadly. We've been trying to penetrate his network for years. With little success, I might add, although we managed to turn one of his agents in Lebanon a couple of years ago. It didn't last long – the woman concerned was found floating in the Mediterranean with a single bullet between the eyes about two weeks after we recruited her. In amongst everything else, Usmanov's been making these weird, occasional day trips to Switzerland. We never figured out why. A few weeks ago, we increased surveillance. On his most recent visit, he met with the headmistress of a glitzy school in the mountains. Took her out for lunch. We thought at the time that Usmanov might have a child we didn't know about there. There's another son of his at an equally smart school in Istanbul. Seems we were wrong. You heard the conversation just now. The kid isn't his – it's the Russian President's. He, naturally, doesn't make the trip himself, so he sends his oldest friend to find out how the kid's doing instead.'

'I wonder who the mother is?'

'Sounds like this DESTINY person. I smell the whiff of a Russian mole in the air.'

'Me too, Herb. The question is, who's she working for? God, I hope it's not us.'

'I doubt it. We've trawled through our dirty linen so many times over the years. My money's on the Israelis.'

'Why?'

'Why else was Yoshi Nathan circling? Perhaps Tel Aviv's become suspicious of someone they think might be a mole.'

'You've got to find out. Talk to this headmistress. Put a little squeeze on if you have to. We've got to know who the kid is.'

'She won't know who the real father is, I bet.'

'Of course not. Look, the President and this woman have a lovechild. It's one huge fucking secret. The mother, DESTINY, is either determined to become a spy – or is somehow persuaded – so she puts her career first and gives the kid up for adoption. I would. How else would they be able to protect the identity of the child? It wouldn't be the first time a political figure gave away her newborn to further her career. It would be useful to learn the adopted parents' names.'

'You think the adoption papers will reveal the identity of the parents?'

'You've got to be kidding! You heard the two Russians. They've gone to huge lengths to protect their backsides.'

'Interesting that the French are sniffing around Usmanov.'

'Never underestimate the DGSE, Herb, they're cunning as hell. It may be some random attempt by the French to ensnare Usmanov, just like we're trying to do. However, if they've got an inside track, I'm much more worried.'

'Perhaps DESTINY is French?'

'Perhaps, but don't forget: Usmanov runs most of Moscow's agent networks from the Balkans to Afghanistan. Every spy in the western world wants a bit of what he's got.'

The two sat in silent contemplation for a while. Eventually, it was Turley who spoke.

'Tell you what. Talk to the Brits. Share extracts of the recording with them. I'd be interested in their take on all of this. In particular, see if they know who this teacher of theirs is, the one who's supposedly screwing Usmanov's wife.'

Chapter 17

A week ago, Moscow

Sergei Borodin was well-acquainted with the Kremlin's imposing corridors. As the President's former Chief of Staff, he knew virtually every nook and cranny of this enormous fortified citadel, a complex of buildings that to this day retained an ability to threaten and intimidate. Now, as the director of the Russian Foreign Intelligence Service – the SVR as it was more commonly known – he was once more a frequent visitor to the historic building. His prior position and current status, although not absolving him of the requirement to be security-screened and body-searched like all visitors, allowed him some freedom of movement within the complex itself. When meeting the President, however, there was only so far that anybody could wander unattended before picking up an armed escort.

Having mounted the sweeping staircase to the upper level, Borodin was saluted at the top landing by a uniformed guard he recognised, and ushered into the first of two long corridors that would lead, eventually, to the President's office. The corridor, well over 100 metres, had both walls and its tall, arched ceiling painted in white. A long ribbon of scarlet-red carpet edged with a simple pattern covered the entire length of the wooden floor underfoot. As Borodin entered, the red carpet disappeared to a thin point in the distance. He strode down the centre line as many important people had surely done before him: past random paintings by various Russian artists; past the occasional door and an infrequent floor-to-ceiling window, the seemingly endless carpet propelling him hypnotically towards the end. Which was an illusion, since this particular end was simply an excuse for another uniformed guard to be standing to attention, saluting, ushering Borodin onwards yet further, this time towards a second corridor to one side. He was closer to his destination now, this corridor slightly shorter. A quick right turn at the end followed by a left, and he was walking into the President's outer office where two more security detail were standing to attention. They, too, saluted as Borodin was ushered into the waiting area. He didn't have to wait long.

'Sergei,' the President said, pulling the wooden floor-to-ceiling doors of his private office wide open, ushering his guest in with a wave of his arm. They shook hands warmly, the President directing Borodin to a sturdy mahogany table immediately behind him. For such a gilded, grand building, it was a stark and masculine presidential office. Beneath a white ceiling and a single, large chandelier, all the walls had been clad in the same dark-coloured wood as the meeting table. To give balance, the carpet was a lighter colour, the eight chairs set around the table also upholstered in a beige that matched a pair of simple curtain swags: however, neither of these attempts at lifting the mood succeeded. It was a dark and foreboding space. Not exactly what one needed having just completed the Kremlin Walk of Death, as someone had once called the long march down the carpeted corridor.

'Thank you for coming.'

'It's always a pleasure to return to the Kremlin. It feels like coming home.'

'One day, it could be your home.'

'I doubt that very much. I am too old – but we digress. How may I help?'

'I have a delicate matter in need of a safe pair of hands.'

'You have my full attention.'

'As you know, one of my oldest friends, Oleg Ivanovich, is a senior officer in one of your directorates.'

'Indeed. And unless you are about to say anything to the contrary, he is highly regarded. Some see him as a more-than-worthy successor to my position.'

'Good. I am pleased. In my position, I have to be careful not to show undue favouritism. Anyway, the matter, as I mentioned earlier, is delicate.'

'Tell me, in what way can I help?'

'Like his father, Oleg Ivanovich runs more agents and informants than most. Like you and I, he's been around long enough to know where the bodies are buried. One or two highly sensitive bodies spring to mind.' He arched one eyebrow in that way of his: part question, part knowing explanation.

'Naturally, he travels widely and is away from his family all the time. He confided in me recently that his wife, the journalist from Rossiyskaya Gazeta, has become somewhat distracted. With a British teacher. I never liked that woman. She has not been on-message with her written word. Oleg is man enough not to display too much concern at this admission of his wife's infidelity – none of us are saints.' He shrugged, openly splaying both hands. 'Anyway, Oleg, the professional that he is, has assured me he is taking matters into his own hands.'

The President looked down at his fingers, scraping a speck of dirt from under one nail.

'Sergei, on occasions like this, perhaps more should be done to protect our very best from themselves.'

'I see,' Borodin said, his elbows on the table and hands steepled together under his chin. 'I infer, from what you are not telling me, that there is a risk that certain information, if it was to be in any way mismanaged by this woman, might reflect badly on more than just himself, would that be fair?'

The Russian President said nothing, pursing his lips and shrugging his shoulders.

'I see. Well, this does indeed need careful handling.'

'Very good. This is a problem neither you nor I need to be wasting our energies on any further. Do we understand each other, Sergei?'

'Certainly.'

'Then get on to it right away. Time is of the essence. It is imperative that there are no Russian fingerprints anywhere near this, do I make myself clear?'

'Crystal.'

Chapter 18

Four days ago, Istanbul

At ten in the morning, Istanbul's Havalimani airport terminal was flooded with natural light and teeming with people. On the main concourse level, a vast glass and steel atrium, passengers bustled back and forth; some shopping, some sitting and waiting, others hastening towards their departure gate. Having cleared immigration and security, Ross was one of those taking a few moments for a final Turkish coffee, waves of sadness tinged with guilt washing over him as he reflected on his departure. He would miss Istanbul, and all that it meant. Regardless of his supposed mission, regardless of his desire to prove himself worthy to his British spymasters: Istanbul, and especially Natalia, had well and truly got under his skin.

Contact had been made only the once, a few days after he and Natalia had crossed red lines together. Ross had been running beside the Bosphorus in the late afternoon when the former soldier with the bad smoking habit appeared from nowhere. Ross's recruiter had listened, congratulated, encouraged, then departed, leaving Ross feeling at the same time comforted and disconnected. Apart from that one, brief injection of moral support, there had been no one obvious who had been sitting in the wings giving stage prompts; no seasoned agent cautioning him not to get too close to his source. Instead, he had felt on his own, compelled to trust his instincts, guilt nagging at the edges, the thought he might be using Natalia troubling him. The fact that he yearned to be with her, craved the smell of her chestnut hair, wanting to feel her skin next to his, whispering confidences and sharing secrets, had also been confusing and unexpected in equal measure. He came close at one stage to 'fessing up to the crime of leading a woman to bed under false pretences but had bottled out. His feelings for her weren't something to be ashamed of; he was guilty of no crime. Their passion was electric, their lovemaking raw and tender. This was, without question, the genuine article, no longer part of any staged performance.

Their last moments together had been an unexpected bonus. An end-of-day staff gathering, to say farewell to Ross and to welcome back the teacher who had been on maternity leave, was over. There had been cake and tea and lots of happy laughter, but after saying his goodbyes, it was time to clear his room. Perhaps even go for a final run. That was until he heard the gentle knocking on his door.

'You should not be leaving, Calum, without first saying proper goodbyes.'

There were tears welling as they crossed red lines for one final time.

'I brought a gift,' she said some time later, reaching into her handbag. It was a small, rectangular package wrapped in brown-patterned paper with a small red ribbon on the outside. Ross unwrapped the parcel to discover a pocket chess set: a wooden box, plain but intricately carved, hinged along one edge and with a flip-down latch on the opposite side.

'Keep it safe, Calum. It's special. One day I'll explain why. Now, open it.'

Inside, besides chess pieces, there was a tiny blue glass amulet on a thin, leather chain.

'It is Turkish good luck charm. A *nazar*. It keeps away the evil eye. You must wear it, Calum. Promise me.'

'Thank you. But I'm now embarrassed. I have nothing for you.'

'You bought me one too,' she said, taking an identical one from her bag to show him. 'See!'

As Ross sipped his coffee, listening to an announcement over the public address system, he touched his jacket, feeling the chess set nestled safely in an inner pocket. The amulet was safe around his neck, the glass cool against his skin.

'Mind if I join?'

If Ross felt any emotion at seeing him after all this time, he didn't show it. His unexpected guest arrived bearing a tray containing two cups brimming with Turkish coffee.

'It's a No Smoking airport, you know that?'

The man was left-handed, the task of depositing each cup and saucer made more challenging by dint of his missing fingertip.

'Today, we have caffeine instead of nicotine. Who gives a shit?'

'I'd given up on you, to be honest.' Ross inspected his onetime recruiter. The man was shorter than Ross, but solid, with lots of muscle. His jet-black hair was slicked to one side, and he wore a beard that was trimmed close by a razor.

'You've done well, matey,' the man said.

'How do you know?'

'We know. We also know that the woman's about to come to London. A final recce before the big leap. Good job, by the way. Everyone's proud of you.'

'I'd have appreciated a bit more support, to be frank.'

'No you wouldn't. Anyway, what you don't know, you can't tell. Besides, you've been doing great. I told you, we've been watching your back the whole time.'

'I never saw you once.'

'We must have been doing a good job, then.'

'What next?'

'No one's contacted you yet?'

'Not that I'm aware. Only you.'

'It won't be long, that's what we think. When it happens, just play along.'

'Have I been paid yet? It's only that I've seen nothing.'

The man reached inside his jacket and withdrew an envelope. It was from a bank in Switzerland that Ross had never heard of, addressed to him personally at some nondescript mailbox number in London that he'd never heard of either. Ross opened the envelope and took out a bank statement. It showed an account in his name with a balance of £60,000 in credit: six instalments of £10,000 monthly deposits.

'Wow!'

'You didn't think we'd cheat on you, did you?'

'I didn't know what to think, to be honest. How do I get this money out?'

'You make an appointment, visit the bank with your passport and some other means of identification, and the rest will be sorted.'

'Tax-free, right?'

The man said nothing, simply looked back at him blankly.

'Should I keep this?'

'No,' the man said, retrieving the statement and placing it in his pocket. 'Remember the bank's name. That's all you'll need.'

'I have a confession.'

'I'm listening.'

'This woman, Natalia. We've sort of become close.'

'We know.'

'Very close, in fact.'

'Like I said: we know. Your point is?'

'Is it a problem?'

'Why the fuck would it be a problem? It makes the chances of success even higher, doesn't it?'

'I thought I was meant to be acting out a part here, that's all.'

'Acting out a part or part of an act: who gives a shit? Nothing beats a true-life drama. Don't be a wazzock, Calum. Fall madly and deeply and shag away to your heart's content. Deliver the goods and we'll love you, regardless.'

'I'd like to be able to contact you from time to time.'

'You can't and you won't. The more you know, the more dangerous it is for all of us. We'll be watching. We haven't let you down yet, have we?'

'No.'

'Well then. Stop being a prat and remember why we picked you. We only choose the very best. You're lucky to be part of the cast for this show, trust me.'

Which was when the man stood, slapped Ross gently on the shoulder, and wandered off into the depths of the terminal. He'd hardly even touched his coffee.

Chapter 19

Three days ago, Shannon, Ireland

The Aer Lingus Airbus A320 banked a sweeping left turn to make its final approach to Shannon airport. Frances Riordan was relieved to hear the landing gear descending in readiness for arrival. She was not a good flyer. Even on these short trips, she found herself eager to be back on *terra firma*. The weather outside was grey and overcast, droplets of rain streaking past the plane's windows as they descended through the last of the cloud.

Despite the longer flight time, for reasons of weather alone she preferred MI6's quarterly trips to the Eastern Seaboard to these ad-hoc meetings in some back-of-beyond location closer to home. The urgent request from Okumura had only been made two days ago. After much shuffling of the diaries on both sides, they had agreed to meet halfway at a CIA safe house that they'd used once before, a bleak and uninteresting property close to the equally bleak and uninteresting County Clare shoreline, about thirty minutes by chauffeur-driven limousine from Shannon airport. As the plane taxied to its gate, they passed several private jets standing in a line on the apron. Riordan casually wondered which of these might have been the one that had ferried Okumura out of Washington's private jet terminal at Reagan National airport.

'Frances,' Okumura said, opening the rickety wooden door at the side of the property to greet her a short time later. Riordan had long ago dispensed with the confusion of whether or not to be kissed by her American business-cousin by always extending a hand in greeting. She was uncomfortable in most kinds of social situation; the handshake she gave was Okumura oddly limp, her unnaturally large hands momentarily lifeless.

'What a perfectly hideous place this is, Herb. I remember it from last time. Miles from anywhere. One blink and you'd miss it.'

'Sounds the ideal place for a safe house, then,' he said with a grin. 'Come on in. The coffee's fresh in the pot and the housekeeper's made a tray of food for us to pick on if you're hungry. Feel free to make yourself comfortable, grab whatever you'd like and I'll be out the back when you're ready.'

The tray of food had been prepared by an American housekeeper, without question. The ready-prepared pastrami sandwiches, at least an inch thick, were crammed full-to-bursting with layers of brined meat. The make-your-own options included rolls and bagels, a plate of sliced tomatoes, a plate of sliced meats, several four-inch squares of processed cheese in different shades of yellow and orange arranged in heap, tiny plastic packs of butter and sachets of ketchup and mustard. To one side, an ice bucket full of sodas and colas of just about every make and model plus a selection of potato crisps – or chips, as they were labelled. Riordan placed two chocolate-chip cookies and a sugar-dusted chocolate brownie on a plate, poured herself a mug of coffee from a large Thermos with its push-down top, and then looked around to assess seating options.

'Where would you like me?'

'Wherever you want.'

She chose a chair that gave a good view over the water's edge. Riordan had two subjects on her list but, since Okumura had called this particular meeting, she let him begin proceedings first.

'I want you to listen to something,' he said, fiddling with a remote-control unit. From hidden speakers came the recorded excerpt from Usmanov's recent secret meeting at the Four Seasons Hotel in Moscow.

'Impressive technology, Herb,' she said at one point. 'To get this level of quality and to have avoided Russian scanners, I mean. It's a credit to the Agency.'

Okumura smiled but didn't respond. They listened right to the end before he stopped the playback.

'Do you have any idea who this DESTINY is?'

'Not at the moment,' he replied, taking a bite out of a pastrami sandwich. 'We wondered if you might, now you've heard it.'

'Sadly, no. But the rest is fascinating. How old is this recording?'

'A couple of days, no more.'

'Are you able to share the transcripts with us? I'm sure one or two people in Vauxhall Cross will find this fascinating.'

'Sure. In the interests of the Special Relationship. For very limited eyes only.'

'Naturally. What do you know about Usmanov?'

'Probably about the same as you, give or take. Why?'

'Because he's become a person of extreme interest to us, of late.' She looked up as she said this, the movement causing both to eyeball the other. 'We have had an operation in planning for a few months, about to kick off for real in the next twenty-four hours.'

'With Usmanov?'

'Concerning Usmanov. Or rather, ORION as we prefer to call him. We're heavily invested. It's all part of an operation we're running called WATCHKEEPER.'

'Does the recording change anything?'

'Strengthens, actually. There's a lot of very sensitive information at stake.'

'Is this teacher that's mentioned part of it? Do you know who he is?'

Riordan didn't reply, instead breaking off a corner of brownie and eating it deliberately slowly.

'Were you planning to invite Langley to join this party of yours?'

'It was actually on my list of things to discuss with you today, Herb. Full and open access to ORION's material – if, as and when. The Special Relationship, in action.'

'We'd sure as hell like to know about DESTINY. In particular, which side of whose fence she's sitting on.'

'I agree. Your recording makes the imperative to recruit ORION only greater.'

'Let me ask you something. Were you aware of ORION's infrequent trips to Switzerland before you heard any of this?'

Riordan took a bite of brownie and wiped her fingers and mouth with a tissue before replying.

'Let's simply say we've been interested in ORION for quite some time.'

'And you've no guesses who the child is?'

'Not at the moment. However, we may be getting close.'

'How?'

'I wouldn't expect you to discuss operational details with me. All I'll say is that it's work in progress.'

'Jeez, Frances, can't we at least help each other on this one? We need to max out our chances of success, surely?'

'Be patient. WATCHKEEPER's a clever operation with several complicated moving parts. Barring unforeseen events, I'd rate our chances as good.'

'I sincerely hope so,' said Okumura. 'I got people back in Langley who are shitting themselves, you'd better believe it. No agency likes a mole hunt. Yours or mine especially. They only ever end badly.'

'Don't we know it. It's old hands like the two of us who carry the scars, let's not forget that.'

Chapter 20

Three days ago, Istanbul

The road from Kapikule on the Turkish-Bulgarian border back to Istanbul had long since been made into a dual carriageway, the traffic at such an early hour of the morning mercifully light. Usmanov had used the outward leg to the border crossing to debrief a Russian agent who'd recently finished an assignment in the Syrian city of Raqqa. The woman had flown into Istanbul airport the night before, from Beirut via Cyprus. With the agent finally installed safely on a night train to Bucharest, Usmanov had slept in the back of the Mercedes saloon the whole of the three-hour return journey. By the time the driver turned into the gated entrance to Usmanov's family residence, it was shortly after four in the morning.

Usmanov slipped quietly into the house, careful not to wake Viktor in the room upstairs. On a circular table in the entrance foyer was a handwritten note from his wife. She was travelling on business to Paris and London and wouldn't be back for four days. She had signed her name without a kiss. Natalia always wrote kisses: whether to friends, the housekeeper – even the gardener: they all received a mandatory 'x'. Oleg Usmanov evidently no longer merited such tokens of affection. He scrunched the note tightly in his large hand and lobbed it angrily into a bin as he made his way towards the back of the house.

At the door to his study, he paused, noticing the tiny pinprick of LED light shining beneath his desk in the dark. It wasn't especially bright, emitting sufficient luminescence to tell Usmanov everything he needed to know. Someone had been inside his special safe. On the assumption they hadn't had burglars, that reduced the number of possible culprits down to only one other person. At least, that was the theory.

Switching on the lights, he scanned the room, checking to see whether the glass cabinets that housed several of his less valuable chess pieces were still intact. He was relieved to see that nothing looked disturbed. Examining the wall safe hidden beneath the large oil painting behind his desk, he found it all perfectly in position: when he swung the painting outwards on its hidden hinge; the safe was closed and locked, exactly as he would have expected.

Next, he went to the corner cupboard to one side of his desk. Inside were shelves full of papers and files, all stacked in neat piles. Usmanov grabbed hold of one particular shelf with both hands, depressing two hidden switches simultaneously. The whole shelf assembly swung outwards to reveal a hidden cavity containing a second, much larger and more complicated-looking safe. This, too, looked closed and secure – as it should have been, given the precautions that Usmanov had taken to keep its precious contents from prying eyes. To open the second safe, it was necessary to use a special key that was kept hidden at the bottom of the first safe. One also needed a code. Only one person besides himself knew the code. The beautiful Svetlana, his confidential private secretary from the Consulate in Istanbul.

Usmanov had taken one other precaution to ensure that the secrets and half-truths that he kept in the safe remained hidden from would-be spies and thieves alike. He had installed a sophisticated motion-activated camera recording system in his study, one that he had used to great personal effect over the years. It allowed him to record, amongst other things, some of his more intimate, private liaisons: not only with Svetlana but also with other women he had the habit of entertaining on the large couch in the corner of the room, usually when his wife was away on business and Viktor was at school. Switching on the desktop computer on the side of his desk, Usmanov stifled a yawn as he logged in to the machine and found his way to the secure website where the camera records were automatically uploaded. The last time someone had activated the recording system was at eight-thirty the previous evening. About the time he had been at Istanbul's Havalimani airport meeting his agent.

He clicked on the link and watched in fascination.

Natalia!

Natalia entering the study. Natalia opening the wall safe. Natalia kneeling on the floor of the corner cupboard, grabbing hold of the shelves and finding the second safe. Then Natalia opening the second safe, using both the special key and entering the secret code. He watched, relieved, as she deliberately ignored his chess collection, including his most prized possession, a Cybis porcelain chess set in its unique wooden box. Finally, Natalia carefully removing a small, black, leather-bound notebook: briefly looking inside; scanning various pages; suddenly noticing the incriminating bank statement that Usmanov had placed loosely inside the cover; and then, finally, closing the notebook, placing it carefully inside her jacket before shutting the safe door.

Chapter 21

Three days ago, Istanbul

Svetlana put down the phone and began to shake. She had been summoned to Oleg's house by the man himself. Viktor, the son, was at school and Natalia was now travelling abroad. Normally she would have been happy, perhaps even excited. A lazy hour of illicit lovemaking with such a powerful man was normally a satisfactory way to pass a long lunch break. Today, she had a sense of dread about it all, knowing in advance that this particular out-of-office rendezvous was unlikely to end well.

What choice had she had? When Natalia had shown her the photographic evidence of her lunchtime liaisons with the handsome Frenchman, had proven to her that he was not the simple businessman he'd pretended to be but actually an agent working for France's DGSE, Svetlana knew that if Oleg found out, she would be bundled off to Moscow in disgrace and brutally murdered. Out of principle, she had refused point blank to open the safe for the woman. That would have been a fundamental breach of protocol and one she had felt unable to do. Instead, she had revealed the codes to both with great reluctance, explaining about needing a key from one to open the other. She might as well have done the deed herself, but it was something she refused out of a warped sense of duty, even under duress. It was, she had told herself, unlikely that Oleg would find out.

In her heart of hearts, however, she had always known that he would. Usmanov seemed to know everything about everybody. Which was why she had begun to shake so badly moments after receiving the call. Only a few hours after he had returned home and most likely discovered the treason. Nothing he'd said had given any intimation to her that he knew, but she was sure he would have. He would never say anything on the phone, nor would he say anything when she arrived at the house. With his wife away, he would drag her either to the couch in his office or, more likely, to his bedroom. They would make love on the super-king-sized bed that he was so proud of. Afterwards, when she would be lying with her head on his shoulder, her neck enveloped by his enormous forearm, that would be when the questioning would begin. He would ask softly and gently why she had betrayed state secrets to his wife. By this stage, her head would be locked in the vice-like grip of his arm. She would deny everything at first, hoping that he would release his grip. However, she imagined him not moving a muscle, instead asking the same question all over again. In time, she would be obliged to confess. She would argue that she'd had no choice, her mitigation that she had not opened the safe herself, only given his wife the ability to do so. Then, most likely when he was saying that she had nothing to worry about, he would twist her neck with brute force, severing the spinal cord in one fluid movement. He was that kind of man. Soft and gentle on the outside, but with a heart of cold steel. Svetlana shivered again.

She gathered her bag and looked at her watch. There was less than an hour before she was due at the Usmanov residence. She slipped out of the Consulate's gated entrance and walked in a numbed stupor along Istiklal Caddesi, the street busy with ambling shoppers. She headed northwards, trying to clear her head but failing, tears streaming down her face. Her mind was made up, but there seemed a yawning gap between theory and practice, like two worlds apart. Then behind her, the sound of an approaching tram. The moment was upon her. If not now, she would never do it. As the tram rang its warning bell, she stepped to one side to let it pass, the tram once more picking up speed as the driver sensed the street ahead was clear.

Which was when Svetlana threw herself to the road, her body hitting the rails a split second before the tram's wheels passed over them. With a sickening sound, the tram lurched to an unsteady halt. By then it was too late. A massive pool of blood was visible beneath the now stationary tram. That, and a pair of legs lying akimbo, not long since attached to the now dismembered trunk of their former owner.

Chapter 22

Two days ago, Moscow

The timing and manner of Svetlana's death had been inconvenient, causing Usmanov to make several abrupt and unplanned changes to his schedule. There were police and diplomatic investigations to be dealt with, all of which took time and were an unwelcome distraction. Despite everything, Usmanov still made the same late-night Aeroflot flight to Sheremetyevo that he'd taken only a few days before. By seven-thirty the next morning Moscow time, he was ready and waiting for his driver, having showered and changed in his apartment, on this occasion without the benefit of a young research assistant to distract him. The email from the courier company that he'd received earlier had confirmed that delivery was expected that morning between nine and ten o'clock that morning. In the Moscow rush hour traffic, it was going to be tight to get to the Ritz-Carlton in time.

Luck was on their side that morning and they made reasonable time, Usmanov once again entering the five-star hotel, reversing his jacket, checking that his driver had departed before slipping out of a side exit. At the Four Seasons hotel a short time later, having made his way to the same suite and after passing through a similarly intensive security check, Usmanov didn't have to wait long for his friend to arrive.

'This is becoming a habit!' The Russian President said, stepping forward to give Usmanov an embrace. 'Your message said there was a crisis. It wasn't easy to fit you in – but for my oldest friend, a few exceptions are possible. Come, sit. Tea? Coffee?'

Usmanov shook his head and produced a slim, folded sheet from his pocket. It was special paper, and Usmanov had used a 3B, soft pencil, writing on a glass sheet on his desk in his apartment that morning. He passed it across to the Russian President in silence, watching as his friend made no sound whilst he read.

'Actually,' Usmanov said, 'I think I'll take a glass of water. Would you like one?'

'No, thank you,' the President said, silently handing the sheet back to Usmanov. The two men looked at each other knowingly. Usmanov folded the paper in half and half again before dropping it into the glass of water he'd just poured. Immediately, the paper reacted with the liquid. In less than twenty seconds it had dissolved completely.

'We have a major problem,' Usmanov began. 'I came to inform you in person and to apologise. My wife, Natalia, has betrayed me, betrayed us all. She has stolen private papers. State secrets. She blackmailed my secretary, Svetlana, to gain access to my secure safe at home. Then she stole one of my most secret files.'

'You'd better not be about to tell me that DESTINY has been compromised.' The President's tone changed abruptly, the switch from friendly to hostile happening in a heartbeat.

'I hope not.'

'Only hope?' came the icy reply.

'It is complicated.'

'Dear God, it will be more than complicated if she has. What's been stolen that was so secret you daren't even keep it in the Consulate?'

'My private notebook. The one where I record the meetings I have with the school in Villars.'

'Imbecile!' the President boomed angrily, slumping back in his chair with exasperation. 'The world is about to learn I have a secret love child, is that what you're telling me?'

'Possibly.'

'Be careful how you answer this next question, my friend,' he said, the menace in his voice audible. 'What is the probability that DESTINY is mentioned in this damned notebook?'

'Almost zero.'

A long and uncomfortable silence followed, the President staring at the coffee table, fingers under his chin, eyes flicking from side to side.

'Almost zero, but not completely, is that what you're telling me?' he said, eventually.

'That is one reason I am here.'

'You're a damned fool,' The President said, standing abruptly and pacing the room. 'I told you, last time we met, that that wife of yours, behaving as she was, was trouble for someone in your position. You promised me you were taking care of matters. It seems you were deceiving me.'

'I wasn't. I am taking care of things, I promise,' Usmanov pleaded, his words fading into another period of uncomfortable silence.

'Should I be relieving you of your duties?' The President was leaning over the back of one chair, his face scowling directly at Usmanov.

'That is your choice. I sincerely hope not.'

'What has the traitor done with this notebook? Am I to read about my love child in tomorrow's Rossiyskaya Gazeta?' There was a chilling calmness to his voice.

'I think she plans to blackmail me. She wants to run off with a British teacher and the notebook is her collateral.'

On hearing this, the President came and sat opposite Usmanov, his face set and empty of emotion.

'She has to be stopped.' The statement was delivered coldly and brutally, both men staring at each other. 'In the meantime, the immediate priority must be to steal the notebook back. Where is it now? Where is she, for that matter?'

'On her way to London, to meet this teacher. The notebook she couriered to Venice in Italy for safekeeping. Why there, I am uncertain. I tracked down the courier company but the delivery address is to a pickup location. She will have someone there, a friend most likely. I am working on it.'

'You'd better be. Your life – indeed, your current position – now depends on you retrieving that notebook. I hope you appreciate the predicament you are in, my friend.'

'I do. I will deal with this, I promise. I am sorry.'

'I am disappointed in you, Oleg Ivanovich.' The President was standing suddenly, his signal that the meeting was at an end. 'We have to do all we can to protect DESTINY. If this isn't resolved quickly, God only knows what damage will be done.'

'I am aware of that. I felt I had to tell you in person. I am sorry.'

'I require a progress report every twenty-four hours,' the President snapped testily. 'An encrypted call will suffice.'

'Very good,' Usmanov answered dejectedly, his friend in a hurry to leave the room. It was only as he stopped by the door to look back that Usmanov felt any small measure of relief. His oldest friend gave him a fleeting wink and a tiny smile before hastily leaving the room.

Chapter 23

Two days ago, Switzerland

Ordinarily, Herb Okumura might have taken the trip himself. He loved fieldwork, and he would have relished a side excursion to the Swiss mountains in the month of May. However, Turley wanted him back in Langley, and for that reason, he'd asked Sarah Warren to visit the school in Villars. She had been part of the original two-person surveillance team who had followed Usmanov to his lunch date two months earlier.

'All I need is the boy's name, Sarah. We can find out everything there is to know about him later.' Okumura had been speaking from the CIA executive jet awaiting takeoff clearance at Shannon airport. 'One more thing. Who's the person who replaced you as the liaison officer at MI6?'

'Alan Murray.'

'I remember. Call him and see if he can find out about an operation the Brits are running, codename WATCHKEEPER. Ask him to do a little snooping around. Nothing that triggers alarm bells. Tell him the operation concerns a Russian SVR agent, Oleg Usmanov.'

'I'll speak to him. How urgently do you want me to head to Switzerland?'

'How about yesterday?'

'Leave it with me.'

*

Warren's taxi from Villars station deposited her at the front entrance of the Collège Alpin Beau Soleil in good time for her appointment at two o'clock in the afternoon. Smartly turned out in a skirt and jacket, her short, brown hair neatly combed, she paid the driver and studied the outside. It was an imposing building, constructed out of stone and painted largely in white, with plentiful windows on every aspect. On either side of the front door, sitting like sentries, were a pair of life-sized stone dogs. Warren passed their watchful gaze as she entered the building, a cheerful Swiss receptionist greeting her and showing her courteously to a side room where a tray of mineral water and two glasses lay waiting. Warren took off her coat and sat down, depositing a slim, leather document case on the table beside her. Her eyes were drawn to a pile of brochures on the table. She picked one up, casually flicking through pages of glossy photographs, skim-reading about the school's various academic and sporting achievements. A bell rang loudly in the corridor outside, the sound catching her by surprise. A few moments later, the door opened and an imposing figure dressed in a navy-blue twinset and skirt entered the room with a flourish.

'Madeleine Simpson,' the headmistress said, her hand extended in a greeting. 'So nice to meet you.' She had straw-blonde hair neatly held up at the back in a bun.

'Good afternoon,' Warren replied, shaking the offered hand. 'Emma Baker.' It was one of her more frequently used cover names.

'My apologies for that dreadful bell,' Simpson said, sitting down at the table and pouring two glasses of sparkling water. She placed one glass in front of her guest and took a sip from the other. 'It sounds so shrill out here in the reception area. Afternoon classes have just started. Now, I believe you asked for this meeting. How may I help? I'm afraid I don't have a lot of time.'

'Thank you. As I mentioned on the phone to your secretary yesterday, I'm a partner in a small law firm, Swaine & Co, based in London. We specialise in the mediation of financial disputes for some of the world's wealthiest individuals, people who find their marriages have come to an end.' She handed Simpson a business card that gave credence to her cover story. Simpson looked at the card and ran an index finger over the embossed blue lettering. 'One of my clients – who, for the purposes of this meeting, I would prefer to keep anonymous – is seeking a divorce from her estranged husband. She suspects him of having numerous affairs over the many years of their marriage – and, as is sadly often the case, has become aware of several children he has fathered along the way.' She paused to see if Simpson felt the need to make any comment, but the headmistress remained impassive.

'One of my client's concerns is that, in pursuing an appropriate financial settlement with her soon-to-be ex-husband, she would like, as an additional condition of the divorce agreement, to see the establishment of a trust fund for any such children sired along the way. Locating and naming these children is not straightforward. It involves a fair amount of detective work, as I am sure you can understand. The reason I'm here today is that I believe you will not only know of the man in question but also be able to identify at least one child believed to be involved. A young adult that my client would like to ensure gains a beneficial interest in this trust.'

She reached into her leather document case and removed an A4-sized photograph.

'This is the man in question. He uses many aliases, but it is our hope and belief that you will recognise him.'

Simpson unfolded a pair of reading glasses hanging around her neck on a gold chain, studying the photograph intently for a few moments.

'Yes, I know this man,' she answered, placing the photograph down on the desk and nudging it back in Warren's direction. 'He's one of our school's most generous benefactors. I know him as Herr Karpov.'

Harley removed a small notebook and began taking notes using a Montblanc ballpoint pen.

'How long have you known this Herr Karpov?'

'Almost five years. We meet every six months. He takes me to lunch and we have a very agreeable time discussing the school, its investment plans and the progress of one young student in particular.'

'What do you believe is Karpov's link to this young student?'

'There is a trust fund for the boy's education that Herr Karpov administers. That, at least, is what I've been told by Herr Karpov, and I have had no reason to doubt it. The boy's fees and boarding costs are always settled promptly.'

'Which may or may not suggest that Karpov is the boy's father. What do you think?'

'I simply do not know. The child in question was legally adopted many years ago. I meet the adoptive parents from time to time, at the start and end of term, that sort of thing. It is not unusual to find a child's natural parents trying to take some kind of interest in their child even when they have relinquished all rights as a parent through an adoption process. To be frank with you, Emma, we have several pupils with parents scattered far and wide: some we never see from one year to the next, many of whose relationships are' – she paused, searching for the right word – 'complicated. At this school, our principal concern is the well-being of the children and in ensuring that there are sufficient financial resources in place to cover the fees. In this particular case, Herr Karpov always pays the fees in advance each year and, as I mentioned earlier, he has been a generous benefactor to the school.'

'Karpov's a very wealthy man. Do you believe he could be the boy's father?'

'To be honest, I do not know and it really doesn't concern me. He never asks to see the boy, if that's any help. That all said and done, I have to confess that I have wondered about it from time to time.'

'What name does the child go by?'

It was the million-dollar question, everything building to this one, crucial ask.

'Alexei. Alexei Perrin.'

'Is that the boy's real name or his adoptive name?'

'His adoptive parents are Swiss. They are Perrins, that's all I know.'

'Would you, by any chance, have a photograph of this young man? It's just that, down the line, we are likely to need more than simply a name before we can proceed. Things such as DNA. A picture would be helpful.'

'I'm afraid we don't keep photographs of pupils in our files. For privacy reasons. Plus, during adolescence, appearances alter a great deal, as I'm sure you can understand. However, I think you might be in luck.' Simpson picked up one of the brochures on the table in front of them both.

'We've only recently had these reprinted. If I am not mistaken . . .' She thumbed through the pages. 'Yes, here we are.' She pointed to a photograph showing a group of three teenagers staring intently at a piece of chemical apparatus. There were two girls and one boy. 'That young man there,' she said, pointing, 'is Alexei Perrin.'

'May I keep this?' Warren asked.

'By all means. Now, if there's nothing else, I'm afraid I need to be at a teachers' meeting.'

'I think for the moment we're done. Thank you very much indeed for your time.'

Later that same afternoon, Simpson was back in her office with the door closed. School had finished for the day and her secretary had departed. She had been thinking a lot about the Baker woman since the meeting a few hours earlier. In particular, whether the visit was significant enough to warrant her contacting Herr Karpov in the manner he'd requested a few months ago. She concluded that it was and, with that decision made, went to locate the special phone number that he'd given her. Opening the bottom drawer of her desk, from within one of the neatly partitioned filing racks, she withdrew an unlabelled green file bearing the school's crest on the front. She laid the file on her desk and turned various pages until finding what she was looking for. She reached for the phone on her desk, dialling the number written in ink on the small piece of paper Herr Karpov had supplied before holding the phone to her ear. After a few seconds of waiting, the line clicked twice before a distant phone rang.

'*Da*,' a gruff voice answered in time.

'Good evening, Herr Karpov. This is Madeleine Simpson calling from Villars in Switzerland. Is this a convenient moment?'

'Yes, Madeleine. How can I help?'

'Some months ago, you asked me to call you on this number if ever something happened in connection with the boy I considered to be unusual: people making enquiries was the example you used. Well, this may or may not be relevant, and my apologies if this is a wasted call. However, I had a visitor this afternoon from London, someone who said her name was Emma Barker, a partner from the law firm Swaine & Co. She claimed to be a divorce lawyer chasing philandering husbands and she arrived bearing your photograph. What she was trying to do was to track down the name of the child. I thought you'd like to know.'

'I see. Did you give her Alexei's name?'

'Yes. I hope I did nothing wrong, Herr Karpov?'

'No, that was what we agreed. This call is helpful, thank you. You don't have her card to hand, do you? If so, is there a contact number on it?'

Simpson recited the number from the embossed business card.

'Do you want me to call again, Herr Karpov, if she returns?'

'I don't think that will be necessary. This call has told me everything I need to know, thank you.' The line clicked and the call disconnected.

Replacing the receiver, she felt slightly disappointed that Karpov hadn't wanted to talk for longer or ask more questions. Whenever they'd met at one of their lunches, he had always spoken effusively about so many things, and she'd secretly enjoyed his company. She put his brevity down to the fact that she must have caught him in the middle of doing something.

Chapter 24

Two days ago, London

The current Chief of the Security Intelligence Services, Sir Anthony Defries, had a modest office on the upper floors of the wedding-cake building more commonly known as Vauxhall Cross. The view behind his desk, assuming he ever had time to look, was across the Thames in a north-westerly direction. The room's large windows provided a sweeping river panorama that included the tip of Big Ben to the right and a surprisingly dull vista to the left, one landmark of minor interest being the newly built American Embassy literally down the road – a building that Defries had privately described as looking like the inside of an anechoic chamber. Close by his uncluttered desk was a small, circular meeting table with four chairs. Occupying one of these was Frances Riordan. Sitting next to her was Margaret Squire, Defries's prim-looking private secretary.

'Tell me, Frances. What do you think we should do about DESTINY?' Defries was an imposing figure, well over six foot three and with hardly an ounce of fat on his lean body. He normally wore a three-piece suit, but within the confines of his private office, he had draped his jacket over the back of his leather chair.

Riordan shuffled her large frame in the seat whilst considering her reply.

'For the moment, nothing,' she said eventually. 'We now know, thanks to the Americans, that there is a highly-prized Russian asset somewhere in Western intelligence. However, at this particular moment, conducting yet another mole hunt would, I suggest, be counter-productive. Especially when we know so little.'

'Perhaps that's what the Russian Premier wants? All of us Western spies preoccupied, chasing our tails. Hardly a novelty, though, is it – a Russian spy in our midst?'

'Agreed. However, this one sounds like a big fish. It was a masterful exposé by the Americans.'

'Yes. I wonder how many hotel rooms around the world Langley and the NSA have been able to compromise? So, you believe DESTINY to be genuine but consider that we shouldn't be trying to find out who she is, is that what you're saying?' He glanced mischievously across at Squire and winked.

'Not exactly.'

'What, precisely, does "not exactly" mean?' He eyed Riordan with a fixed stare, making Riordan look away. The Chief had a squint in one eye, and it invariably made colleagues feel unsettled.

'We have a small operation underway that might, just might, allow us to get more information about DESTINY without pulling up the carpets and burrowing beneath the floorboards.'

'Yes, I remember. Project WATCHKEEPER.'

'Correct.'

'Do you want to say anything more?'

'If I did, it should be for your ears only.'

'I see.' Defries considered this for a moment, then turned to his private secretary. 'Margaret, I think Frances is politely telling me she would prefer to speak alone with me. Would you mind?'

'Of course not,' Squire said, picking up her notebook and quietly leaving the room.

'Did you know Margaret is a fluent Russian speaker?' Defries continued once they were alone.

'I confess, I did not.'

'She was a professional translator before she joined the service.'

'What are you suggesting? That she might be DESTINY?'

'Don't be ridiculous. She's been cleared more times than any of us. No, she's not a Russian mole, of that I'm 100 per cent certain. Anyway, she's not exactly man-friendly. It's unlikely that she would ever have been the Russian President's type.' He smiled thinly, but then saw the look of discomfort on Riordan's face. 'We digress. Tell me. WATCHKEEPER. What's going on?'

'The President's friend, ORION as we refer to him within the WATCHKEEPER protocols, is an SVR spy with many secrets. Our operational game plan is to turn him to work for us.'

'Are we talking entrapment, extortion or a voluntary changing of sides?'

'At this stage, more a fishing expedition – with a strong whiff of entrapment in the air. ORION lives with his increasingly estranged wife in Istanbul and travels hugely. His wife, a journalist, has a reputation for being, how shall I put this, a little on the promiscuous side. For the last four months, she's been very close to a British teacher by the name of Calum Ross. ORION's wife appears to be infatuated and she's planning to escape her husband and come to London to live with Ross, bearing secrets that she hopes will ensure her safety.'

'How do you know this?'

'Some of us are reasonably competent in our day jobs,' she said with an attempt at dry humour. When this was met with a frosty silence, she felt obliged to say more. 'The Americans are not the only ones able to listen in to conversations in hotel bedrooms.'

'I see. You think a jilted Russian spymaster will be seeking revenge on a faithless wife, is that how the plotline goes? This all sounds tenuous, Frances. What sort of secrets might we be talking about? Even a journalistic wife's not likely to be able to access her husband's SVR files, is she?'

'That's why this is a fishing expedition, at the moment. ORION's not your ordinary Russian spy, though. He happens to be one of the Russian President's oldest and closest friends. He's also the one who's been secretly visiting the school where the President's illegitimate son, courtesy of DESTINY, has been hidden away. ORION knows a lot of very interesting secrets. We think there is a high probability his wife will be able to discover certain incriminating material in the family home. Secrets that could prove helpful in persuading ORION to work for us. The sort that ORION wouldn't risk being entrusted to SVR files and archives, either electronically or those that might be held physically in, say, the secure vault at the Consulate in Istanbul.'

'You're confident that some of this material is kept at home, are you?'

'That is our strong belief. His confidential secretary brings papers to his Istanbul house regularly.'

'Where does Ross fit in?'

'We want Ross to get close enough to this Russian woman so he can share any secrets she finds with us.'

'Why would he be interested in ratting on his newfound lover?'

'Because we are in the throes of persuading him to work for us.'

'He doesn't at the moment?'

'No.'

'It all sounds a bit iffy, Frances.'

'I haven't troubled you with all the details. I'm confident he'll do what we ask.'

'What's Ross's background?'

'Mixed. Not perfect, but not bad, on balance. He was in the Special Forces for a while, so he's more than capable.'

'Did he leave in good odour?'

'Reasonably.'

Defries took a few moments to consider what he'd heard, for a while the only sound being the muted hiss of the building's air handling system.

'You know the Americans are actively sniffing around WATCHKEEPER? Langley's liaison, the new person who replaced Sarah Warren. What's his name?'

'Alan Murray.'

'That's the one. Well, after your little tête-à-tête with Okumura, Murray tried poking around our databases in a quest to learn more about WATCHKEEPER. It came up on the 'access denied' report that crosses my desk each morning. Sounds like they want ORION as much as we do.'

'I don't find that altogether surprising.'

'It's disconcerting if they're now trying to spy on us.'

'I'll have a quiet word with Murray.'

'Look, for the record, Frances, verbal only, but here's my conclusion. This whole operation worries me. We have a wonderful new source of intelligence, thanks to the Americans, telling us about a top-ranking mole somewhere in the West. Besides the Russian President, arguably the one person who might know more than most about DESTINY is ORION. This fishing expedition of yours is flaky. There's no other word for it. We don't know yet whether we can persuade Ross into working for us. More's the point, we don't know, even if Ross were to agree, that he'll be able to get his hands on whatever ORION's wife might bring with her. Finally, and here's the nub, we're not even sure whether she'll discover anything significant enough to enable ORION to be turned. Frankly, I think you need to go back to the drawing board and start again. This operation is all far too speculative.'

'What if it succeeds, though?'

'I would not waste any further time on it, Frances.'

'Is that a direct order or is that your counsel, Sir Anthony?'

'For the moment, that's my counsel. Be very wary, Frances. Our ministerial lords and masters will not countenance us wasting resources on speculative projects. Especially operations that do not deliver value for money. If you ignore my advice and still convert ORION to our cause, there will be nothing but praise for you in high places. Higher than in this room, certainly. If you fail, however, then you cannot say that you were not advised along the way. Do we understand each other?'

'Perfectly.' Riordan got up and headed towards the door.

'One more thing, Frances.'

'Yes, Sir Anthony,' she said, turning, her deep husky voice sounding weary.

'If you do continue, against my best advice, then for God's sake don't allow the Americans to get to ORION before us.' He looked at her with a half-smile. 'To avoid any doubt, that is a direct order, not simply wise counsel.'

THE DAY OF NATALIA'S ARRIVAL IN LONDON

Chapter 25

London

When Lauren McIlvoy woke with the alarm shortly after six-thirty, the interview with Calum Ross was still front of mind. Well, not so much Ross, more her own failure to contact Brendan North following Ross's arrest. She checked her alarm, resolving there and then to call North as soon as she got into the office.

As she worked her way through a snatched bowl of muesli, she tried to prepare herself. What was she going to say to North? The bare minimum. Facts not emotions. No 'long time, no speak, Brendan. How are you?' That would be a disaster. He would want to brag and boast. Tell her about yet another promotion. How they should go out again, perhaps for a drink. For old times' sake. McIlvoy shuddered.

By the time McIlvoy was at her desk, it was shortly before eight in the morning. The open-plan office space was largely empty: her desktop, however, was not. Crammed with manila files and reports, there was barely enough room for a keyboard and mouse, let alone a mug of tea. It was her one guilty pleasure, a daily ritual. McIlvoy liked hers black and strong. Brendan North would have added one of his innuendo-laden quips to that statement. She checked her watch. It was time to call the ghastly man. With luck, he wouldn't yet be at his desk. She'd leave a simple message. Just the facts. No need to call back unless there was a problem. Please, dear God, may there not be a problem.

To her dismay, he answered on the third ring.

'Brendan, it's Lauren.'

Keep it simple, her analyst would coach her. *Breathe in and out, slowly. Remember, if you have to speak, less is more.*

'Princess!' he purred in that camp, syrupy manner. 'How simply divine to hear from you. So early in the morning too.' She could hear his lascivious smile. A victorious grin. He'd won a fictitious wager: she'd rung him first. The princess label had started as a joke; over time, the joke had worn thin. Now it was in danger of making her feel nauseous.

'Do *not* call me that, Brendan,' she said in as even a tone as she could muster. However, it came out somewhat nervously, more like an apologetic whimper.

Breathe, smile, say your piece and then hang up.

'This is not a social call. We arrested a man yesterday at Green Park tube station. A dog unit picked up the scent of cocaine. We took him in for questioning and found a brick of C-4 in his possession.'

'And the man's name, darling?'

'I am not your darling. His name is Calum Ross.'

'Let me run a quick check. Not about to run off somewhere, are you?'

Less is more. Do not rise to the bait.

She waited in silence. It didn't, in fairness, take long.

'Here we are,' he said shortly. 'Never heard of him. Not on our radar at all. Any clues why he'd had both drugs and plastic explosive on him when he was arrested?'

'We're still investigating. Nothing obvious. He says he was stitched up.'

'They all say that. What was his story?'

'A man left a bag on a Victoria line train yesterday. The man got off the train, Ross picked up the bag and tried to find the man. Unfortunately, he bumped into a dog handling unit at the station exit and got himself arrested.'

'That was careless. Pity he didn't think to check the rucksack first. Before doing his good Samaritan act. Have you run prints? Just to make sure he is who he says he is.'

'We ran them overnight. His prints are not in the system. He's an unknown.'

'Good. Then we are officially not interested. Is that all?'

'That's all, just going by the book. Liaising when we have to.'

'You know, Lauren, you and I ought to try another go at liaising. We had such a lot of fun together. Before it all went wrong. I'm sorry if I ever offended you. Perhaps we should meet and make amends? I'd like that if you're game.'

'Are you crazy?' hissed McIlvoy, lowering her voice. 'Our relationship was a fucking disaster from start to finish. Don't ask me again, do you hear? After all that happened, I'm simply not interested.' She slammed the receiver back into its housing triumphantly. Shaking, but jubilant. She had faced her demon and not made a fool of herself.

There was something she'd learned, however. One small but crucial detail. In his desire to be pompous and dominant, he'd said something. Whether it was a genuine guess or a small but crucial miscalculation, she didn't know. He'd mentioned the rucksack. She'd only referred to it as a bag. If it wasn't a guess, how had North known about that?

Chapter 26

London

Ross woke early. Pushing the hotel's two queen-sized beds to one side, he spent fifteen minutes completing his early morning routine. Ligament and muscle stretches followed by a high-intensity static workout. Then a long shower, a ritual as much part of his routine as the exercises. Finally, nursing a mug of bland, instant black coffee and sitting in the room's only comfortable chair, he checked his watch. Natalia would be calling any minute. In a few hours, her train would arrive in London. He would go to St. Pancras and meet her off the Eurostar. As if on cue, his phone rang. It was a number he didn't recognise.

'Hello.'

'Hello,' was all she said in reply.

'Not long now.'

'I am happy. Is everything in order?'

Ross explained that his flat had been burgled. He skated over the previous day's other events. It wasn't the time to tell her about being arrested. Or his afternoon and evening spent in Savile Row police station.

'That sounds like my husband, I am sure of it. Is my arrival still convenient?'

'Very. We might need to stay in a hotel. Until I get the flat sorted.'

'A hotel is fine. Naturally, you have spoken to the police. What did they say?'

'Not yet. I'm about to call. I only discovered I had a problem late last night. The police wouldn't have done anything at that hour. Not in London. They've got bigger things to worry about than a small robbery in a tiny basement flat.'

'I am excited.'

'Me too.'

There was a pause.

'Did you discover anything?'

'I found treasure.'

'That's amazing! Are you certain?'

'Positive.'

'Is it what we hoped?'

'More than.'

'Is it safe?'

'Completely.'

'Are you still on time?'

'Yes, I will be on time.'

'I'll be there.'

When the call ended, he was about to phone McIlvoy when he checked the time and paused. It wasn't yet eight in the morning. McIlvoy might not be in. It would be a complication to talk to an underling. Then he wondered about the lawyer, Jonathan Richards. Perhaps it would be wise to speak with him first? The two incidents on the face of it weren't related, but there again, the rucksacks said that they were. Ross didn't want to screw up due process. He fished Richards' card from his wallet and dialled his number.

'Richards,' a tired voice in Ross's ear rasped.

Ross quickly went over the events of the previous late evening.

'Did you touch anything?'

'Sure. I had to check what was missing.'

'And?'

Ross told him about the missing passport and money in his secret stash.

'What about the rucksacks?'

'They were all empty.'

'You mean you checked? Did you wear gloves?'

'No.'

'That might have been a mistake. Especially after yesterday. You did the right thing calling me. Can we meet at your flat, say, at noon today? I'll contact McIlvoy and get her to meet us at the same time. She'll want to come, I'm sure. Especially because of the rucksacks. It's a pity you had to touch everything.'

'Noon should work for me. I need to be away soon after, that's all.'

'Okay, unless you hear from me, I'll see you then.' The line went dead.

Ross was suddenly hungry. With the lack of food these last twenty-four hours, the all-inclusive buffet breakfast sounded tempting. He rode the lift down to the lobby and went in search of breakfast. On the way, he had to pass directly in front of the reception desk. An elderly couple were checking out, but one of the two receptionists on duty was free. Ross stepped forward.

'I'd like to extend my stay a few days,' Ross began. The male receptionist took Ross's details and checked his computer screen. Yes, Ross's room was indeed available for the next five days at the same promotional rate. Ross handed over the card he had tried the night before. Again, it was rejected.

'I'll have to get some cash and come back to pay you later,' Ross said, irritated. 'If it's not until this afternoon, will that still be okay?'

The man assured him it would be fine. Ross, appeased for the moment, turned and headed to breakfast.

Chapter 27

Istanbul

Oleg Usmanov's mobile phone was buzzing. The Russian finished reading the final two lines of the report he was reviewing before answering the call. It was a Moscow number, most likely someone at Yasenevo.

'Hello.'

'Is the line secure?' the voice at the other end asked. Usmanov instantly recognised the caller's voice. It was Sergei Borodin's chief of staff, someone Usmanov had known for years. He was a trusted friend and an ally.

'Yes, I'm on my office mobile.'

'Good. I'm going to have to be quick.'

'Okay, what is it?'

'Your old friend, Nicolai Kozlov. He's sniffing around.'

'What in particular?'

'Cash expenditure reports. He's asking for information from all the *rezidentura*, but he's particularly focused on Istanbul. On you, in particular, be in no doubt. There was a large cash withdrawal that was made a few months ago. Kozlov's on the case.'

Usmanov felt an icy cold feeling form in the pit of his stomach. It was happening, just as he feared it might. He struggled to keep his composure.

'That's interesting, thank you. What else do you know?'

'At this stage, not a lot. I just wanted you to be aware. The man's acting as if he's on a mission. There's an operation underway in London that he's working on.'

'Kozlov? He's not an operational guy.'

'That's what's so odd. He's been asked to do something by Borodin. It's all ultra-hush hush.'

'Okay, my friend. I appreciate the insight. If you hear anything else, let me know as soon as possible.'

Usmanov abruptly ended the call and leapt out of bed, heading for the shower. Kozlov was definitely up to his old tricks again. The last thing that Usmanov needed right now was an investigator like Kozlov conducting a line-by-line audit of Istanbul residency's accounts. Especially given the two hundred thousand dollars that he had withdrawn. If he wasn't careful, Kozlov might very well jeopardize everything. Perhaps as a precautionary measure he might just need to have a private word with his oldest friend?

Chapter 28

London

The roads around the hotel were snarled. After the previous night's rain, large potholes full of dirty water were slowing traffic down. On the pavement, Ross found himself sidestepping large puddles. Close to Camden Underground station was a branch of Ross's bank, two ATMs set in the wall, the machines next to escalators leading up to a banking hall on the floor above. Ross inserted his debit card and, when prompted, entered his PIN. The screen showed an inverting egg timer symbol for several seconds before the following message appeared:

Card retained. Please contact staff at one of our branches for more details.

With an ominous feeling, Ross rode the escalator to the banking hall. A uniformed meet-and-greet person pointed him to a side cubicle where a manager, he was informed, would soon be with him. A short while later, a bank employee by the name of Winston came and introduced himself. He was tall and when they shook hands, Ross felt the man's long fingers engulf his own with room to spare. Winston took a seat behind a computer screen and Ross explained the predicament with his card. Winston asked if he had any identification on him. Ross shook his head.

'Not even a driving licence? Utility bill?'

'I'm sorry, no.'

'I'm not meant to discuss details about your account without first proving your identity, I'm sorry.'

'Winston, I'm not asking you to disclose details. I'd like you to tell me what's going on, that's all.'

'Let me take a look. Do you have your account information?'

Ross recited his account number and sort code and Winston typed them into his machine.

'Your name, address and date of birth.'

As Ross rattled off these details, Winston checked them against entries on his screen, his eyes moving from side to side as he read. After a while, he stopped and looked up.

'I can see the problem,' he said gravely. 'Your account's been frozen.'

'Frozen? It should be in credit at the moment. How can the account be frozen?'

'The money in your account was all withdrawn yesterday. In two lots. One large transfer and a second, lesser amount that took you overdrawn. That's the reason.'

An icy chill that started in the pit of his stomach began inching its way throughout Ross's body. Stealing his money was a declaration of war.

'Who authorised the withdrawals?'

Winston looked down at his screen and clicked on the relevant entries.

'You did, sir. Online.'

'At what time, precisely?'

Winston again scrolled through his screen to check the details.

'At 1.32 yesterday afternoon.'

Ross received this news in silence. Things were suddenly clearer. Everything that had happened these last twenty-four hours, these were acts of retribution. Clumsily executed, maybe; irritating as hell, certainly.

'That's impossible.'

'The evidence points to the contrary,' Winston said, tapping the side of his computer screen as if to make the point. 'You logged on to your account at 1.25 yesterday afternoon. You logged out nine minutes later, having successfully authenticated the two withdrawals I mentioned.'

'Bullshit.' Ross stared blankly at the other man, leaning back in his chair with his arms crossed. The two eyeballed each other in silence.

'The reason it's bullshit,' Ross continued in time, 'is that from eleven in the morning yesterday until nearly ten o'clock at night, I was in a holding cell at Savile Row police station, being interrogated for crimes I didn't commit. It wasn't me who entered and authorised those payments. Your systems have been hacked. Someone else cleaned out my account yesterday. Check with the police, they'll corroborate my story. Speak to Detective Chief Inspector Lauren McIlvoy at Savile Row police station. Now, while you try to recover my stolen money, I urgently need some replacement cash. Are you able to help me or do you need to take this to higher authorities?'

Chapter 29

London

By the time Ross left the bank, he only had fifteen minutes remaining before his scheduled meeting with McIlvoy and Richards. On a whim, he ran back to his rented apartment. It was faster and more reliable than waiting for the bus, and he desperately needed some exercise.

Dodging pedestrians as he headed north, Ross reflected about the painful and protracted conversations he'd endured. Winston had eventually found a more senior manager. She had felt unable to decide anything without first informing the bank's fraud department. They – in denial, initially – had called Lauren McIlvoy's office, the duty sergeant confirming that, yes, Calum Ross had been in their custody the whole of the previous afternoon. Which in turn got the fraud department agitated, since it made it more likely that someone had indeed hacked their systems. The problem was then escalated within the bank. Ross, by this stage impatient if not angry, had decided it was the moment to thump the table. He requested an emergency loan of £500 from the bank, his rationale being that his account had been fraudulently depleted of all funds and he needed the money. After yet more deliberations back and forth, they granted the request. Ross signed his life away on several official-looking documents before Winston was finally able to count out £500 in crisp twenty-pound notes, laying them triumphantly on the desk in front of Ross.

He completed his run home with two minutes to spare. As he turned the corner of his street, slowing to a walking pace and adjusting his breathing, he spotted McIlvoy waiting on the pavement up ahead. There were two others with her he didn't recognise.

McIlvoy shook hands with Ross and introduced two junior officers from her team. Just then, a black London taxi pulled to the curb and Richards climbed out. Introductions over, Ross led them down the small flight of stone stairs to his flat.

'No forced entry, then?' McIlvoy asked as Ross unlocked the front door.

'Not that I could see. Your team will be better able to judge. I was able to lock the door as normal when I left.'

'Who else besides you has a key?'

Ross shrugged. 'This is a short rental. I got my key from the landlord. He'll have another, for sure. I don't know about anyone else.'

'When you say short, how short?'

'One month. Cash in advance.'

'Do you have a cleaner?'

Ross shook his head.

'Okay. Do you mind if my team take a look around?' McIlvoy asked once everyone was inside and they could see the chaos for themselves.

Ross looked at Richards briefly. He shrugged, which Ross took as an affirmative gesture. 'Sure. Feel free. I've nothing to hide.'

McIlvoy, Ross and Richards stayed together in the hall, talking, while the other two searched the rooms.

'What time did you discover this last night?' McIlvoy asked.

'I came straight home after leaving Savile Row,' Ross said. 'I was here shortly before eleven.'

'Why didn't you call the police?'

'Seriously? At eleven o'clock at night? It was a house burglary. No lives were at risk. The perpetrators had fled the scene. Whoever I called would have told me to wait until morning. Which is what I did. After I had first rung my solicitor here,' he said, nodding at Richards.

'You could have called Savile Row. We'd have come.'

'I figured that, like me, you'd have been heading home for some sleep.'

'Did you stay here last night?'

He shook his head. 'No, I checked into a chain hotel up the road. Shortly before eight this morning, I rang Richards. He wasn't free to meet before noon.'

'Yes, sorry about that. I had to be in court,' Richards said.

'It was a good job, in a way,' Ross went on. 'I went to get some cash out this morning. Discovered that my account has been hacked and all my money cleaned out.'

'I'd heard something to that effect. The bank called the station this morning. How much did you lose?'

'A few thousand. I'd just completed an assignment, working abroad.'

'Banks usually compensate customers, in cases like these. Assuming you weren't negligent, such as writing your passwords somewhere obvious.'

There was a shout from the bedroom. All three turned and hurried into the next room. One of McIlvoy's team was on his hands and knees, next to the loose piece of skirting. The board was on the floor, the young officer peering into the void with a torch.

'See this,' he said carefully, reaching into the cavity and extracting a small brick-shaped object. About the size and shape of a bar of soap. Wrapped in greaseproof paper.

'Well, well, well,' McIlvoy said sarcastically. 'Not seen one of those for a few hours, have we?'

'That wasn't there earlier,' Ross said defensively.

'Oh yes? How do you know?'

'Look, this is a cheap rental. There's nowhere secure for hiding bits and pieces. So, I found this loose piece of skirting in the bedroom and prized it away from the wall. Behind it was – is – the cavity we're all staring into. It's where I hid my valuables. You know, passport, spare cash, notebook computer and the like. Last night, when I saw that someone had trashed the apartment, the first place I looked was this cavity. The skirting was undisturbed. However, when I checked inside, it was empty. They had stolen everything. Trust me, I made sure. Very carefully.'

'It's not empty now, sir,' the officer on his hands and knees was saying. 'There's at least one, if not two, more of these blocks down here, by the look of things.'

'I need you to return to the station to make another statement.' McIlvoy was cold and clinical as she spoke. Ross caught a look that he hadn't seen before. He concluded it was her angry look but, for one fleeting instant, he wondered if it might have been something else.

'I'm sure my client will be happy to,' Richards said before Ross could respond.

'I think you need to show us the rucksacks,' McIlvoy said. He turned and headed to the hallway where the small coat cupboard was located. He opened the door and stared in amazement. All the rucksacks were gone. Ross stood aside to allow McIlvoy to see for herself.

'How many did you say there were earlier?' McIlvoy called out from within the cupboard.

'Five. I checked and counted them all. I also looked inside every one. They were all empty.'

'Meaning your prints will now be all over them,' she muttered to herself. 'Well, there's nothing here now. I'll need Forensics to give everything a thorough going-over. I could get a search warrant. Or, you and your lawyer could grant me full permission and access rights, here and now. You make the choice.'

'I have nothing to hide,' Ross said without even consulting Richards. 'I'm happy for your team to do whatever they want.'

She looked at Richards. 'Can you send me a brief note for our files.'

Richards let out a deep sigh. 'Sure,' he said, removing a smartphone from his pocket. 'Will an email suffice?'

'That'll work.'

'I'll send it now.' He began typing.

'Are you about to arrest me again?' Ross asked.

'It's tempting. There are plenty of grounds. For the moment, I need you to make a voluntary statement under caution. As long as your solicitor is happy.'

'I'm happy if you are, Calum,' Richards said without even looking up from his phone.

'Sure. I guess. Can it be later this afternoon? I have to meet someone at St. Pancras first. They're arriving on the Eurostar.'

'It would be better if you came right away.'

'I realise that. However, it would save my life if we could make it around four this afternoon. The way I understand it, I'm not technically under arrest at the moment. That is correct, isn't it?'

'Technically, that's correct. Okay, here's how we'll do it. Ordinarily, I'd ask for your passport. I guess that option's out the window given everything that's happened. Instead, come by the station later today. By four o'clock at the latest. If you are so much as a minute late, I'll be issuing a warrant for your arrest. Is that clear?'

'Thanks,' Ross said. 'To be honest, nothing much is clear to me, at present.'

Chapter 30

London

McIlvoy announced that she had seen all she needed to see. Richards was also eager to leave. Natalia's train wasn't due for well over ninety minutes, so with time in hand, Ross went in search of a few items of clothing from the detritus scattered around his bedroom floor. Lying on its side on the floor, next to an upended bedside table, was Natalia's gift to him, his treasured pocket chess set. Ross checked that there was no damage, relieved to find no pieces missing either, and put it to one side. Locating a clean shirt and underwear, he changed quickly, keeping the cardigan he'd been wearing earlier. Natalia had said she liked him in that. He'd been wearing it that first day she'd spotted him at the chess club. Next, from the cupboard under the stairs, he selected a thin, burgundy-red waterproof jacket. He placed the chess set inside a zippered inner pocket and put the jacket on. With little need to hang around the apartment any longer, it was time to get going. One member of McIlvoy's team had been ordered to stay behind keeping vigil until McIlvoy's forensic team arrived.

Outside, it was drizzling, the traffic around Archway junction now gridlocked. With Northern Line trains running directly to the Eurostar railway terminus six stops to the south, it was going to be simpler to take the Underground rather than a bus. Ross ran across the busy road at the end of his street and ducked out of the rain into the station entrance.

That day's problem on the Underground system only began once Ross got off the train six stops later and was standing on the escalator leading from platform level to the station concourse above. In point of fact, it was two problems. Both different manifestations of the same problem. One in front. One behind. He didn't see the problem behind until he had been staring at the first problem in front for several seconds. In total disbelief.

The person in front had the same rucksack.

There was no doubt. Same make. Same model. Same colour. The wearer was a woman. Curly-blonde locks, the hair scraggy. Slender, trim waist, small butt, nothing much to make her stand out – other than the rucksack. He stared at it, inches from his nose. It wasn't empty, that was for sure. But it wasn't crammed full either. It was déjà vu. By definition, all over again.

What made him turn to look behind him, he didn't know. They were one-third of the way to the top by that stage. Turn he did, however, which was when he saw the second problem. This one was male, standing sideways on the tread, looking across at passengers heading down towards platform level. Youthful face, acne scars, mirror sunglasses. Plus the same rucksack. This one also not completely full. However, not empty either. Ross turned to face the front and by this stage, the woman in front had spun around to face him.

'Please don't make a fuss. Someone wants to talk. Follow me as we leave the escalator. All will become clear, I promise.'

Hindsight is a great tool in theory. For the practically minded, however, it is mostly useless. In hindsight, Ross might have done several things differently. Run away, for starters. Perhaps straight-arm tackle the spotty youth behind, pushing him down the escalator so that it was just him and the woman in front remaining. He actually did none of these things. When the escalator reached the main concourse, like a stray lamb sandwiched between two sheepdogs, Ross followed the woman out of the station. Through the ticket turnstiles, they headed left, where there was an underground pedestrian cut-through leading directly to St. Pancras mainline station. Riding another, smaller, escalator up, they arrived on the main concourse. They walked in a thin line, Ross behind the woman, with the spotty youth at the rear. Like this, they traipsed through the entire length of the shopping mall towards the end of the station nearest to Euston Road. Past the Eurostar arrival doors, where taxi and limousine drivers waited patiently, some holding name cards. Past food shops, bookshops and gift shops by the dozen. Past an old, out-of-tune piano, left on the concourse to invite passers-by to play their favourite tunes. A small crowd was listening to an elderly man playing Sinatra's 'My Way'. Finally, to the very end where there was a small pavement café belonging to a big branded food store. A stern-faced woman was sitting at a table. She was on her own, a teapot on a tray before her with two cups of tea already poured. Ross's line of three came to a halt. The blonde turned, indicating one of the vacant chairs beside the woman with the tea. Ross took this to be his cue to sit down.

'Ah, Calum. Nice of you to come.' She spoke in a deep, husky voice. 'Please take a seat. I won't keep you. I thought it might be helpful if the two of us had a little chat. If you don't mind, that is?'

She was a large and formidable woman, in possession of a masculine-looking face set on a frame shaped like a barrel. Ross considered that she might easily have been transgender. The voice, for starters, was husky enough to have been male or female. She had a sizeable bosom, squashed beneath a tweed jacket done up tightly over an ivory-coloured blouse with a ruffled neckline. She didn't stand when Ross arrived. Nor did she offer a hand for him to shake. The two rucksack-clad guides had already vanished.

'Do we know each other?' Ross said testily. Then, emboldened, he continued with a similar level of aggression. 'Are you the one responsible for getting me arrested yesterday? For stealing my money? For trashing my apartment and wasting my time?' The venom in his voice was genuine, the anger quickly bubbling to the surface.

'I poured some tea for you,' she said, deliberately ignoring Ross's rant.

It was a smoker's voice, the words rasping in her throat.

'Now, Calum, I don't want to take up too much of your time. I believe you're here to meet someone off a train shortly. Let me, therefore, be brief. My name is Frances Riordan and I am a humble civil servant working for people you need not be troubled with. Amongst the many things that my team and I do is follow closely the actions and intentions of numerous people of a different nationality to ourselves. People we believe are doing or might be planning to do things against our national interests. All right so far?'

Ross shrugged indifferently and said nothing. He drew one of the two teacups towards him and took a sip. The tables were positioned outside, on the concourse itself. There was a constant hubbub of noise, the sound echoing under the enormous curves of the steel and glass roof high above them. It was a good place for a discreet conversation. Even shoppers passing back and forth into the food store inches from their table would have been hard-pressed to hear their conversation.

'One character who has been of acute interest recently to the British government is a Russian by the name of Oleg Usmanov. The name is probably familiar to you. He is a spy, working under the cover of being a Second Secretary at the Russian Embassy in Ankara. A very important spy, as it happens, since we believe Usmanov controls a considerable network of agents across the Balkans, Turkey and into the Middle East. Usmanov is married, I hardly need tell you, to a journalist by the name of Natalia Borisenko.' Riordan took a sip of tea at this stage and peered at Ross over the rim of her teacup to see if there was any reaction. Ross remained impassive. He was playing this very cool, a point that Riordan registered. 'Usmanov also happens to be close to the Russian President,' she went on. 'They were at school together. That fact, together with the importance of Usmanov's role as a spy, puts him firmly on our radar.'

'Can we cut to the chase? This is all very interesting, but several things have happened these last twenty-four hours to make me decidedly grumpy. If you are about to hint that you might have had a hand in some or all of them, I will be extremely pissed off.'

'Calum. You find yourself in a unique position. You have a relationship with Usmanov's wife, a person of acute interest to us. She, more than anyone, is closest to Usmanov and his secrets.'

'I don't think you've been doing your homework. Natalia hates her husband. He abuses her, treats her appallingly and she can't wait to be able to escape from his odious clutches.'

'Quite, Calum. So why doesn't she?'

'Well, she's trying to.'

'Precisely. But she hasn't yet succeeded, has she?'

'What are you getting at?'

'The point is, Calum, that if she did simply walk, she knows that the chances are very high that her husband would have her killed. You too, I suspect. Am I right?'

Ross fiddled with his cup as he contemplated his answer.

'Possibly,' he said at length. 'Though why on earth do you think she's on her way to see me today? The answer is because she has already decided to run. It is going to happen. This trip is her one final check before the big leap.'

'Our analysis is that if Natalia comes to live with you, wherever in the world the pair of you set up your new life, she will only be confident in walking away if one of two conditions are fulfilled. Either she starts a new life with a new identity, one she feels Oleg will never discover. Or, and we think this to be the most likely, she brings with her some kind of collateral. Something that can protect her – and you – from Usmanov's vengeance. Secrets that can be used against her husband to keep him at bay.'

'Maybe you're right. Who can say?'

'Calum, I have a proposition to put to you today. Are you prepared to listen?'

'That depends on what it is.'

'It's very simple. I – we all, in fact – would very much like you to be working for us. In secret, naturally. Life otherwise to go on as normal. No one – especially Natalia – is ever to know. We pay well. All we ask in return is that, assuming that our premise about Natalia having access to her husband's secrets is correct, then we'd like your help and connivance in having sight of these.'

'You're asking me to spy on Natalia?' He laughed scornfully. 'Why should I want to do that, for God's sake?'

'Well, hopefully for several reasons, Calum. One of them might be patriotic, another might be financial. There is, of course, your liberty to consider.'

'Meaning what, exactly?'

'You are in a somewhat difficult predicament with the police at the moment, so I understand. We find ourselves arguably in a unique position to make all that disappear for you, if we were to find ourselves all working on the same team. If we leave events to their own devices, the chances of you escaping a custodial sentence currently look, from where I sit, slender.'

'You bastard. Are you blackmailing me?'

'Heaven forbid, Calum. I'm trying to be helpful. We want to be friends. Friends help each other. If you were on board, all I am saying is that we could apply a little pressure in one or two quarters to allow certain charges, assuming they were ever formalised, to be dropped.'

'Answer me one thing.' Ross was standing, the anger in his voice inescapable. 'Were you or any of your team responsible for trashing my apartment yesterday and for hacking my bank account?'

'Absolutely not, I promise. My team were not in any way responsible. I'm proposing solely to find a way to get you off the hook. Think about it, Calum. Don't take too long. Let me give you my card.' She handed him a plain white business card that had her name and a London telephone number on it. 'Call this number at any time, day or night. Tell me you want to join our team and I'll take care of the rest. You have my word on that.'

Ross snatched the card from her hand and walked away without saying a further word.

The train was due within the hour. Ross, still angry about his conversation with Riordan, had time to kill. He wandered into a bar across the road from the station and ordered a steak and ale pie, plus a light beer from a bored-looking server behind the bar. He paid in cash and carried his beer to a seat in a corner cubicle. As he waited for his food to arrive, he telephoned the hotel to ask how much it would cost to have flowers delivered to his room. The concierge was polite but unable to offer any help. The hotel had no valid credit or debit card on file. As a result, they were unable to make purchases on Ross's behalf.

His food arrived and he ate hungrily, wondering how Natalia was feeling. She'd chosen to travel via Paris to meet a source for an exposé she was writing about the role of organised crime in funding elections in Turkey. It was a sensitive subject and one that required a face-to-face meeting. It also gave her a reason to be that much closer to Ross in London. He'd offered to meet her in Paris, but she'd wanted to come to London. She was going to be excited and not a little nervous about meeting again, this time away from Istanbul. Their last snatched conversation had suggested she had found something. Ross hoped it really was a treasure trove full of secrets. It would be welcome news on so many levels.

He checked his watch. Twenty minutes before her arrival.

He pulled out Riordan's card from his pocket and examined it. Could this British spook have been responsible for putting him through the wringer these last twenty-four hours? Or had it been, as he'd become more and more convinced until now, Oleg Usmanov acting out of revenge? Both parties had their motives. Riordan had strenuously denied any involvement: *my team were not in any way responsible.* That statement had contained a certain amount of wriggle room. A civil service maxim came to mind: *believe nothing until it is officially denied.*

Chapter 31

London

In the days and weeks of self-doubt, introspection and denial that would follow, the next hour of Calum Ross's life was usually cited by those in the official clandestine agencies of the United Kingdom as either undeniable proof of his guilt, or incontrovertible evidence of his innocence. Lawyers for the prosecution – for there would be many hovering in the wings – would argue that the tradecraft shown by Ross during this one particular hour went further than was ever envisaged in any teaching – or athletics – training curriculum. Counsel for the defence would argue that those assertions were speculative at best and largely malicious conjecture. That the talent-spotters might have missed such a fine potential candidate was seen not as a failing on anyone's part, more a credit to Ross's latent talents as a potential future recruit. Whether this was an actual defence or a mere vindication of their previous failings was never argued. What was undeniable, they would suggest, was that his actions and behaviour both before and especially during the ensuing episode proved *beyond reasonable doubt* that he was perfect for the job. *Quod erat demonstrandum.* Game, if not set and match, to the defence.

*

Ross, his lunch eaten and beer finished, crossed the road towards St. Pancras station and checked his watch. There was enough time to complete a circuit around the station perimeter. Just to make sure there were no familiar faces lurking. No olive-skinned Caucasians or men wearing Yankees fleeces. No stern-faced women drinking tea alone whilst watching passengers arriving on the Eurostar.

From that moment, life is going to get complicated.

He knew what he had to do. Someone like him didn't need spy school.

He headed along the pavement that ran the length of the station terminus, aiming for the busy Euston Road up ahead. He passed black cabs, disgorging passengers and their large suitcases. Weaved between tourists coming in the opposite direction, dragging luggage on wheels. Narrowly avoided a collision with one – a woman carrying a bulging rucksack with a foam bedroll tied underneath, her head in a mobile phone, unaware of Ross bearing down on her. Before he reached Euston Road, he ducked back inside the terminus building, through an archway to the right. It was an interior walkway that led to the rear entrance of the station concourse a short distance up ahead. Bringing him a circuitous back way into the shopping concourse, close by the set of three tables where he had recently had his cosy chat with Frances Riordan. If Riordan were still in situ, she would most likely be looking away from him. Towards the Eurostar Arrivals area, several metres in the other direction.

This time, however, the tables were empty and Riordan was gone. He slowed his pace and scanned the crowded concourse. There were retail outlets to the left and retail outlets to the right. Besides the hubbub created by shoppers and passengers alike, there were intermittent sounds of arriving and departing trains, their wheels screeching as they rolled in and out of the platforms one floor above. Distant passenger announcements and the occasional train whistle added to the cacophony. Periodically, the pedestrian flow along the centre aisle of the shopping concourse was interrupted by a set of stairs or a glass-fronted elevator leading to and from the platform level. The areas around these obstacles was where travellers gathered to wait for their trains. In one, tucked under a staircase, was the piano Ross had heard earlier. This time, it was silent, the small crowd dissipated, now only a handful of people loitering. Most were on the phone, consulting paper maps or scanning mobile devices. Further along, two ATMs filled a similar space. Ahead was a café with yet more tables set outside. All were busy, probably occupied by people like Ross: waiting for friends or loved ones to appear through the secure Eurostar arrival doors positioned immediately opposite.

As Ross meandered, he saw nothing that twitched his radar. Nobody he recognised. He walked the length of the mall, up to the end where several fast-food outlets were enjoying a brisk trade. It was only as he spun around, deliberately sharply, that he noticed the woman. She had been ambling along behind, about fifteen paces to his rear and to the left. Short, curly dark hair, scuffed leather bomber jacket and a cavernous black bag slung over a shoulder. It was the head movement that Ross spotted. No eye contact, no sudden change of direction, only a slight movement that caught his eye. He carried on, senses heightened. One of Usmanov's people? It was always going to be a risk. Close by the Eurostar check-in area, shy of the Arrivals door, he spun 180 degrees on his heel once again. Just to make certain. There was no sign of the woman. His eyes rested on a beefy chauffeur type: muscles bulging under a tight suit jacket and a thick neck. What made him stand out was his reaction to Ross's turn. He made a slight misstep. A boxer's shuffle, as if an adjustment was required given Ross's course correction. Again, no eye contact, no other signs of recognition. Ross stopped by a chocolate shop and peered in the window, waiting a short while before stepping inside. A sales assistant came forward with a tray offering a sample. Ross turned slightly towards the window as he selected a glossy-looking chocolate. The bomber-jacketed woman was staring at the shop window opposite. Ross thanked the assistant and walked out. He checked his watch. The train should be arriving any moment now.

He and Natalia had previously agreed an arrival protocol. In case Usmanov's watchers happened to be looking. No intimate affection. Not even a kiss. Just a friendly wave and a handshake. This was to be Viktor's chess teacher welcoming his private tennis pupil to London. Ross took up his position in the centre of the concourse. In one of the loitering areas. Along with the meet-and-greet squad of chauffeurs holding cards with passengers' names on them. Within eye contact of the beefy guy with the thick neck and bulging muscles standing ten metres away. But not looking at him. As indeed he was not looking at Ross. Yet.

Chapter 32

London

Brendan North had a team of 'bloodhounds' at St. Pancras station. According to the Security Services' unpublished but universally recognised Turf War Convention, the code that delineated the boundaries between his bloodhounds in MI5 and what North liked cheekily to refer to as Riordan's "assassins" in MI6, any operation of a non-analytical nature conducted by the Security Service within the United Kingdom was for MI5's bloodhounds alone to deal with.

Project WATCHKEEPER had been a strange example of interdepartmental co-operation almost from day one. Strange, because it had not been thoroughly examined, reviewed or vetted by anyone in MI6's chain of command. Instead, operational planning and purview had been kept tightly under the sole responsibility of Riordan and her small but highly effective team of assassins. Strange also because, despite this somewhat unconventional approach, Riordan had felt no qualms or hesitation in eliciting the private support of North and his bloodhounds when the Usmanov operation was beginning operational manoeuvres in the UK. Successful co-operation on WATCHKEEPER relied on the small but important matter of trust between all parties, that rare and special commodity that allowed the formality of turf war conventions either to work or be cast aside. Despite their fifteen years' difference in age, North and Riordan seemed to share similar views on many things in life, perhaps not surprising given that neither fitted the more traditional norms of either gender or sexual proclivity, increasingly an asset these days within their respective organisations. It was a good basis on which to build trust. Which, in turn, only benefited WATCHKEEPER.

North's bloodhounds at St. Pancras that afternoon numbered three in total. One, a man in his fifties sporting a well-worn cloth cap and padded jacket. A second was a chauffeur, standing near the Arrivals area holding a piece of card with the name of a randomly chosen passenger inscribed upon it. The third was a woman up at platform level, leaning down over the balcony. Dressed in a train company's livery, she had a bird's-eye view over the entire shopping mall. All three spotted Ross and called his position into WATCHKEEPER's London control centre, set deep underground at Millbank House, MI5's headquarters in Westminster.

Also on the station concourse that afternoon were two of McIlvoy's plain-clothed officers, people who had not yet met Ross but who, by now, knew all about him. A station sweeper, armed with a long-handled dustpan and brush and pushing a small cleaning trolley; and a young recruit fresh out of police training college at Hendon, wearing a mustard-coloured sweatshirt. McIlvoy had specifically asked for this young constable. He was rumoured to be fast on his feet.

'One more thing. Find out why the dog unit was at Green Park station yesterday,' she'd asked her deputy over the phone once she'd made the surveillance request. 'They're usually sent for a specific purpose. I'm curious why they were there at that particular time. Was it simply a lucky break or had someone tipped them off?'

PRESENT DAY

Chapter 33

London

DCI McIlvoy began watching the live CCTV camera footage at St. Pancras station as much out of professional curiosity than any foreboding that something was about to happen. She was, at that stage, blissfully unaware of the concurrent surveillance operation being conducted by Brendan North and his team at Thames House. DC Frank D'Souza had four different computer monitors on the go. McIlvoy was standing, leaning over D'Souza's shoulders, watching each of them avidly.

'There's Ross,' she said, pointing to a man in a dark red waterproof anorak wandering into the shopping mall. 'He's a cool customer,' she went on, more to herself than to D'Souza. 'If he wasn't a schoolteacher, I'd have reckoned he was casing the joint. What do you think, Frank?' She put her hand on D'Souza's shoulder for a moment. 'Can we hear audio from the team on the ground?'

'Sure,' D'Souza said, unplugging his earphone from a jack on a console in front of him. Immediately a background buzz from the station was audible. He rotated a small dial and the volume increased.

'Where's the new grad? The one who's the sprinter?'

D'Souza pointed to a blond-haired individual in a mustard-yellow top.

'Not exactly blending in with the crowd today, is he? It'll be good training for him, though, if nothing else. Hang on, what the heck happened there?'

Ross had, moments earlier, performed a rapid 180-degree turn on one heel.

'Do they teach counter-surveillance manoeuvres at teacher training college these days? It got a reaction, though, look!' she said, pointing to a large man following in Ross's wake. 'Can you rewind a few seconds? There.' They stared at the screen. 'Well, well, well. Our friend appears to have a tail. Calum Ross, what the hell's been going on that you haven't been telling us about?'

They watched the different camera feeds until Ross arrived outside the Eurostar Arrivals entrance.

'That's our other person on the ground,' D'Souza said, pointing to the cleaner with the dustpan and brush. Sure enough, they could hear her muted voice over the desktop loudspeaker.

'*Subject now in position for the Eurostar from Paris. I'm wandering past now.*'

McIlvoy smiled as she watched the feed.

'That's more like what I call undercover.'

D'Souza pointed to a different screen. It was from a camera at platform level, immediately above where Ross was now standing. It showed a train conductor, leaning over the balustrade, looking down at the small crowd in front of the Arrivals gate.

'This person intrigues me. She hasn't moved for at least the last five minutes. It's a prime surveillance position.'

'Interesting. Another one. Who the hell is Ross meeting? Why this sudden attention, for heaven's sake?'

'Passengers are coming out now,' D'Souza said, indicating another monitor. They watched the screen together in silence. The camera, positioned within the secure area, recorded people as they filed past Customs Officers and UK Border Agency personnel moments before stepping out onto the concourse. In time, they noticed Ross greeting someone. The young trainee's voice was excited over the radio.

'Subject's making contact with a woman. One wheelie bag and a rucksack. I'm going to follow.'

'Zoom in on the woman,' McIlvoy said, eager to see the person who appeared to be the centre of so much attention. An attractive female, perhaps mid-to-late-thirties, swivelled around to face Ross. She offered him her hand in greeting and he, all smiles, pumped hers with enthusiasm.

'More friends than lovers, perhaps?' D'Souza muttered.

'Could be an act.' She leaned forward, staring in sudden disbelief. 'Now, wait a minute. What's that she's carrying? For God's sake, is that one of those rucksacks? You know, I think it is. She's only carrying one of those bloody rucksacks! Well, that just about does it for me. Do you know what? I'm sick of all this bullshit Ross's been spouting. Let's haul them both in for questioning.' She tapped D'Souza briefly on the shoulder. 'Call our team on the ground. I want Ross and the woman under arrest and back here, pronto!'

*

Two miles away as the crow flies, Brendan North was watching the same video feeds as McIlvoy – and several more for good measure. The operation was being monitored step-by-step by a small team within the MI5 operations room at Thames House on Millbank, a subterranean room colloquially known as the Bunker. Ross had taken hold of the woman's rucksack and the pair were walking briskly away from the Arrivals area. A different camera allowed them to watch the same scene viewed from the front, close to where one of North's team in a flat cap and quilted jacket was positioned. Another showed Ross and the woman as they walked away from the Arrivals area as viewed from the rear.

'Nice-looking rucksack Ross is carrying, don't you think?' North said.

Bronwyn West, an analyst standing next to North, didn't react, instead pointing at a different screen with a tiny green laser pen.

'Notice the sudden interest in Ross and the woman.' West spoke in an even tone. 'This person here in yellow is an easy-to-spot tail,' she said, indicating with the laser. 'Almost too easy, in fact.'

'Probably one of McIlvoy's,' North sneered.

'Then, besides our own officers both here and here' – she again pointed – 'there's this woman in a leather bomber jacket. She's definitely following them. As, it would appear' – she moved the laser to a different screen – 'is this one here.' The green dot was focused on a muscular, thick-necked man dressed in a tightly fitting suit jacket.

They watched the next thirty seconds in growing alarm and disbelief. Ross stepping to one side, disarming the knife from the woman, the thick-necked muscle man pointing a gun at Natalia, Ross attempting to disarm him, their brief tussle, the weapon firing whilst the woman ran away, stabbing the journalist.

'Holy fuck! Ross has killed the man! Where the hell are our people?'

'One's there,' West said, pointing to the screen as a man dressed in a chauffeur's uniform drew a gun on Ross.

'Under no circumstances, I repeat, no circumstances is he to risk a shot that hurts the woman, can we be crystal clear about that?' North cried out anxiously. A man at a nearby desk, a half-headset clipped to his head, spoke rapidly into a mouthpiece.

'Message acknowledged,' he came back seconds later.

'Shit! Is she okay?'

'Ambulance is on its way. ETA thirty seconds.'

'Fuck, this is out of control! The proverbial is going to well and truly hit the fan.'

'I think Ross is going to do a runner,' West said solemnly.

'Explain?'

'Look at his body language.'

'Tell that man with the gun not to open fire. I repeat, he is *not* to use his weapon.'

'Order acknowledged,' came the affirmation across the room moments later.

'At least the paramedics are there.' They watched as Ross laid the gun down on the floor. 'Let's see if you're right. Can someone get me Frances Riordan on the phone? I need to speak with her urgently.'

Chapter 34

London

McIlvoy was worried. There were now two men on the concourse with guns and one woman had just been stabbed. The risk to life had become too great. She grabbed D'Souza's phone and dialled the designated senior officer of the day. It was time to declare a critical incident: for this, she needed authorisation. Within the command protocols developed for rapidly developing events of this nature, the purpose of the call was to appoint McIlvoy in a temporary role granting her total authority to direct all the emergency response teams on the ground. It took next to no time for the Duty Superintendent to listen to, and then grant, her request. Next, she rang the Duty Officer at the Met Police's Special Operations facility in Lambeth, requesting immediate live surveillance and intelligence analysis on the incident that was unfolding at St. Pancras. Tommy 'the Hutch' Hutchinson, one of the Met's longest-serving officers and something of a legend in tracking fugitives successfully, was immediately available and assigned to the case. McIlvoy had worked with him only twice before and felt privileged to have him on the team.

'Hutch, we have one female down, abdominal stab wound. Plus, one male perp either dead or with a serious gunshot wound. Ambulances are required immediately at the northern entrance to

St. Pancras station. Another perp has fled into Pancras Road. Female, dark hair, leather jacket. I need her tracked and placed under arrest. She may be armed. There's another man on the concourse right now with a gun. I need to know who he is and have him brought in for questioning.'

'I understand that there are already two ambulances on their way, Mac. ETA in less than a minute.'

McIlvoy smiled momentarily. Few people called her by her old nickname these days.

'Hold on a moment,' McIlvoy said, staring at the screen on D'Souza's desk. Ross had, only moments earlier, been putting down the gun he'd been holding. She watched, mesmerised, as he bolted from the scene. 'Shit! We now have another suspect on the run. Male, red anorak, fast on his feet, heading north also into Pancras Road. Name of Ross. Calum Ross. There's an undercover officer wearing a mustard-yellow sweatshirt in pursuit. Ross is unlikely to be armed, but we can't be certain.'

'We have them,' Hutch responded.

'Can we order helicopter surveillance from NPAS as a priority?' The National Police Air Service provided air support to police operations nationwide from any of fourteen airbases around the country.

'One unit is already airborne out of North Weald. ETA in less than five minutes. Another's being diverted from south of the river.'

'Good. One more thing. There's a roll-on suitcase and a small, black rucksack on the station concourse, both belonging to the woman who's been stabbed. I need them both recovered. I want to know urgently who she is and what's in them, the rucksack especially.'

'Are you coming here, Mac? It's usually best.'

'Yes, I'll be over right now. Call me back on my mobile.' She gave him the number. 'Then we can stay in contact whilst I'm in transit. Oh, and while we're at it, call Brendan North at Thames House, will you? I need him to join us at the Command Centre in

Lambeth. Tell him that's an order, not a request.' She smiled as she put the phone down, waiting for her mobile to ring. It was nice to be able to pull rank over Brendan North just once in a while.

Chapter 35

London

Calum Ross burst out of the side entrance to St. Pancras station and turned right, directly into a one-way street, the traffic rushing straight towards him. In the distance, approaching at speed, were two police cars, lights on full-beam and flashing, sirens blaring. This was not a good start. He contemplated reversing direction, but ruled this out when he swivelled his head. The plain-clothed policeman in the mustard-yellow sweatshirt was already hot in pursuit. Thirty metres away and closing fast. Behind him, the other man with a gun was struggling to keep up. The chances of collateral damage from a stray bullet were arguably still too high for him to be risking a shot.

Ross raced across the road and darted down a quiet, residential side street. He was a good runner, especially over middle distances; however, the young lad on his tail seemed something of a sprinter. Ross checked again as he took a corner: the distance had reduced to less than twenty metres and was closing. At his running club in Istanbul, the Hash House Harriers, his pursuer might have made a good hare for hashers – the hounds – to chase after. Always assuming that alcohol didn't impede the running process, which today was not going to be an issue. Ross ran with a pounding headache, the result of having head-butted the killer on the station platform, the pain jarring with every step he ran.

Dear God, he hoped Natalia was going to be all right.

There had been a lot of blood gushing from the knife wound to Natalia's stomach even before the paramedics had arrived. Evidently the woman who'd stabbed her had escaped the station without being caught.

Unfamiliar with the neighbourhood and desperate to avoid running into a dead end, he zigzagged right and then immediately left at the next junction. The steady rhythm of pounding footsteps echoed off the tenement blocks and terraced houses along the street. Neither man had the perfect gear for running. Ross was thankful that he, at least, was wearing trainers. A T-junction loomed up ahead, and he decided to take another right-left combination once again. He snatched a quick glance behind, sensing the separation between the two men had reduced further. Perhaps, though, not by as much as Ross feared. Consciously, he began lengthening his stride, using his experience as a distance runner to increase speed little by little. Sure enough, a short while later, as the road curved gently to the right, he sneaked another glance over his shoulder. This time, the gap had increased. He tore through a set of bollards designed to prevent cars from cutting through to the busy road up ahead. He veered left onto the wide pavement, immediately sensing an opportunity to escape his pursuer. Two double-decker red London buses were stationary in traffic a short distance in front. Coming the other way, heading back in the direction he'd just come from, were various cars, a glazier's van, and another double-decker bus. These, too, were slowing to a crawl, a set of traffic lights at a busy intersection nearby slowing everything down. Ross put on a burst of speed, overtaking both buses before ducking across the road to the other side. For a brief moment, he was going to be invisible to his pursuer.

*

Lance Kenny was having the time of his life. Fresh out of training college, he'd always fancied undercover police work. Here he was, week three into the job and already hot-footing it around the streets of London, chasing after a suspect. When DCI McIlvoy had asked for him in person, he had felt especially proud. He would not let her or the team down. The DCI had said that the suspect was a good runner. Well, so was he. Especially good out of the starting blocks.

Ross had made a strong start, the unexpected nature of his flight catching Kenny momentarily off guard. By the time Kenny was off and running, heart thumping, thigh and calf muscles pumping, Ross was as much as thirty metres in front. That gap closed as Kenny's faster sprinting technique kicked in. With Ross weaving this way and that around the back streets, the gap kept gradually reducing. Kenny estimated that it had dropped to as low as fifteen metres or less when, after nearly two minutes or more of intense effort, he found his energy levels starting to flag. They maintained the separation for a short while before Kenny was disappointed to see Ross edging ahead once again. It spurred him to run faster, but with limited noticeable effect, Ross already weaving around a traffic bollard and then veering left onto the pavement alongside the major road up ahead. The traffic was stationary, two London buses nose to tail amongst other traffic that was no longer moving. Unexpectedly, Ross darted across the road to the right, immediately in front of the two buses. The angle of Kenny's approach, twenty metres in Ross's wake, meant that he lost sight of Ross for several seconds.

Which was unfortunate since, by the time he felt able to cross the road, Ross had vanished. One moment he'd been there; Kenny had blinked; then he was gone. Frustrated, Kenny glanced around frantically, hands on knees, drawing breath heavily. There were a few retail outlets on this side of the street, but no sign of Ross. A bus was heading back the way they'd come, but he instantly dismissed this. If it had been an old Routemaster, with its open rear deck that people could use to jump on and off, then fine. The one he was looking at needed to come to a halt and open its doors before anyone could clamber aboard.

So, how in hell's name had Ross managed to lose him?

The glazier's van, a white lorry with a sloping rack on the passenger side, was perfect. Normally full of outsized panes of glass strapped to the side, the rack was empty today. No sooner had Ross crossed the road in front of the lead bus than the van was alongside, crawling towards a set of traffic lights up ahead. Ross grabbed one of the webbing straps, stepping up onto the rail and flattening his body against the side. Remembering his athletic training, he adjusted his breathing, inhaling and exhaling slowly, the pounding in his head and tension in his neck diminishing as he forced himself to relax. Precious seconds later, the van began to move, crawling through the traffic lights before picking up speed as it headed towards the clear road beyond.

Chapter 36

London

Long before Ross had time to feel safe, another crisis loomed. The one-way system that skirted the railway terminus meant that the glazier's van was being directed down Pancras Road, back towards St. Pancras station itself. The strident sounds he could hear getting closer by the second – jarring blends of out-of-sync, two-tone sirens – were a wake-up call. The van was heading back towards the very place he had recently fled! They were already slowing, traffic grinding to a gradual standstill because of the incident. Sensing an opportunity to jump off the rail and head down a different side street, he stopped himself just in time as two police motorbikes, their blue lights flashing, rapidly approached the van from the rear. Ross held his breath as the bikes hurtled by without stopping.

The van, still inching its way forward, was now beside the entrance to St. Pancras Gardens. Ross slid to the ground, careful to avoid alerting the driver. He took off at a run, passing through a pair of gold-crested wrought-iron gates framing the entrance. The gardens were misnamed: the place consisted mainly of areas of poorly maintained grass interspersed with crisscrossing paths, mature trees and the odd tombstone over-spilt from a churchyard next door. Ross ran towards a distant exit on the far side, checking his tail along the way, satisfied that the runner in the mustard-yellow sweatshirt wasn't following any longer. He was grateful for being fit – and for the many hours he'd spent hashing around Istanbul. He was back in familiar territory. So far, the hounds were out of sight. He had to hope that his knee didn't give up.

He veered around a small monument in the centre of the gardens and could hear a helicopter buzzing like an angry hornet. How near it was, it was difficult to tell. He realized, arguably too late, that his red anorak would be easily visible from a helicopter. Spotting a litter bin close to the exit up ahead, he jettisoned the garment as he ran past, first removing the chess set from its inner pocket and placing it securely in the deep pocket at the front of his cardigan.

Emerging onto a minor backstreet close to the railway, he turned left and ran towards a building site up ahead. Cranes towered across the skyline, while several identical apartment blocks in various stages of construction stood on either side of the road, plywood walls painted in blue keeping the area secure. Despite the road being almost deserted and with no pedestrians, the sound of helicopters overhead and distant sirens made him anxious. Which was when he remembered his mobile phone, as good a tracking device as anyone might ever need. He withdrew it from his pocket and pressed various buttons to ensure that it was no longer connected to any network or hotspot. Rounding a corner to the left, desperate to find a way to escape undetected, he saw something that made his heart soar. It was a bridge over a canal. Where there was a canal, there was likely to be a towpath. If he could find a way down there unseen, he might even stand a chance of slipping away from the area unnoticed.

Chapter 37

London

'I've lost contact!' came Kenny's despondent voice in McIlvoy's earpiece. 'I can't see him anywhere.' McIlvoy was being driven at high speed, full blues and twos, towards the Command Centre south of the river. 'He stepped in front of a bus, crossed the road, and then vanished. I've searched everywhere. I'm sorry, everyone.'

'Keep looking. Check every shop. He can't have gone far. Is there CCTV footage available, Hutch?'

'Not in that part of the world, it's a black spot. Listen up, everyone.' McIlvoy could hear him addressing the wider team assembling in the Lambeth control room. 'We have live feeds coming directly from the two NPAS choppers circling the area above the station. I want everyone who's available to sift through the footage. We have two targets. Target One is female. Short, black hair, leather bomber jacket. She exited the station into Pancras Road. How she made her escape is not known. Sanjay,' he called out to one of his team, 'I need all relevant CCTV footage at or around the station taken apart with a toothcomb. See if you can find out where she went. Target Two is a bit easier. He's male, dark red anorak, most likely a fast runner, with a young police officer in pursuit. I want all eyes on the live footage. Let's see if we can find them both. They won't have gone far.'

'What about Ross's mobile phone?' McIlvoy chipped in.

'We lost it from the grid a short while ago.'

'Is there any other way to locate him?'

'I've got someone running his bank details. We'll put a trace on his cards.'

'I wouldn't hold your breath. He told me earlier that an ATM ate his debit card this morning.'

'Well, he might have others. We'll know soon.'

'His bank account was hacked and cleaned out of funds yesterday. That's what he claimed, at least.'

'Interesting. That'll make it hard for him to get cash. That could be very helpful. What do we know about Calum Ross's friends and networks? Anything?'

'Nothing that I'm aware.'

'Fine, let's get to work on it, then. Amy,' he called out to another colleague, his booming voice echoing in McIlvoy's ear. 'Drop what you're doing and focus on Calum Ross's social media accounts. I want to know his friendship groups, school friends, the works. We need chapter and verse on the man as quickly as you can. Anything that might give clues as to where he might be heading. Mac, does he have a valid passport?'

'Yes, but according to Ross, it was stolen yesterday.'

'Fine. We'll run a stop on it and see what happens. Now.' Hutch paused, and McIlvoy imagined him surveying the control room. 'It doesn't look as if we're having much luck in locating anyone at present. Tell me, what do we know about Target One?'

'Absolutely zilch. No name or anything.'

'Toby, see if you can get any facial recognition off the station CCTVs for Target One. I want to know who she is, where she came from, what she had for breakfast. Run her visuals through every database you can think of. Let's pull some rank here. And Toby, while you're at it, do the same for the dead man on the concourse, the one who was shot. I need to know his life history as fast as you can, too. Mac, what about the woman who was stabbed? Who is she?'

'We don't yet know. Recently off the Eurostar from Paris, that's all we know. How she knows Ross is still a blank.'

'Right, listen up. Who's not busy? Fine, Sunita – I want you to focus on the injured woman. Who she is, where she came from, how she knew Target Two, the works. Also, find out her condition and which hospital they're taking her to. Mac, should we be assigning her some protection?'

'That's a good thought, Hutch. Can you fix that?'

'Sure. Sunita, make that a priority. So, Mac, a quick update. Target One remains missing and we're having no joy spotting Target Two at the moment either. He may even have ditched the anorak.'

'How are we going to find him, Hutch?'

'We'll find him, trust me. We usually do. How far away are you?'

'About two minutes.'

'Plenty of time then. See you shortly.'

Chapter 38

London

'Frances, it's Brendan. We've got a situation. Where are you?'

'In a car, on the way back to Vauxhall Cross. What's happened?'

'WATCHKEEPER's going pear-shaped. The Usmanov woman's been stabbed, Ross has fled the scene, there's a dead body on the concourse and St. Pancras is in fucking meltdown.'

'That's disappointing.' Riordan's voice was unnaturally calm. 'Tell me about the woman?'

'The paramedics are doing their best. I've been summoned, apparently, so we'll find out shortly.'

'And the dead man?'

'He was waving a gun at Ross, the two men got into a fight, the gun went off, the man died, Ross walked away.'

'That was fortunate. Who was the man with the gun?'

'We don't know.'

'And where's Ross now?'

'AWOL. One other person fled the scene at the same time.'

'Tell me more.'

'It was a woman we'd not seen before. She's the one who tried to stab the journalist.'

Riordan paused. 'I smell the lingering odour of Russians in the air.'

'You might be right.'

'Of course I'm fucking right, darling. The bear's chain has been well and truly rattled. We need to find Ross. Especially if the woman's life is on the line. Why's he gone AWOL?'

'Because his fingerprints were on the murder weapon, most likely. Plus he was almost arrested twice these last twenty-four hours. Even before the Usmanov woman turned up with yet another of those rucksacks in her possession. Running was probably the easiest option. Even for a schoolteacher.'

'The rucksacks were a lovely touch, you know, Brendan. You're always so clever at the operational details.'

'How did your conversation with Ross go?'

'Let's wait and see. The fact that he's chosen to cut and run will prove helpful, I feel sure. Who's in charge of the police operation, by the way? You say you've been summoned.'

'Lauren McIlvoy. Life can be full of interesting turns and twists, don't you think?'

'My dear Brendan! What a delightful surprise! I bet the two of you can't wait to see each other.'

'What do you think we should tell her?'

'Where are you meeting?'

'At the Command Centre in Lambeth.'

'Why don't I come over then? Let me be the one to explain things. That way, you can deny all and any involvement in the matter. How does that sound?'

'That, my friend, would be perfect.'

Chapter 39

London

The Command Centre control room was smaller than McIlvoy had imagined, but no less impressive. Multiple screens filled one wall of the windowless room: three rows comprising eight televisions to a row, each showing different live images. Scattered in places around the room, in an approximate horseshoe, were twenty or more workstations positioned so that each occupant had a line of sight not only to their own screens but also to the images on the bank at the front. Standing in the centre, like the conductor of an orchestra, pacing, shirtsleeves rolled up, was Hutch.

'Mac, welcome aboard. Good to see you again,' he said, bounding forward and shaking McIlvoy's hand. 'Listen up, everyone, this is Lauren McIlvoy. She's Gold Commander on this one, in case I need to remind you all.'

'Thanks. No standing on ceremonies, just call me Mac. I appreciate everyone's efforts. What news?'

'We may have a couple of breaks. First, a man fitting Ross's description has just been spotted. No red anorak, but otherwise we're sure it's him, caught on CCTV running north on a back road leading away from the station. Camley Street. The good news is that this particular road is a dead end.' A street map appeared instantly on one screen. 'The bad news is that there's a pedestrian cut-through at the end here,' he said, pointing towards the top, 'that links the northern end with Tufnell Park and beyond. Isn't that close to where Ross lives?'

'Close. Further north, towards Archway actually.'

'There we go, bingo! He's heading to familiar territory. They always head home in the end. Okay, with your permission, we'll send units up ahead to block him in. Your young lad who lost him earlier. Is he still on the line?'

'I'm here,' Kenny called from afar.

'Good. Ross has been sighted on Camley Street, heading north. That's close to where you are. He's no longer wearing the red anorak. We'd like to use you to try to box him in from the rear. You might have the edge on us if you're on foot. Think you can handle that?'

'Sure, I'll do my best.'

'What about the two NPAS helicopters?' McIlvoy asked. 'Can't one of them help locate Ross?'

'That was the plan. We've hit a snag. Sod's law. The good news is that Alex over there,' he said, pointing to a nearby workstation, 'reviewed camera footage from outside the station. The woman in the bomber jacket was picked up by a stolen white Ford Transit, currently weaving its way in and around the back streets to the south of Euston Road. One chopper is currently on the van's tail, with multiple police units closing in as we speak. That's the good news.'

'And the bad?'

'The other helicopter has had to return to base. Engine malfunction.'

'Then we have to hope Kenny can catch Ross. What news on the victim's bag and rucksack?'

'The woman's name is Natalia Borisenko. Married to one Oleg Usmanov. She has a Russian passport and from credentials in her bag, she's a journalist. There was nothing in either the rucksack or her other bag of any concern. No drugs, explosives, weapons or anything like that. Simply clothes, books and a few personal items.'

'That's a shame.'

'No point chasing rabbits if there are none out there.' McIlvoy's mobile phone was buzzing. It was DC D'Souza back at Savile Row station.

'Frank, what is it?'

'Sorry to trouble you. You asked about the dog handling unit, yesterday at Green Park. In particular, why they were there. I thought you'd like to know. They had a tip-off. It was an anonymous caller.'

'Are you sure?'

'Yes, but wait, there's more. I checked the electronic call logs. Whoever rang in knew exactly who to speak to.'

'I don't get what you mean.'

'They direct-dialled straight through to the right department. Anonymous tip-offs usually come through the switchboard. This one didn't happen that way. How many folks out there know those kinds of numbers?'

'Very interesting,' McIlvoy said slowly. 'Well done. Great work. If you learn more, let me know immediately.' Hutch caught her staring at the floor for several seconds.

'Everything all right?'

McIlvoy looked up, momentarily embarrassed.

'Sorry, something else entirely. I was wondering, is it possible to watch the Ford Transit in real time?'

'Sure. Hitesh, enlarge the image, will you?' Four individual monitors at the centre of the bank in front of them suddenly merged into one large screen, two panels square. The white van in question was zig-zagging its way around Fitzrovia, the oblique camera angle shifting constantly as the orientation of the helicopter relative to the van kept changing. On a smaller screen to one side, a street map showed the van's location as a pulsing, red dot.

'I wonder where they're heading.' McIlvoy was mesmerised; the clarity of the images was amazing. They watched as two police motorbikes caught up with the van. One hung on the van's rear whilst the other bike pulled alongside the van, trying to overtake.

'Shit! Did you see that?' Hutch cried out a few seconds later.

The van had swung deliberately to one side, wedging the police outrider in a sandwich between it and vehicles parked on the edge of the street. Too late, the motorcyclist tried to brake, the front wheel catching the rear of the van, the bike and its rider slamming into one of the parked cars at speed. The second biker narrowly missed his fallen colleague, braking and swerving out of trouble only just in time, the bike sliding to the ground as the Transit accelerated away.

'I need an ambulance right now! On Margaret Street, beyond the junction with Great Titchfield Street. There's a police motorcyclist who's hit the deck and collided badly with a stationary vehicle. Another is also down, condition uncertain. Right, everyone, we can focus on Ross in a minute. This is personal. I want that van stopped and everyone inside it banged to rights.'

'We might be in luck. Traffic up ahead is at a standstill. Look!'

The helicopter camera feed showed the van grinding to a halt. Four cars were stationary in front and a panel van had tucked in behind. A police patrol car had got stuck in traffic at a junction a few metres behind, but two officers were already out of the car and making their way cautiously towards the van's rear doors. In a pincer movement, another pair of police motorcyclists were heading down the one-way street in the wrong direction, straight towards where the van was stopped. Suddenly, the passenger door of the van was flung open and a white male wearing a back-to-front baseball cap jumped out, sprinting away from the scene through a pedestrian-only side street. In the control room, they watched helplessly as the man raced towards one of the many entrances to Oxford Street Underground station.

'Shit! The bastard's getting away.'

'Should we be stopping all the trains?' McIlvoy asked.

'He won't be taking a train. He'll pop in one entrance and out another. Ditch the baseball cap and boom! – he'll be gone. At least the woman should be in the back of the van. That's something, at least.'

Except it wasn't. The moment the two police officers grabbed the rear door handle and opened it, they stared inside with disbelief. The van was empty.

Chapter 40

London

Ross's luck was in. Over the canal bridge was a small supermarket. Even better, tucked away behind it, a set of concrete stairs led down to the towpath itself. Risking a momentary detour, he hurried inside the shop in search of paracetamol and some water for his throbbing head, emerging a short time later and taking the steps down to the canal two at a time. He paused at the bottom, long enough to open the water bottle and down two tablets. Ahead lay a route that would lead back to King's Cross/St. Pancras and then onwards, east towards Islington; the opposite direction was going to take him towards Camden and then Regent's Park beyond that. Ross chose the latter: anything to increase the distance from the pandemonium at the station. He resumed running, this time at a slightly less frenetic pace.

*

Lance Kenny had been feeling despondent. It had felt harsh, having to admit defeat. A black mark against his name so early in his career. He'd been chastising himself for wearing unsuitable clothing, realising too late that a mustard-yellow sweatshirt made him stand out rather than blend in. Unlike Ross, he hadn't ditched the garment. Instead, it was tied around his waist, hanging down at the back and flapping like a skirt. Mollified at being given a second chance, he could hardly believe his luck when, rounding a sweeping bend, there was Ross – minus red cagoule – emerging from a supermarket and quickly ducking down a set of stairs out of sight. Kenny slowed to a walk as he crossed the canal, risking a downward glance and finding Ross taking a swig of water from a bottle before setting off running once more along the towpath.

'Can you hear me?' Kenny spoke quietly but with urgency into his neck microphone, realising too late that a wire must have become disconnected when he'd removed his sweatshirt. Hearing no reply, he cursed, deciding to take the initiative on his own and follow Ross. He would deal with the electronics later. This was his big opportunity to make amends for his earlier cock-up.

*

Ross felt instantly more relaxed beside the canal. His throbbing head eased and his mind switched to thoughts about the recent events at the station. Especially about Natalia – in particular, her injuries and where they might have taken her.

Just keep the woman safe.

There were any number of hospitals, the most likely being the Whittington, close to his flat at Archway, or University College London Hospital close to Euston. What he needed was a burner phone. He found the image of the dead man pervading his thoughts. He hadn't needed spy school to tell him how to cope with death. He'd seen more than his share of bodies during his time in the military. In any event, Ross hadn't been the one who'd pulled the trigger, even if the police might try to see things differently. He imagined McIlvoy's incessant questioning, glad to be on the run and not wasting time pointlessly with police procedure.

If things go to plan, somewhere along the journey contact will be made.

He felt in his rear trouser pocket for the card that Riordan had given him, feeling strangely comforted by the promise that had been made earlier. A 'get out of jail' card might indeed be a lifesaver.

Play hard to get. If more slack is needed, let the line out a little.

Well, he was certainly playing hard to get. What was really bothering him was Natalia. God, he hoped she was going to be okay.

It was a different, almost parallel universe beside the waterway, the pace of life considerably slower. Boats and pedestrians sauntered, most of the time unseen and unheard as they passed stealthily below the bustling neighbourhoods above. In places where the current appeared hardly to be moving, the water was covered in a thin layer of green algae. There were a few runners out that afternoon. Otherwise, apart from an occasional dog walker or an ambling pedestrian, the towpath was largely deserted. The canal ran mostly in a straight line, the path beside the water meandering gently. Only once did Ross check his tail, spotting a lone runner in his wake some way behind. Someone not, this time, in a mustard-yellow sweatshirt.

Close to the outskirts of Camden, he passed under a cast-iron road bridge. To his right, a set of brick stairs led up behind to a busy road above. On a whim, Ross made a U-turn, charging up the stairs, his knee instantly complaining. Instinct told him he needed to check his tail. Having survived undetected during many deep-cover reconnaissance missions, he knew better than to ignore those little radar twitches. The bridge parapet would be an ideal hiding place to discover whether anyone was following him.

Chapter 41

London

'What have we got?' The surgeon, his old gown discarded and a new one in the process of being tied behind his back by an orderly, was at the sink, scrubbing furiously.

'White female, we believe Russian, aged about mid-thirties, name Natalia,' said the senior paramedic, rattling off the condition report as part of his patient handover. 'Laceration, a knife wound, presumed deep, to the lower abdomen on the right side. The wound's been under compression all the way here. BP is ninety over sixty, pulse variable, currently hovering at around 120 and still only sixty per cent oxygen saturation. Generally fit and healthy, clearly in shock, she is struggling to be coherent. She understands English and states that she isn't pregnant.'

'We'll see about that in due course. How much blood's she had?' the surgeon asked, his back still turned as he nudged the long-handled taps to the off position with his elbows.

'One unit, O positive. Plus, she's been on saturated oxygen for the last ten minutes.'

'Any pain relief?'

'None.'

'Okay, thanks. Your team did a great job, as ever. Let's see if we can save this one. Right side, you said?'

'Correct.'

'Let's hope the knife missed the liver, then.'

Gowned, masked and gloved, he turned towards Natalia, who was being attended to by four nurses busy attaching wires, tubes and monitors in various places. Overhead, banks of yet more monitors, television screens and lights crowded the space above.

'Natalia,' the surgeon said. 'My name's Anand, can you hear me?' He touched her gently on the shoulder. Natalia's eyes opened briefly and she gave the briefest of nods. 'Good. Now listen, I don't want you to be at all anxious. You're in safe hands. I'm the chief surgeon in the best Accident and Emergency unit in London. My job is to make you better. Are you in pain?'

Natalia nodded a small amount.

'We'll be taking care of that for you. Try to relax if you can. I will firstly explain a few things. Just to confirm upfront, I've been told that you are not pregnant, is that correct?' She nodded. 'Okay, that's helpful. So, here's what we are going to do. You have been stabbed in the stomach. Not a great place, but trust me, there are plenty of worse places to suffer this type of injury. I'm about to put you to sleep for a short while. I need to widen the incision in your abdomen, to find out what's been damaged and see what needs to be sewn back together. While you are sleeping, it'll be my job to repair anything that's bleeding. Then, in no time at all, you should be waking up, your pain will be under control and if all goes to plan, you'll be on the road to recovery. Is that clear?'

She nodded.

'Very good. Okay, let's get this underway, everyone. Natalia, if you could hold the nurse's hand for me. Now then,' he said, nodding at the anaesthetist, 'why don't you count down slowly from ten?'

*

It was a long time later before Anand was able to take a much-deserved break.

'How did it go?' a senior registrar was asking. The two of them were waiting for vending machines to dispense strong, black coffee into personalised ceramic mugs. Both men were still in their scrubs.

'Touch and go. Knife wound to the lower right abdomen. She had this massive haematoma inside her abdominal cavity. Once that was out of the way, there was a lesion in the abdominal aorta and, to make matters worse, the knife had pierced the left lobe of her liver.'

'Shit!'

'Had to be seen to be believed.'

'You managed to stop the bleeding?'

'Only just. She'd lost so much blood, I couldn't get her to coagulate at first.'

'Last time I saw a perforated liver, it was a nightmare.'

'It's never easy. It's like trying to fix a broken tap when the mains pressure hasn't been disconnected. For the arterial repair, I roped in Sam Foley. She's the best vascular surgeon in London.' He shook his head.

'Brutal day in the office. What do you rate her chances?'

'No better than sixty-forty. She's in Critical Care for a while yet. Drains are in and she's on antibiotics. Let's pray she doesn't get an infection.'

Chapter 42

London

If Lauren McIlvoy had realised what was about to unfold when she'd swung out of bed that morning, she might have been tempted to call in sick, retreating under the duvet with just her cats to provide solace. As she would later reprimand herself, she only had herself to blame. Who else would have been stupid enough to invite the wretched man so brazenly back into her life? And why? Simply because, momentarily, she had the power and authority to command his presence. Wanting to humiliate him by summoning him to her court and to do her bidding.

Her psychotherapist would be having a field day.

Deep down, Lauren, it wasn't that, was it? Why do you think you summoned him?

She heard North before she saw him. That felt strange, since his wasn't a booming, deep voice. More of a medium-pitch, slightly resonant sound. A confident oiliness that, even to this day, allowed him to exert a chilling authority in a manner that oddly haunted her. Which probably explained why she had heard him so clearly. Subconsciously, she would have been listening out for him.

Secretly, is there a possibility that you might have been excited?

'Lauren, my dear. How heavenly to see you. After all this time. You look divine!' McIlvoy had been all stiff and clumsy, a hand thrusting out awkwardly for a handshake, her manner abrupt and cold. North was having none of it. Like the consummate professional he aspired to be, he took the offered hand in both of his, holding her fingers in his palms and drawing her inwards with a gentle, but not forceful, tug. He didn't kiss her, which was the surprise.

Or perhaps the disappointment?

She gave an involuntary shudder, looking beyond North to find another woman approaching, someone she didn't recognise.

'Now, Lauren, I'd like to introduce someone from our sister operation with whom you may not yet be acquainted. Frances Riordan, meet Lauren McIlvoy.' The two strangers shook hands, Riordan several inches taller than McIlvoy. She was an imposing figure in a tight-fitting tweed jacket and skirt combination.

'It's a pleasure to meet you, Lauren,' Riordan said in a deep, gravelly voice.

'Let's go to a side room. Hutch, can we use that one over there?' McIlvoy asked, pointing to a glass-panelled conference room, empty save for several large-scale maps strewn on the desk.

'Sure. Let me clear the detritus for you.'

The room was ordinary in the way that a cheap government-funded meeting room can only ever be, the exception being that the standard-issue, foam-filled chairs looked new. Their unsullied, shiny royal blueness was in stark contrast to the scuffed and peeling grey laminate of the meeting room table. Lauren took a seat at the head with North and Riordan sitting opposite each other on either side of their host.

'Forgive my intrusion, Lauren,' Riordan began once Hutch had closed the door. 'I know you are up to your neck in an operation at the moment.' She double-patted McIlvoy on the arm, a gesture meant to make McIlvoy feel relaxed. Given how hyper-vigilant the detective was through sitting so close to North, the effect it had was the exact opposite.

'Brendan, here, said that you'd asked him to join you. I thought it might make sense if I said a few words first, by way of background. I can then leave, allowing the two of you to get on with other matters.' She smiled thinly, glancing across the table at Brendan, winking with the one eye that McIlvoy could not see. North glanced away quickly, staring at imaginary papers in front of him, stifling a smile.

'It concerns the woman at St. Pancras station,' Riordan began. 'Natalia. At this stage, we have to declare an interest.' She paused long enough to allow this confession to sink in. 'It so happens that Natalia, a journalist by profession, is married to a Russian of extreme interest to the Security Intelligence Service at present. The reasons for this, I need not bore you with.' She said this with a benign authority that was capped by a thin smile. North simply nodded soberly. McIlvoy knew a rehearsed storyline when she heard one. These two actors were delivering lines in a play that was well beyond the dress rehearsal stages.

'What you may not be aware of is that this woman, Natalia, had recently become *intimately* involved with another man,' she said, looking at McIlvoy to gauge her reactions. 'A British teacher by the name of Calum Ross.'

Another pause, this time for longer. McIlvoy momentarily felt North's knee brushing hers under the table. It was as if a live wire had touched her skin.

'I understand from Brendan that you know Ross.'

'That is correct,' McIlvoy replied, adept at the less-is-more technique of question-answering.

'It is our understanding – and we only have anecdotal evidence on this so far – that this journalist may have been planning to leave her husband and hoping to move in with Ross. Hence her arrival in London. All right so far?'

McIlvoy nodded and again felt another jolt of electricity touch her leg. North's knee was hovering close to hers. She could sense it, almost feel the radiating heat, trying desperately not to move hers in case it accidentally touched his again. She shuffled in her seat, swivelling her legs in Riordan's direction.

'Because of this, and because we knew Natalia was coming to London on the Eurostar, I asked Brendan to mount a little light surveillance upon her arrival on the train earlier today. We were particularly interested to find out whether she was being followed. As it transpired, she evidently was, although we did not understand it would take the turn it did. Otherwise, naturally, we would have alerted the police authorities.' More pauses and another thin smile. 'Brendan tells me that Ross has recently been implicated in various crimes. If that's so, it's our belief that this could all be related. Natalia's husband is a powerful man. We always thought he might be vindictive, but never quite in this way. He must have found out about her *affair*,' she said delicately, as if embarrassed by the very word. 'How is she doing, by the way?'

'Still in theatre.'

'What about the woman who got away?'

'For the moment, we've lost her. She gave us the slip. We're on the case.'

'To put down a marker, as and when, we'd be keen to speak with her too. Well, Brendan and his team would, isn't that right, Brendan?'

North nodded.

'What about the dead man?' Riordan continued.

'The one Ross shot, you mean?'

'I doubt that was technically how it happened, but no matter. Who was he?'

'We've no idea. He wasn't one of yours, Brendan?'

'Certainly not.'

'There was another man on the concourse, however.' McIlvoy turned directly to face North. 'Someone also waving a gun all over the place. Any ideas on that one, Brendan?'

'Well, I confess, that particular person was one of ours, yes,' North said, elbows on the table, hands waving in the air briefly, head lowered. '*Mea culpa*. In a perfect world, we would have briefed each other in advance. Especially – and you have to understand this, Lauren – especially if we ever believed that someone's life was at risk. We simply had no idea. Neither did Frances and her team. We presumed that Natalia's husband might, possibly, have got to learn about the affair. It didn't cross our minds that he might try to kill her. Let alone set this Ross guy up in the way it appears he has.'

'When I rang this morning, Brendan, I specifically asked you about Ross. You told me categorically that you had no interest in the man. In fact, you said you'd never heard of him.'

North was all smiles, the oily charm exuding everywhere.

'Lauren, darling, don't go chasing ghosts. You rang me at eight. I told you what I knew at eight. Frances here, she rang me at about ten. Two hours later. At the time, she'd only recently learnt about the journalist arriving on the 2.30 Eurostar from Paris and needed urgent help from my team. I didn't know before. I do now. It doesn't alter the basic conclusion one iota. We believe that Ross was – is – being framed by Natalia's husband. Russian retribution at its very worst. Some Russians are crazy, crazy people.'

Riordan was on her feet.

'I won't take any more of your time. For what it's worth, I agree with Brendan. I strongly suspect the teacher's been set up. He may actually be key to encouraging the journalist to be co-operative. Assuming she makes it. So, all I ask is that you go gently on him.'

'I don't buy what you say about Ross,' McIlvoy said. 'His fingerprints are all over a whole load of weird shit at the moment: drugs, explosives and not to mention everything that happened at the station. I warned him earlier in the day. I was going to throw the book at him if he wasn't co-operative. Now he's become a fugitive, that's his choice. Every hour he's evading capture makes it more difficult for him. He's on the run and I'm determined to catch him. It so happens that I've got the best team of trackers in London here to help.'

'Well, do whatever you have to. I've asked Brendan to hang around for a bit, if that's all right with you? He can report back as soon as anything comes up that may be of interest.'

'I promise not to get in the way,' North smiled. 'Besides, I'm sure in the quieter moments we'll have plenty to catch up on.'

The door closed behind Riordan, leaving the two of them sitting side by side uncomfortably.

'Who'd have thought we'd be back together again?' It was the confident oiliness speaking. McIlvoy was hardly breathing.

Isn't this what, all along, you really wanted?

He reached across, gently, and stroked her hand. It felt weird, though perhaps not as creepy as she was hoping it might feel.

'Brendan, this has got to end,' she blurted, standing abruptly. 'There's an operation to be run and people's lives are on the line.' She was about to raise her voice, then composed herself. 'Don't be a prick. Leave me alone and stop messing with my fucking head.'

Chapter 43

London

Cristina Marinca jumped out of the van the moment it turned off the busy Euston Road, thumping loudly on the interior wall directly behind where the driver was sitting, and yelling for him to stop. She slipped out in seconds, closing the door behind her and banging the rear panel twice to signal the van to race away. It quickly disappeared, at the next junction turning right, out of sight. Overhead, there was the sound of a hovering helicopter, the noise louder by the second.

She swiftly removed her distinctive leather jacket, wincing at the pain in her shoulder where the man who'd attacked her had twisted her arm. Wrapping the knife inside the lining, she folded the coat onto itself and jettisoned the entire bundle into a skip next to a building site she was passing. From her large black shoulder bag, she withdrew a blue headscarf and wrapped this around her head and neck. The woman from the station concourse had, for the time being, disappeared.

A former member of the Romanian Intelligence Service, the SRI, Marinca was these days an independent contractor working for anyone who paid enough money to allow her the lifestyle she had become accustomed to. Dependable and clear-headed under pressure, she was a highly trained and hugely resourceful operative, often used by certain SVR controllers when they needed agents not attributable to Russia's intelligence network. Outwardly calm, inside Marinca was seething as she walked at a brisk pace through the back streets towards the Underground station at Euston Square. She hated failure and, although she believed that she had seriously wounded the Russian journalist, she wasn't 100 per cent certain that her stabbing would have been fatal. She had also lost a colleague due entirely to his stupidity. He should have simply shot and killed the teacher and then escaped. He had failed, and for that he had lost his life. It was a waste. She had known and used him on many an occasion over the years – a fellow Romanian, who had lived as peripatetic and confused a life as she did. There was nothing that could link him to her, and for that she was grateful. However, she would miss him. He had been a like-minded, free spirit, someone content to live from day to day; or, as in her case, from contract to contract. Proof, if it were ever needed, that one simple slip in their business could cost them their life.

She took the Underground train to Lancaster Gate, changing trains once along the way. From there, it was a short walk to the cheap hotel she'd checked into the previous day. Satisfied that she hadn't been followed, she entered the hotel and went straight to her room. It was time to change her appearance. The woman at the station had been dark-haired. Marinca was about to become blonde. Half an hour later, her short hair rinsed and dried, she admired the effect in the mirror and was pleased. When she took a pair of tortoiseshell-framed spectacles from her handbag and donned those as well, even she hardly recognised herself in the mirror. She removed a recently purchased burner phone from its packaging and switched it on. First, she needed to find out which hospital they had taken the journalist to. When she had that information, it was going to be time for Marinca to resume her nursing career.

Chapter 44

Istanbul

The Russian Consulate in Istanbul was an imposing courtyard building, the main block and its two wings embracing an immaculately manicured grass turning circle on three sides. Usmanov's driver, having negotiated his specially reinforced Mercedes through the double layers of cast-iron security fencing, deposited his charge by the main entrance. Usmanov quickly hurried inside. The SVR offices – a rudimentary open-plan attic space with several workstations, two meeting rooms, a secure filing room and a single fully-enclosed, lockable office which Usmanov claimed as his own – were on the top floor, tucked at the back of one wing, hidden behind its own security paraphernalia. It was an arrangement that could hardly be described as luxurious. However, as Usmanov told his agents regularly, no one was being paid to mope around the office in luxury all day.

The mood in the office since Svetlana's suicide two days earlier had been sombre, Ankara immediately assigning a new confidential secretary to support Usmanov and his activities in Istanbul. Ludmilla was several years older than her predecessor, and less pleasing on the eye, as Usmanov noted to himself privately when she first arrived. Today, as he marched imperiously into his office, Ludmilla was standing sombre like a sentry, waiting for him outside his office door, a large pile of correspondence in her hands. When he took these from her and carried them to his desk, it surprised him to see that she had followed him into the room.

'This, too, has just arrived.' She handed him a secure email that, only moments earlier, she'd printed out. Usmanov scanned it quickly and then sat down, gripping the document tightly whilst reading it again, more slowly.

'Where is my wife now?'

'In a London hospital.'

'Do we know which one?'

'Not yet. This only just came in.'

'Find out from the British. Get onto it right away. While you're at it, I need to speak with Mikhail Luzhkov urgently on a secure line.' She left the room and closed the door behind her.

Usmanov slumped his heavy frame into the large, leather chair and pinched the bridge of his nose in an attempt to keep a lurking headache at bay. This was his fault. He had revealed Natalia's unfaithfulness to his friend. Once, six days ago. And then again, the previous day. He'd known, both times he'd said it, that it was risky. He'd been an idiot.

Usmanov would get Luzhkov involved. He was excellent on damage limitation. Plus, there was one other thing that now needed taking care of. Urgently.

The Bakelite phone on his desk rang.

'Da?' he said.

'Mikhail Luzhkov on the secure line for you.'

Usmanov hit a button on the top of the phone and a light came on to indicate a secure connection had been made.

'Mikhail! Where are you?'

'London, as always.'

'Good. I have a critical problem that needs sorting. My wife's in London and someone's been trying to kill her. She's alive, apparently, in some London hospital but I know little else.'

'Leave it to me. I will find her.'

'I need to know who did this.' The two men spoke in hushed tones for several seconds.

'Consider it done, my friend,' Luzhkov said a short while later. 'That particular problem is going to disappear, I promise.'

Usmanov put the phone down and was deep in thought when his phone buzzed once more on his desk. He snatched the received angrily.

'Da?'

'I have Nicolai Kozlov holding for you from Moscow. He says that it's urgent.'

What did that bastard, Kozlov, want? In truth, Usmanov had been expecting this call, ever since reading about Kozlov's reappointment a few weeks ago.

'I'll take it,' he said wearily, dreading what might be about to come but needing to face the facts. Could it be really be a coincidence that Kozlov was calling so soon after hearing that his wife had been stabbed?

Chapter 45

London

Ross hid beside the bushes at the top of the steps, invisible from the towpath below. Well over a minute passed before the jogger appeared, heading in the direction Ross had been running. It was the same young policeman, no question, his mustard-yellow sweatshirt now tied around his waist. Ross imagined the conversation the man would be having with McIlvoy and others.

He's heading along the canal towpath toward Camden.

Can you see him?

Not currently. I know he's ahead of me. I lost sight of him a few moments ago.

Is he wearing the red anorak?

Not anymore. He's a good runner. He should reach Camden any minute.

Okay, we'll be waiting. You continue your approach from the rear. Let's try to box him in.

Which, either consciously or otherwise, was when Ross heard the helicopter swoop in low overhead. It was following the canal towpath. He stayed in the shadows until it had passed. When he emerged, a London black cab was coming his way, its orange 'for hire' light illuminated. Ross immediately flagged it down and climbed aboard.

'Paddington Station,' he said. There was no clear plan in his mind other than to escape the immediate area. Plus, he figured, he should be able to buy burner phones at a railway station.

'The traffic's congested up ahead, mate. You happy me doing a detour?'

'Sure. What's happened?'

'Some sort of argy-bargy at St. Pancras station. We'll be better off going around the top of Regent's Park.'

Some sort of argy-bargy! One man dead and Natalia critically injured. Two police cars suddenly burned past at high speed.

'They seem in a hurry!'

'There's a manhunt underway. Some bloke's been shot, another woman's been stabbed and there are these two nutters on the run. I've just caught it on the radio. They've even got a helicopter chasing around, can you hear it?'

Ross feigned interest.

'It's like being in the middle of one of those television shows.'

'Let's hope they get whoever it is before they do any more damage.'

'You and me both, mate.'

They made Paddington in good time, Ross asking the driver to drop him in one of the streets near the station. He wanted to alter his appearance, choosing a navy-blue 'Visit London' sweatshirt to wear over his other clothes from one vendor and a sunhat in the same colour from someone else. On the station concourse, there were several mobile phone vendors to choose from. Ross bought two burner phones and sat on a bench installing SIM cards before discarding the packaging into a station cleaner's wagon as it passed by. All the while, his mind was whirring, working out what to do next and how. What he needed was a base, somewhere to regroup and plan his next moves. He had more than enough cash for a cheap hotel room for the night. However, his biggest worry was avoiding being spotted. He imagined McIlvoy circulating his newly-taken police mugshots across the internet and subconsciously tugged the brim of his hat lower over his face. Plus, he needed to conserve money as much as possible. He had no credit or debit cards, and already the £500 the bank had given him was disappearing.

Which was when he remembered Stephanie, a former girlfriend who lived not far away. Ross kicked himself for not thinking of her before. Steph would help, he was certain. They'd been an item for quite some time – before life had got in the way, Ross drifting off to foreign parts and she finding another man. They had kept in vague contact. When he'd been in Istanbul, she'd even threatened to come and visit, but it had never happened. She was an artist, and her top-floor flat in South Kensington, light, airy and cluttered, was where she painted. Her abstract paintings – big bold pictures with bright colours that had done little for Ross – seemed to do well in the salerooms. He selected a burner phone at random and dialled her number, smiling briefly when he remembered the sequence of digits correctly.

'Hello,' a familiar voice answered.

'Steph, it's Calum.'

'Oh my God! Calum, how amazing! Where are you? Are in London? What are you up to?'

It was her typical catalogue of questions.

'Just back from Istanbul. I'm sorry to be calling out the blue. To be honest, Steph, I'm in a bit of a bind and need to ask something cheeky.'

'Sure. Ask away. How can I help?'

'Can I cadge some floor space? It'd save my life if you said yes.'

'Tonight?' She sounded surprised, maybe even a little put out. 'Yes, I guess, if you don't mind kipping on the sofa in the studio?'

'You're sure it's not inconvenient?'

'No, really, it'd be great to see you again. Wow, well, you'll be able to meet Tyler as well. Did I tell you about him?'

'A bit.'

'He's the divine new man in my life. He designs websites and stuff I can't even get my brain around, they're so technical. When are you coming around?'

'How about in around thirty minutes?'

He could hear a deep intake of breath at the other end of the line.

'Sure, that would be amazing. I'll have time to tidy up and put the kettle on.' With Steph, the kettle was always on. 'I can't wait to see you.'

'Me you too,' he said, and ended the call. He checked the time. The incident had happened too late to have made the front page of the evening paper that day. Which was a positive development. For the moment, his biggest worry would be CCTV cameras and vigilant police officers. A route to her house that took him across Hyde Park would keep his contact with either to a minimum.

Chapter 46

London

Kenny stopped a little way short of the bridge, unaware that a few metres away, Ross was hiding in the bushes above. He could no longer see his quarry and that was bothering him. He reached behind to locate the stray wire from his microphone that had been bobbing against the back of his shirt, struggling to insert the jack into its slot on the transmitter unit attached to his belt.

'Can anyone hear me?' he blurted, running once more.

'We thought we'd lost you, Lance.' It was Hutch's voice. 'Where are you?'

'On the towpath, beside the Grand Union Canal, heading towards Camden. Ross is ahead of me. The canal's no longer straight and I've lost sight of him for the moment.'

'Good work! Okay, we'll get the chopper to divert and give you support. How far from Camden are you?'

'I've no idea. I've covered a fair distance already, and I'm about to pass under a major road overhead. Do you want me to carry on?'

'Yes, keep going. The helicopter will be with you shortly.'

*

Back in the control room, Hutch was ruling the roost whilst McIlvoy held her side discussion in the conference room with the two spooks.

A young man, shirtsleeves rolled up, stepped forward.

'I may have something on the dead man. Although he's not on our police records, we have a possible match with biometrics from Border Force's passport system. A Spanish passport, name of Raoul Roca. There were no cards or driving licence on the body but we have at least a seventy-five per cent probability match.'

'Interesting. When our friend Brendan is finished in there with Mac, we'll get him to see if he can find out any more about this Roca. What news on the woman who was stabbed, Sunita?'

'We know her name: Natalia Borisenko. She's a journalist, married to a Russian diplomat, Oleg Usmanov, based in Turkey. As to her connection to Ross, apart from the fact that he was working in Istanbul until recently, we don't know a great deal.'

'Okay, pedal to the metal everyone. Hang on,' he blurted, waving a hand for silence as he clutched his earpiece. 'Damn! That was the pilot. No sign of Ross along the towpath. Amy, we need those insights into Ross's friends and family pronto. How are you getting on?'

'Not a lot so far, I'm afraid. Ross doesn't appear to be active on social media.'

'Is someone checking mobile phone records?'

'I'm on it,' someone shouted from the far side of the room. 'He's hardly used his phone since coming back to the UK.'

'Web browsing history?'

'We're about to get a data dump from his network provider.'

'What about the address book on his phone? It's got to be backed up in the Cloud, surely?'

'Web browsing history we can do easily. Accessing Cloud backups is problematic.'

'Keep chipping away. Ross will be heading somewhere. What about before he went to Turkey? Do we know what he did then? Where he lived? Girlfriends, boyfriends, that sort of thing. Come on, let's see what we can find.'

He turned to wave at Frances Riordan who, having left the meeting room, was on her way out of the building. Mac and North were still engrossed in their conversation. Hutch went across to where Hannah, his media specialist, was quietly busy in one corner.

'Hannah, have we sent pictures of our missing pair to the media yet?'

'Already in hand.'

'I knew you'd be one step ahead,' he said, beaming. 'I want their faces plastered all over the news channels. We should be in time for the six o'clock news bulletins. Plus the front pages of the national papers tomorrow. What do you think about offering a reward?'

'I was going to suggest it. It often works.'

'I agree. Let's post that to social media right now. Fifty thousand pounds if a confirmed sighting leads to an arrest.' He looked across to the adjacent desk. 'Rachel, can you organise for the helpline to be set up and manned? It's time to crank the emergency response team into action.'

McIlvoy emerged from the conference room with North following behind. She looked white, as if she had seen a ghost.

'Any news?' she asked as she came across to rejoin Hutch.

'We've had the Foreign Office on the line,' one of Hutch's team was explaining. 'Apparently, the injured woman is the wife of a Russian diplomat. Her husband has found out about her injuries and wants to know what's being done to protect her.'

McIlvoy raised her eyebrows.

'How much more complicated does this need to get? Hutch, have armed protection units yet been assigned to wherever she's been taken?'

'Already in hand.'

'What news on the injured woman?'

'Out of surgery, but critical. She'll be in intensive care for a while yet.'

'And Ross?'

'His picture is all over social media. There's a £50,000 bounty offered to anyone giving information that leads to his arrest. Give us a couple of hours and let's see where we get to. We might also get lucky with CCTV. The new facial recognition software we're trialling is excellent. The dead man appears to be a Spaniard by the name of Raoul Roca. Put it this way, we've had a positive match from passport biometrics.' Hutch turned to North. 'Can someone in your team see if anything more is known about him?'

'Sure, but I wouldn't hold your breath. More than likely he'll have been using a fake passport.'

Hutch's face grimaced as he digested this news.

'Okay, I hear you.'

'Riordan just informed me that Ross and the stabbed woman, Natalia, have been in a relationship these past few months,' McIlvoy said.

'Not surprising, but useful to know. This episode hardly has the hallmarks of a typical jilted husband, though, does it?'

'From what I've heard, he's hardly the typical husband. It explains the link between Ross and the woman. Once Ross's in custody, we can put him through the wringer.'

'Surely we need to focus on finding the woman with the knife?' North interjected. 'Ross isn't a murderer. He only killed the other man in self-defence.'

'Sorry, Brendan, but I disagree. Watch the video and see for yourself. I would have thought Frances Riordan and her team at

Vauxhall Cross might have been all over this like a rash. Ross is recently back from Turkey. For all we know, he may have become radicalised whilst he was there, converted to Islam and vowed to become a martyr? Or, at the very least, got himself mixed up in all kinds of other weird shit. Witness the drugs and explosives. Perhaps he became pals with a bunch of sickos who want to inflict terror onto the streets of London once again. The man's chosen to avoid being arrested and in my book that makes him guilty as charged.'

'Just a thought, Mac,' Hutch intervened. 'This journalist is Ross's girlfriend, you say? He'll be desperate to make contact, won't he? To find out how she is and all that. I would, in his shoes.'

'Well, he's hardly likely to barge into a hospital ward, hold her hand and have a quiet chat with her whilst the rest of the world is trying to arrest him,' North flared.

'Got any bright ideas, Hutch?' McIlvoy retorted, her eyes livid.

'Perhaps we need to monitor phones on whatever ward she's on,' Hutch said placatingly. 'Plus, the same with the hospital switchboard. If he calls around, trying to find out where she is, maybe even trying to speak with her, we ought to be tracing those calls.'

Chapter 47

Venice, Italy

Claudia Cuccinelli stepped out of her front entrance and into the late afternoon Venetian sunshine, the small courtyard that greeted her bathed in gentle shades of colour. Terracotta pots and hanging baskets adorned the square on two sides, randomly planted azaleas and bougainvillaea giving a dishevelled vibrancy to the brick and cracked-cement-covered buildings in the pedestrianised neighbourhood. Cuccinelli had spent the day on her laptop, researching an article for La Stampa about corruption within the Italian police system. She had written over 1,000 words of polished prose when the email came in from UPS telling her she had a parcel ready for collection. The pickup location in the Rialto Mercato area was across the lagoon from her apartment on the island of Giudecca.

There was an hour and a half remaining before closing time, more than enough for Cuccinelli to take the *vaporetto* across the lagoon before changing to a different waterbus that would meander its way northwards up the Grand Canal to Rialto. There were no cars on the island of Giudecca, the alleyways in her neighbourhood often barely an arm's width apart, the walls on either side at least several metres high and made of old, red bricks. Apart from an occasional door or an unmarked entrance to another alley off to one side, the main interest in the tunnel-like walkways was vegetation from unseen gardens on the other side: either window boxes or foliage and flowers peeking over tops of the walls, the slanting afternoon sunlight catching occasional blooms and providing small bursts of colour.

Cuccinelli had lived on Giudecca for several years. Like her good friend Natalia Borisenko, she had originally studied journalism at the London School of Economics before the two had gone their separate ways, Natalia back to Moscow and Cuccinelli to her home city of Milan where, as an aspiring political reporter, she had joined the Corriere Della Sera, Italy's largest daily newspaper. The two had kept in touch, largely by email, but marriage and life had got in the way. At the time that Natalia was moving to Istanbul, Cuccinelli's marriage was on the rocks and she was feeling sick and tired of the Milanese, who seemed only too happy to blame her for her husband's adulterous behaviour. With little money of her own, she had escaped to a new life in Venice, scraping a meagre living as an independent journalist whilst writing pieces on commission. It didn't earn a huge amount but, basing herself away from the central area with its tourist prices, she could still live reasonably frugally. She loved the Venetian way of life, especially the privacy and space her rooftop apartment gave her, tucked away as it was from the prying eyes of the cruise ship tour parties who thankfully never made it across the lagoon to Giudecca. What had been nice was that her old friend Natalia had once more reconnected, sometimes on WhatsApp, sometimes by video. Cuccinelli was happy to lend an ear to someone who appeared to be suffering the same marital issues she had once faced. Although, judging from a recent phone call, Natalia now had a British teacher keeping her attentions occupied.

It was a five-minute walk to Palanca, the nearest *vaporetto* stop. Strolling through the narrow alleyways, for a moment she was struck by a sense that she was being followed. However, every time she checked over her shoulder, there was no one she could see in her wake and she dismissed the notion. When reaching the ferry pontoon, she validated her season pass and waited in the warm sunshine for the next *vaporetto* to arrive. The sky was blue, the waters calm, and that day there was very little wind: it was perfect for taking a boat trip. In time, a number 2 boat heading to San Marco sauntered across the water towards them, the man at the helm expertly guiding the vessel to a controlled halt alongside the pontoon, the *vaporetto's* boatman deploying a simple flick of the wrist to secure a rope to the jetty before sliding open the small access gate to let passengers disembark first. Then, together with a few tourists and one or two locals she recognised and nodded to in silence, Cuccinelli and everyone else hurried aboard. Moments later, with a brief rev of the engines and a crunching of ancient gears, the *vaporetto* began to move. Cuccinelli found a seat at the bow of the boat, a prime position for watching the comings and goings of waterborne traffic, the ferry wallowing its way sedately across the lagoon towards where St Mark's Campanile dominated the far shoreline. A short, stocky man she didn't recognise was seated in a vacant seat to her right, and the reporter in Cuccinelli immediately noticed that he was missing the tip of one finger: the index finger on his left hand.

At San Marco, she made her way to Rialto on foot rather than take another ferry up the Grand Canal. She knew the pedestrian thoroughfares and alleyways like the back of her hand and had learnt from experience that walking often proved to be quicker. That said, she was in no great rush: there was at least an hour before the UPS pickup location closed for the day. There were crowds in the Piazza San Marco despite the early season, many taking photographs, a few queuing to enter the Basilica or to take a later afternoon tour of the Palazzo Ducale, the Doge's Palace. Cuccinelli dodged pigeons as she walked across the piazza and slipped into a very narrow pedestrian street beyond the Basilica that was lined with shops and restaurants on either side. She sauntered through the twisting alleyway, skirting slower-moving tourists, some with baby buggies, others eating cones of fresh *gelati*. She wove her way purposefully, her route passing over Rialto bridge which was teeming with people and street vendors, eventually reaching the Rialto Mercato area where the UPS Access point was located. Once or twice she checked behind herself for reasons she didn't quite understand. It must have been the WhatsApp message from Natalia the previous day that was making her jumpy.

C I need an immense favour I've sent a parcel UPS it's not big *PLEASE keep it safe do NOT open hand back ONLY to me or* *my British teacher friend he should be carrying two gifts I gave* *him one I also gave you trust NO ONE else all my love and* *thanks XXX N*

Collecting Natalia's parcel proved straightforward. In the small shop that was also the UPS location, Cuccinelli showed her *Carta di Identità Elettronica* and this was scanned and verified. The female assistant then disappeared out the back for a few moments, soon returning bearing a padded envelope about A4 in size which she made Cuccinelli sign for before handing it over. Cuccinelli placed the packet within the depths of her shoulder handbag and left the shop.

This time, for her return journey, she took the *vaporetto* directly to Giudecca, squeezing onto a nearly full number 2 boat that arrived at Rialto Mercato heading in a slow, anti-clockwise direction. Once the *vaporetto* had passed the main station at Ferrovia, she even managed to get a seat outside on the tiny, horseshoe-shaped rear deck, the shoulder bag clutched firmly to her body. She gazed idly at the passing scenery as the boatman steered the vessel around the western side of Venezia, past the area where the cruise boats usually parked in summer, the gentle setting sun behind them casting warm shadows everywhere. She wondered what trouble her friend might be in for her to be sending such cryptic messages and parcels by courier. Maybe she might now get to meet this mysterious new man in Natalia's life? That would indeed be interesting.

She stood and made her way to the mid-section as the *vaporetto* began its gentle approach to the floating pontoon at Palanca, the shoulder bag tight against her body as she joined a small crush of people getting off the ferry. It was then that she saw the same man she had sat next to earlier. He wasn't disembarking with her, nor did he look in her direction. He was in the forward section, on his own, his gaze averted elsewhere. She was certain it was him. The same stocky build. Panic suddenly rising, Cuccinelli knew what she was going to do. No sooner had the boatman thrown open the gate to let passengers disembark than she hurriedly stepped onto the jetty and almost immediately broke into a run. She never once looked behind. Instead, clutching her shoulder bag, she zigzagged her way at speed through the back alleys, taking a circuitous route back to her tiny apartment. Only when her front door was closed, both deadbolts in position and the cylinder lock secure, did she feel the panic subside. As she slumped against the door, gasping for breath, knees shaking and heart thumping, she considered what might have just happened.

Was she simply being paranoid? Or might this person have been following her all the way to Rialto Mercato and back?

'Dear God, Natalia, what are you getting me into?' she said to herself in a low voice, clutching the bag that contained the couriered parcel close to her chest.

Chapter 48

Istanbul and Moscow

'Oleg Ivanovich!'

'Hello, Nicolai,' Usmanov answered, deliberately not using the patronymic. 'I was wondering when you might call.'

'I presume you've heard the news. About your wife, that is.'

'If I hadn't, you would doubtless be about to relish in being the first to tell me.'

'The reports state that she's injured but not dead.'

'Don't sound so disappointed.'

'I wanted to say how sorry I was to hear the news.'

'Thank you. I'm sure it is not the reason you called.'

'Maybe not, but she's quite the controversial figure, your wife. It's not altogether surprising that someone took a pop at her.'

'I suddenly have a lot on my plate, Nicolai. How can I help?'

'You heard about my appointment?'

'Yes, congratulations. I am sure the Director will be well-served by having you ferreting around in the background.'

'We are all obliged to feel some oversight. Even you, my friend.'

'Can we get to the point?'

'Four months ago, you requested two hundred thousand dollars in cash. From Istanbul Consulate banking section. That was an extraordinary amount of money for anyone to draw down. Even for someone as well-connected and respected as yourself.'

'What of it?'

'There is no record in the system as to what it was used for.'

'That is correct.'

'Well, this cannot be appropriate. I am instructed to ask you to supply full details, including how, and on what, it was spent.'

'These are state secrets. It is an operational matter. You are not cleared to know anything of this operation, I am sorry.'

'That is regrettable. The Director has asked me specifically to report back to him on this matter with utmost urgency.'

'Then, I shall be delighted to talk to the Director himself. Unfortunately, you do not have the required clearance to allow you to be in possession of this information.'

'Then I shall make the necessary arrangements with the Director to get the appropriate clearance.'

'Very good.'

'I have the sense that you are trying to be uncooperative. That would be unwise. Especially with so much money unaccounted for.'

'*With respect*, Nicolai, it is possible that some in Yasenevo forget what it is like to run agents in war-torn parts of the world like the Middle East. Without cash, nothing much can ever be achieved.'

'Don't take me for a complete fool, Oleg Ivanovich. It's one thing for a senior SVR agent to have a philandering wife screwing her way around the school teaching staff. It's quite another when the agent in question is suddenly spending hundreds of thousands of dollars with no accountability whatsoever. Given your wife's recent behaviour, you were already under additional scrutiny. Because of your unhelpfulness in this matter, I shall now lead the investigation into the missing money myself.'

'Are you threatening me?'

'Only if I find you are guilty of abusing state funds. Be under no illusion: if you are hiding something from me, it won't be kept hidden for long.'

Chapter 49

London

'Calum!' the woman said, opening the door wide and flinging her arms around him. For several long seconds she hugged him close, he breathing in the familiar perfume, she gripping him tightly. 'Oh, it's so good to see you again,' she whispered in his ear.

'You look great, Steph,' he said, admiring her short blonde hair. 'Love the new look. It suits you.' She was wearing a simple navy top and white trousers, her cheeks flecked with specks of paint.

'Do you think so? You are sweet. Come in. Tyler will be home shortly. How are things? How was Istanbul? Are you home permanently, or is this a flying visit?'

Ross laughed.

'One at a time, Steph, one at a time. Things are fine but, right this moment, a bit complicated. Istanbul was great and, yes, this may or may not be a flying visit, that remains to be seen. Did you say you had a brew on? I could murder a cuppa.'

Over tea, he gave her a quick summary of the last twenty-hour hours. 'Bloody hell, Calum,' she said. 'Are you on the run from the police?'

'It's all a fabrication. I've been framed, had my money stolen and now, apparently, I'm a wanted man.' He shrugged and smiled. 'Not bad for a simple teacher, heh?'

'It's not funny. Sounds like you need a good lawyer. What are you going to do?'

'I have to find Natalia. Where she is, whether she's all right. She was stabbed, for God's sake.'

'Who is this woman?'

'A friend,' he said sheepishly. 'Someone I met in Istanbul.'

'Are you going out together?'

'Sort of. She's married.'

'You're in love with her, aren't you?'

'It's complicated.'

'What do you mean?'

'It just happened. I didn't mean to, I wasn't supposed to. As I say, it's complicated.' He smiled, sheepishly. 'Took me by surprise, to be honest, Steph.'

'My poor darling Calum. I should never have let you go to Istanbul. Have you tried calling the hospitals?'

'Not yet. I haven't dared to use my phone.'

'Come on, bring your tea. We can head up to the studio and search online from there.'

The upper floor was her workshop: various canvases stacked against each other, a line of them leaning against a wall; a half-completed picture on an easel in the middle of the room. Off to one side was a desk with a substantial computer screen.

'Excuse the mess,' she said. 'I've an exhibition next week and I'm desperately trying to get organised. Failing miserably, but what's new? Pull up a seat and let's see what we can find.'

The news about the incident at St. Pancras station was everywhere.

'Oh my God!' she said at one stage. 'It says here you killed a man.' Her tone was incredulous.

'He was about to kill Natalia. I deflected the gun, struggled to get the weapon from him, the gun went off and the bullet hit him, not me. Hardly murder, but there we are. Welcome to my former soldiering world.'

'This is appalling. God, Calum, look at this!' she said, pointing at the screen. 'There's a £50,000 reward being offered for information leading to your capture. Bloody hell! That's a lot of money.'

'Maybe I should turn myself in! I could use the money at the moment. They cleaned me out, Steph.'

'Who did?'

'You tell me. Probably the angry Russian husband. See if you can find out anything about where Natalia is.'

'What's her last name?'

He told her and she began typing on her keyboard.

'Where's the exhibition?'

'Sloane Square. Look, there's no mention of your woman on any of the main media websites. Why don't I call around some hospital switchboards?'

'I have a better idea. Let's go for a walk in Hyde Park and make the calls from there?'

'Why?'

'I'd hate them to trace any enquiries back to here. I don't need you embroiled in any of this. Besides, I've two burner phones we can use. See if you can find the right numbers for us to call and then we can take a walk.'

A short while later, she was handing Ross a piece of paper with phone numbers of various hospital switchboards written on it.

'I'll come with you,' she said. 'It'll be less obvious if it's a woman who's doing the asking.'

There was a shout from downstairs and the sound of a door closing.

'That's Tyler,' she said, bounding to her feet. 'Hi, honey, I'm up here. I've got a visitor. Why don't you come and say hello?' She blew Ross a small air kiss and ran downstairs.

Tyler had been to the gym and was apologetic for not yet having showered. Tall, lean, but with strong muscle tone, he was wary of Ross from the outset. When Stephanie explained that she and Ross had briefly gone out together, Tyler became even more closed.

'Tyler's a web designer, aren't you, darling?' Steph said, trying to diffuse the coolness between the two men. All three were nursing bottles of beer taken straight from the fridge.

Tyler nodded, taking a swig from the bottle but saying nothing.

'That's an alien world to me,' Ross said. 'Is it a good business to be in?'

'Pretty shit, actually,' the other man muttered. 'I lost a fucking huge potential client today. I'd been designing mock-ups for this massive new business venture. At my expense, naturally. The work had taken me days. Everything was looking good, I kept being told that it was a slam dunk they would pick me, then suddenly, bam! Someone else gets the contract. Bastards. What do you do with your life, Calum?'

Which was when Stephanie filled him in.

'Holy shit! I've just seen something about all of that on Facebook. So, we're now harbouring a fugitive, is that it, Steph?'

'Only if someone finds out, Tyler. I don't see how anyone will ever know he's here.'

'Fifty thousand's a lot of money.'

'Look, I don't want to cause any problems. If it's not convenient, I'll find someplace else to go.'

'Of course you can stay here. Tyler, don't be such an arse.' She stood and grabbed a fleece jacket and green baseball hat from a hook next to the kitchen door. 'Come on, let's see if we can locate this lady friend of yours. Honey, we'll be back in about half an hour. We're heading to the park to make a few calls. There's some pasta in the fridge if you feel like knocking up one of your amazing sauces?' She blew him an air kiss as she and Ross were on their way out the door.

From a bench in the Flower Garden, a long, paved walkway festooned with shrubs and rose bushes, they sat side by side whilst Stephanie made calls to several hospitals. It was a slow and tedious process. Five calls later, and no hospital was claiming to have a patient by the name of Natalia who'd been admitted that afternoon. Neither a Borisenko nor an Usmanov.

'Do you think they're deliberately not saying anything about her, even if she is there?'

'More than likely,' Ross said. 'I don't know what's going on, to be honest. I was starting to feel I had my life all sorted. Until I got back here, that is. Now, everything seems to have been turned upside down. Come on, we should walk. Is your phone off?'

'Mine? No.'

'Do me a favour? Turn it off. It's one less thing to worry about.'

'I'm sorry about Tyler. I thought he would be more understanding, but . . .' She was staring at her phone. 'Oh shit! What a complete and utter pillock!'

'Who?'

'Tyler. He's only gone and called the police helpline. He thinks fifty thou is worth more to him than the risk of us both harbouring a fugitive ex of mine. He wants me to bring you back to the flat. What an unbelievable arse.'

'Turn your phone off.' It came out as a terse instruction.

'It's off.'

'Do you mind if I check?' He settled his growing paranoia by satisfying himself that it was indeed no longer active. 'Steph, this is my fault. You'd better go back. I don't want to screw things up for you and Tyler. I can sort myself out.'

'Bollocks. You need someone to help you. I don't want to go back to the gallery and find myself dealing with the police and all their dumb questions. This is Tyler's fault, he can deal with it. It was his idea, after all. Where shall we go?'

Just then, they heard police sirens on Kensington Gore, the busy artery linking Knightsbridge and Kensington that bordered the south side of Hyde Park.

'Are you up for running?' Ross asked, checking her shoes, noting that she wore canvas flats.

'Sure.' The sirens were growing louder.

'Then follow me. Shout if you find it hard to keep up.' And with that he set off, heading north across the park.

Chapter 50

Moscow

Kozlov ended the call thoughtfully, wondering how best to conduct the next phase of his investigation.

'Irina,' he called out, waiting until she had scuttled into his office and sat down in front of his desk before continuing. 'I need you to drop everything you're working on.' She was young and wore plenty of make-up, badly applied such that it hid what Kozlov secretly believed to be a pretty face underneath. 'I want certain information found quickly. Firstly, I want to discover how much physical cash Oleg Usmanov has drawn from banking section at the Consulate in Istanbul over the last twelve months. I'd prefer it if you went digging electronically rather than calling anyone at this stage. I'd like dates and amounts of every withdrawal.'

He watched as she made detailed written notes on a notepad she held firmly in her lap.

'Second, either from Usmanov's driver's logbook, the Consulate travel section or from whatever other resources you can think: I want to know Usmanov's exact movements over the last four months. Where he's been to, who he's met with. Again, go digging with great care. I don't want anyone to know the reasons or that Usmanov may be under investigation. Do I make myself clear? Is he likely to have an electronic diary?'

'I'm positive Usmanov's secretary will have kept one. Whether it contains every appointment is doubtful. However, we might have a problem.'

'What is it?'

'Usmanov's secretary committed suicide a few days ago. She threw herself under a tram in Istanbul.'

'That's intriguing. Why wasn't I made aware of this before?'

'I wasn't aware of your interest in such matters. It's only came to light in the last day or so.'

'Someone from the embassy will be conducting a thorough investigation. I'd like to speak that person, please.'

'Very good.'

'Has Usmanov been assigned a new secretary?'

'Yes. An experienced operative has transferred from Ankara.'

'Good. So, why not speak to this person and befriend her? Try to get her to share Usmanov's diary going back four months. Tell her that this is an order coming directly from the Director.'

'Very good. Will that be all?'

'For the moment. Let's talk again in two hours, before you head home. I'd like to know how far you've got.'

Chapter 51

London

'Great work, Rachel. This,' Hutch announced to the room at large, 'is going to be our big breakthrough. Where's the NPAS chopper?'

'Refuelling at Battersea heliport,' someone called out.

'Right. The woman's an artist by the name of Stephanie Gately, more commonly known as Steph. Mid-thirties, we're getting photos emailed right now. She's blonde-haired, five-six, just happens to be Ross's ex. Were you aware of that?' he asked the young constable charged with trawling social media for links to Ross's past.

'News to me, sir.'

'Doesn't matter. We're on the case now. According to the current boyfriend, she's wandering around Hyde Park with Ross as we speak, making phone calls, trying to find the whereabouts of Ross's injured Russian girlfriend.'

'What she's wearing?' McIlvoy asked.

'The boyfriend had no idea.'

'Typical,' McIlvoy said, shaking her head and glancing sideways at North.

'What about her phone?'

'Off the grid. The last data we have suggested she was near the Albert Memorial.'

'Okay. Who do we have in the area?'

'Several on the ground by the southern entrances to the park, cars on standby at each. Ditto to the east, close to the Serpentine. We're thinner to the north, but more units are on the way. The good news is that the helicopter is refuelled and airborne once again, and we're about to get live video any moment. In fact, here we go.' The middle four screens merged once more, the wide expanse of green known as Hyde Park instantly recognisable.

'Okay, everybody, eyes front. Let's what we can find. This time we're going to bring Ross in.'

*

North's mobile was vibrating. He looked at the screen and stepped away to a meeting room at the side to take the call. It was Frances Riordan.

'What news?' Frances asked.

'He's somewhere in Hyde Park.'

'Are you sure?'

'Fairly.'

'It's a big place. They may not find him.'

'The team here are throwing the kitchen sink at it,' North reported. 'I rate his chances as slim.'

'That's disappointing.'

'He hasn't rung yet?'

'Not yet. If he's trapped, it gets more likely.'

*

Ross heard the helicopter and immediately stopped running. Moments later, Steph slowed to a walk beside him.

'Those police cars,' she said, gasping for breath. 'They were there for us, weren't they?'

Ross nodded, his mind calculating.

'And the helicopter. It's why I stopped running. It's less obvious if we're walking calmly. We have to split up, Steph. I'm sorry for dragging you into this. There's a far greater chance of getting caught if we're together, trust me.'

'Bloody Tyler, this is all his fault. I don't particularly want to leave you, Calum.'

'You must. Be prepared for some aggro from the police later. Tell them that I forced you to come with me. Say that I ran off towards Marble Arch and abandoned you. If they ask what I'm wearing, invent something. Anything but blue. Now go. Oh, one thing. Can I borrow your baseball cap?'

'Sure,' she said. 'Assuming it will fit.'

'You're an angel,' Ross said, adjusting the plastic strap at the back and trying it for size.

'Not bad. The green colour suits you.'

'You can have my blue hat if you like?'

'I'll keep it as a souvenir.'

'Now, don't get mad at Tyler. Head home and forget all about me. I suggest you run back the way we've just come from.'

She was about to go, when, in a moment's spontaneity, she turned and delivered a huge kiss on Ross's lips.

'For old times' sake. I still miss you, Calum.'

'Be gone!' he tried to say in reply, but by then she was off and running.

Chapter 52

London

Marinca was predictably thorough. Her first task was to make a list of all major hospitals with an Accident and Emergency department within a five-mile radius of St. Pancras station. She then located the relevant switchboard numbers off the internet before calling each in turn, enquiring after the injured journalist by name. After drawing a blank with every call, she moved on to the second phase of her approach: contacting the Critical Care units at each hospital directly. This took longer, busy ward staff often not answering a ringing phone for several minutes. Again, she found no one prepared to admit that the journalist was on their ward.

Which meant one of four things. The hospitals might have been deliberately lying; the Russian journalist might have died; she might still be in surgery; or they might have sewn her back together and simply discharged her. If she had died, there would have been reports about it in the media – which there hadn't been. It was thus increasingly likely that the Russian was still alive. The last option didn't sound feasible, either. Marinca couldn't imagine the wife of a Russian diplomat being so quickly discharged. It was much more probable that the police would try to shield the Russian from the person who had been trying to kill her. Which brought a smile to Marinca's face: they simply had no clue who they were up against.

Looking at the list of hospitals once again, she thought briefly about calling the ambulance control room to learn which hospital the injured woman from St. Pancras had been driven to, before quickly dismissing this idea. Not for nothing did the emergency services not publicise their direct-dial phone numbers. It did, however, give her an idea. She would visit the nearest major hospital to St. Pancras, UCLH, and ask one of the ambulance crews at the A&E drop-off point where the woman had been taken. They would be bound to know.

Many years earlier, under pressure from her parents, she had trained as a nurse in Bucharest before walking out after only two weeks. She had learnt some rudiments of the job, however. Not least, how easy it was for anyone so minded to walk into almost any hospital, acquire a uniform and a hospital pass, and then roam the corridors without attracting undue scrutiny. Since that time, she had had reason to pretend to be a nurse on many an occasion, always reverting to the same basic techniques.

Before leaving her hotel room, she first removed a small atomiser from the inner recesses of a roll-on suitcase, holding the glass bottle to the light to check that it was still full. Satisfied, she slipped this carefully into a less capacious black handbag that she also took from her case. She quickly scrolled through her secure smartphone to check for urgent messages. Seeing none, she placed the phone back inside an inner pocket of the suitcase, instead putting the untraceable burner phone into her handbag along with a credit card and some loose change. Finally, donning her blue headscarf and sunglasses, she was ready to head outside.

*

'We've got a second hit on the UCLH switchboard number,' someone called out. 'Another female caller, asking after Natalia Borisenko.'

'Brilliant,' Hutch said, happy to be momentarily distracted from the search for Ross. 'Have you traced the number?'

'It's another burner. The caller's been ringing around hospitals. The voice doesn't sound English. Central European, more like.'

'Bingo!' Hutch cried out. 'I wonder if it's the woman who tried to stab the Russian?'

'Why?'

'Checking to see whether she succeeded, maybe.'

'That's clutching at straws, Hutch. It's more likely to be this Gately woman, phoning on Ross's behalf.'

'Not unless she's good at accents.'

'It could be a reporter, snooping around. Where's this burner located?'

'Between Paddington and Lancaster Gate. See – it can't be Ross and Gately – they're on the south side of the park.'

'So we think.'

'Can we see the phone's position on the screen?'

'Sure.'

Seconds later, a map appeared of the area close to Lancaster Gate, a large red circle pulsing around a small area to the north of the Underground Station.

'We could send someone to investigate.'

'It's a big area. I wouldn't be optimistic about finding anything.'

They stared at the screen, searching for ideas or inspiration until moments later, almost in unison, they both cried out: 'Look!'

The circle was on the move. Slowly but definitely.

'What are you hoping for? Foot, bus, Tube or taxi?' Hutch asked.

'Oh, I see what you mean,' McIlvoy said eventually. 'I'm hoping bus or taxi.'

'Why?'

'Better chance of stopping either. What about you?'

'I'm hoping foot or Tube.'

'Why?'

'Plenty of CCTV.'

'Any news on Ross?'

'Nothing yet. Eyes peeled, everyone.'

*

Mikhail Luzhkov wasn't wasting a second. One of the SVR technicians at the Yasenevo headquarters, to the south of Moscow, was immediately instructed to hack the CCTV camera systems at St. Pancras station. Video images of the knife-wielding woman in the bomber jacket and black hair were soon discovered and quickly sent back to Luzhkov in London. When he opened the secure zipped file, he laughed out loud.

'Well, well, well. Cristina Marinca! It's been a long time!'

Luzhkov had last commissioned Marinca to work for him in Ghana three years ago. There had been a senior Russian diplomat at the Embassy in Accra under suspicion of trading secrets for sex with an attractive Nigerian woman suspected of having links with Beijing. Luzhkov had been sent to investigate and had used a honey trap of a different kind to see whether the diplomat was susceptible to entrapment. He had hired Cristina Marinca, a Romanian freelance with no links to Moscow. Posing as a Romanian air hostess, Marinca swiftly proved able to determine the man's guilt. However, in a sad twist of fate, the diplomat had died in her arms moments before Luzhkov burst into their bedroom in an attempt to catch the pair *in flagrante*. They had lost the chance to extradite the Russian for further interrogation. In the back of Luzhkov's mind, he still wondered whether Marinca might have had a different agenda.

He dialled the number he had in his address book for Marinca's mobile. It rang, with the ringtone sounding as though the phone was in the UK, but the call went unanswered. He dialled Moscow again, asking the same technician in Yasenevo for an urgent trace on the location of Marinca's mobile. Less than ten minutes later, Luzhkov received an email with the address of a hotel close to Paddington. He checked his desktop computer. From his office, in the basement of the Russian Embassy, it would, at most, be a fifteen-minute walk.

*

'Looks like you were right, Hutch. Tube it is.'

They watched as the red circle vanished from their screens close by Lancaster Gate station.

'Okay, everyone who's available, let's check the CCTV cameras. We should have had someone following on the ground able to follow.'

'There'll be cameras on the platform.'

'Good point. Can we hook into those, please?'

They stared at various screen images. Down at platform level below ground, several people were waiting for Central Line trains, either heading east or heading west. No one immediately stood out as looking like the bomber-jacketed murderer from earlier. On screens to one side, street-level camera recordings of the moments before the signal was lost were being played and replayed.

'There, look at that woman in the headscarf,' the woman called Amy said.

'Nah, she's blonde. The woman we're looking for has dark hair,' McIlvoy replied.

'That's cosmetics. It could be her. She's about the right height. The headscarf makes it more likely. I'd be keen to keep my profile hidden if I was her.'

'Where is she now?'

'Eastbound platform.'

'Anyone else fit the bill?'

'Well, these two men further along the platform look highly suspicious. See them? One here,' Amy pointed, 'and the other here.'

'You think she could have switched the burner and handed it to one of them?'

'Well, they look the type. They're also heading eastwards.'

'Where are they likely to be going?'

'Back to the hospital? To make sure the Russian woman's dead?'

'That's what the Americans call a wild-assed guess, Amy.' McIlvoy smiled thinly.

'How would they get to UCLH, if that's indeed where they're going?'

'Change at Oxford Circus, three stops down the line. Then Victoria line north one stop to Warren Street.'

'Let's get the transport police working on this,' Hutch said. 'I want officers down at platform level at Oxford Street station covering both Tube lines. If any of our three try to change trains, we'll be on to them. Especially if they head to Warren Street. Meanwhile, any new leads on Ross, anybody?'

*

Marinca noticed the increased police presence on the platform of Oxford Street station as soon as she got off the train. She meandered through connecting tunnels, surprised to find several more police officers standing around, surveying passengers as they chose either the northbound Victoria or Bakerloo lines. They seemed particularly interested in passengers taking the Victoria line so, in a spontaneous change of plan, Marinca chose the northbound Bakerloo line instead. Her decision was influenced by two men slightly ahead of her who had been on the same platform as her at Lancaster Gate. They had opted for the northbound Victoria line and had instantly been stopped and questioned by several police officers. Marinca would now have to make an additional connection at Baker Street, catching a different train to nearby Euston Square instead of Warren Street. It was no big deal, both stations being roughly equidistant from the hospital.

The moment she walked into the lobby of the hospital, she realised that her task to find the Russian woman would not be so hard. Armed police were everywhere. This had to be the place they had taken the injured Russian woman. She wasn't going to need to talk to one of the ambulance crew to find that out. Avoiding the direct gaze of the armed officers, she followed a group of three nurses towards an elevator bank and rode with them to the fifth floor, all three disappearing through a 'staff only' door. One of them even held the door for Marinca, who smiled at their kindness. The female showers and changing rooms were to one side. Within minutes, Marinca was walking back out again, dressed this time as a staff nurse, a borrowed name badge and electronic door key slung around her neck on an authentic blue lanyard with white 'NHS' lettering emblazoned in a repeating pattern. In one pocket, she carried the small atomiser. In the other was her burner phone, credit card and money. She had already noted the floor she was looking for as she'd stood waiting for the lift a few minutes earlier. Critical Care wards were two floors down on the third floor.

*

Luzhkov had an ace up his sleeve. It was a Moscow-built, short-range scanner that would detect the location of Marinca's room by pinpointing her mobile phone. The detector was bulkier than he would have liked, meaning that he'd needed a small shoulder bag to carry it in as he walked across Hyde Park. However, using such a device allowed him to bypass the need to ask awkward questions of hotel receptionists as he searched for Marinca's room.

The police presence in and around Hyde Park that afternoon was pervasive. Emerging through an exit gate close to Paddington, he was scrutinised carefully by two police officers before being allowed to pass by. Unfazed, five minutes later he was walking into the entrance lobby of a small boutique hotel, confidently striding towards a staircase at the back and climbing three levels to the top. It took several attempts to adjust the dials on the scanner to the correct settings, but finally, with one of the indicator lamps glowing bright green and an LED display showing signal strength, Luzhkov began slowly walking up and down the corridors. The signal was strong outside one particular room on the third floor, but Luzhkov wasn't convinced the signal might not be coming from the floor below. With the detector still in his hand, he descended the stairs to the second floor and went in search of the corresponding room on that floor, pleased and annoyed in equal measure to find a housekeeping trolley parked outside the room in question. The good news was that door was open and Luzhkov found that he now had 100 per cent signal strength. The bad news was that the person servicing the room was still inside.

'Hello,' Luzhkov called out, secreting the scanner back in his bag before entering the room.

A large woman in a tight-fitting, pale-grey uniform emerged from the bathroom.

'I'm just finishing,' she said, her accent Jamaican. 'Is this your room?'

'My wife's, I hope,' Luzhkov lied. 'I've just arrived,' he said, lifting his shoulder bag and placing it next to the roll-on bag on the rack. 'Yes, that's her bag.'

'Do you need the bed turned down?'

'No thanks.'

'In that case, I'll empty your bin and be gone.'

She squeezed her way past Luzhkov with a bin full of rubbish when Luzhkov stopped her.

'Tell you what,' he said, grabbing the bin, ushering her towards the still-open door. 'Let's leave all that for now.' He smiled apologetically. 'I need to use the bathroom urgently. Bins we can do another time.' He placed the bin on the floor and closed the door, checking through the fisheye lens in the door to make sure the maid was moving to another room. In amongst the trash, the used packaging of a burner phone had caught his eye. With luck, it would have the burner's telephone number printed on the outside.

*

'The phone's active again.' The red circle was back on the screen, this time close to Euston Square.

'I guess we were unlucky,' Hutch asked. 'CCTV footage anybody?'

With half the monitors showing live camera footage from the helicopter circling Hyde Park, images of Euston Road appeared in a different corner of the big screen.

'Whoever it is, it looks like they're heading towards the hospital.'

'We should make doubly sure there's a total lockdown on the Russian woman's room,' Hutch said. 'No visitors, no strange nurses or doctors, nothing. I have an ominous feeling about this.'

'Me too,' McIlvoy said.

'Amy, please can you get that in place with immediate effect?'

'Sure,' Amy said. 'Now, Hutch, changing subjects, I want your opinion about something. What do you think about this person here?' she said, pointing to a frozen image of a man in a blue sweatshirt sitting on a park bench with a green baseball cap.

*

Natalia Borisenko was being kept in the Critical Care ward under strict infection control procedures, in a section of the ward completely sealed off. No one was allowed in or out without a sterile mask and gown. Two nurses were permanently stationed inside the unit, checking the vital signs and well-being of the six patients, and two armed policemen stood guard on either side of the entrance. Marinca wondered for a moment whether she was going to be able to pull this off. However, as she felt in her pocket for the small atomiser, she quickly reassured herself that she was here as a staff nurse: in a place like this, it was going to allow her access anywhere.

Halfway down the ward was a sluice area, where Marinca found a cardboard carton of disposable gowns and sterile face masks. She quickly donned a blue plastic gown before taking a clean mask and tying the cords behind her head. She looked at herself in the mirror, unrecognisable even to herself in this garb. Finally, she pulled on some latex disposable gloves, checking that everything was in position, before making her way out of the sluice towards the secure area a few metres away. One of the two policemen peered at her name badge as she approached Natalia's door and put his hand out to stop her.

'No one is allowed in under any conditions,' he chided her. 'New orders.'

Marinca was about to reply when an unexpected sound caught her off guard. The burner phone in her pocket was ringing. She turned, retrieving the vibrating instrument from under the plastic gown, feeling an icy chill inch in the base of her stomach. It was her own phone number on the caller display. How on earth could she be calling herself?

Chapter 53

London

Ross sat on a bench, watching the police operation unfold around him. Buzzing like an angry insect, a helicopter performed continuous circuits in a wide loop overhead, and he subconsciously pulled the peak of his borrowed green baseball hat lower. Already two uniformed policemen had hurried past, close to where he was sitting. Ross was taking a pause, a monumental decision pending. In one hand was a burner phone. In the other was the card that Riordan had given him earlier. It felt like the moment was upon him. The moment when he would find out whether his get out of jail card was going to work or not. Literally.

Listen, Calum. The moment she arrives in the UK, secrets galore stuffed in her knickers, that'll be when it's time for us to re-emerge from the shadows and offer the pair of you protection. That's a cast-iron commitment, by the way. However, we have our suspicions that others may beat us to that particular offer.

Well, they had been right on that last count. What the hell was going on?

Slowly and deliberately, he keyed in each of the digits on Riordan's card, his thumb hovering over the green button. Finally, a decision made, he pressed hard and held the phone to his ear.

*

North looked at his phone, noted the caller ID and quickly disappeared to the side conference room, speaking as he went.

'What news?'

'He's made the call. He needs extraction. Can we do it?'

'There's a diplomatic protection vehicle that's been commandeered. It's currently tucked behind Kensington Palace, on Palace Avenue. Can Ross make his way over there?'

'I imagine so. He's on his own, he tells me.'

'Good. Do you have a contact number?'

Riordan gave him the information.

'Excellent. I'll stay here and misdirect traffic if required.'

'Tread carefully, Brendan. Your policewoman friend has you in her sights.'

'Tell me about it.'

*

'Hello.' Her voice was quiet, tentative.

'Accra, Ghana, three years ago. Remember?'

'Yes.' This time she was hesitant.

'Is your current operation still active?'

'Yes.'

'Then I have a message from the highest levels. Your contract has been terminated. With immediate effect. Do we understand each other?'

'Yes.'

'Full compensation. NFA and return to base.'

'Why?'

'Just do it.' The line went dead.

*

Ross began meandering idly towards Kensington Palace, as he'd been instructed. To do this, he had to circumvent Round Pond. Which was going well until he saw a uniformed policeman bearing down on him. Ross, pretending to take a call on his phone, walked off the asphalt path and onto the grass. It felt soft underfoot. The policeman initially ignored him, but something evidently made him suspicious, since Ross heard the man swivel on his feet as he turned in his direction.

'Excuse me,' the policeman called out.

Ross, head now firmly down, phone glued to one ear, waved a finger in the air to signal that he was busy taking a call.

'You, sir! The man in front with the mobile phone. Please turn around.' His voice was deliberately loud, full of assumed authority.

Ross continued ignoring him and carried on walking. Directly ahead was Kensington Palace Gardens, about 200 metres away. He was going to have to sprint for it. Which was the exact moment his phone began vibrating in his hand.

'Red police car, north-western corner of Kensington Palace Gardens. ETA?'

'I said turn around.' The policeman was now walking rapidly towards Ross's position.

'About a minute. There's an angry copper on my tail.'

'Run for it. We'll try to intercept, make it appear like we're arresting you.'

Ross chose his moment and bolted, the policeman with his heavy protection jacket and all the paraphernalia strapped to his belt struggling to follow. He'd be calling for reinforcements, but Ross had the edge. As he ran across Broad Walk, the wide avenue that cut across the park, people were stopping to stare. Ross could hear the approaching police helicopter coming in low overhead. From the Bayswater Road end of the park to his right, three police officers were also running to try to cut Ross off in a pincer movement. He sprinted onwards, seeing a red Mercedes van with the word Police on its bonnet careering directly towards him. When it was about five metres away, the car drew to a halt and two armed policemen leapt out.

*

'I reckon that's him,' McIlvoy was saying.

'I think you're right. Who's nearest, at the moment?' Besides the live images from the helicopter, there was a large map showing the location of various police units on the ground in and around the park. One police officer was within thirty metres of the bench where the man McIlvoy suspected might be Ross was sitting.

'This fella,' said one of Hutch's team, pointing. 'Let's get him to investigate.'

'Should we alert a few others?' McIlvoy asked a few moments later, looking around for North and finding him once more on the phone. Something was niggling her about his behaviour. She couldn't quite put her finger on it.

'Let's listen to the man's microphone.'

They watched the policeman begin his approach, the man on the bench already on his feet and moving in a different direction.

Excuse me. In the Command Centre, they could hear the words clearly. Followed swiftly by *You, sir! The man in front with the mobile phone. Please turn around.*

'No room for ambiguity there,' Hutch said, staring, as the man thought to be Ross ignored the police officer. 'The chap on the phone's got balls, I'll give him that.'

I said turn around – which was the moment the man on the phone suddenly bolted. Even though it had been half-expected, the movement still surprised them.

'That's Ross!' Hutch cried. 'Airborne, and all units do you copy? Confirmed sighting of Ross, now running westward from Round Pond towards Kensington Palace. All units close in and apprehend. This time he's ours.'

They watched as Ross veered towards the northern side of the palace and then rapidly came to a halt as a diplomatic protection car skidded to a standstill in front of him. Two armed officers were out of the red Mercedes van, Ross raising his hands in surrender. Three other uniformed police officers brought up the rear. They had him!

McIlvoy glanced sideways again and noticed that North was back in the room finally, his phone still glued to his ear. He appeared to have one eye on the screen as Ross was being bundled roughly into the back of the van, the vehicle performing a rapid U-turn and heading back the way it had come.

'Bloody brilliant. Great work, everyone.' Hutch, quick to enjoy the moment, was high-fiving everybody. 'A little over three hours. Not bad, wouldn't you agree, Mac?'

'Great job. Well done to you all. I want Ross taken to Savile Row straight away,' McIlvoy said, turning to stare back at the screen. 'He can stew in a police cell for a while until we've caught the other woman.'

'That's a bit more problematic,' the woman called Amy replied.

'Why?'

'Because the burner we were tracing has vanished completely.'

*

Luzhkov hated waiting. It was the bane of any agent's life. Ninety-nine per cent waiting, one per cent action, as someone had once described being a field agent. Especially when someone like Oleg Usmanov was calling the shots. Literally. As one of Usmanov's go-to guys, Luzhkov had got used to a certain amount of waiting. Smartphones helped. In the old days, goodness knows how they passed the time. Nowadays they could play games, watch pornography, read a book even. It was a struggle sometimes not to fall asleep. Especially when lying on a comfortable bed.

Luzhkov was old-fashioned: he preferred to sit and listen. There was a lot to listen out for. The maid with her trolley, completing the turndown service, slowly progressing along the corridor. Then there was the lift. The one in this hotel was old and made a grinding noise each time it moved. It was possible to hear when it stopped on this floor, Luzhkov instantly rolling off the bed, the silenced Makarov 9mm weapon in his right hand, about to assume a two-handed grip the moment the door was opened. He could also tell when someone used the stairs. The fire door was the giveaway, opening with a 'whoosh' and closing with a 'bang', the sound sufficient warning to allow Luzhkov to be on his feet once again. When the door to the room opened, Luzhkov would be tucked out of sight, visible only when she came inside, the door behind her already closed. He'd chosen frangible bullets, made from sintered metal powder that disintegrated to nothing on impact. It would reduce collateral damage, which, in a hotel with thin walls, was a consideration. The silencer would also help, although he suspected the maid could still hear the sound. Assuming she was on the floor at the time. All that remained was the waiting. Marinca would be back soon. On her way to pack her bag and spend her well-earned fee. Not yet aware that Luzhkov was waiting for her.

Chapter 54

London

For a place in a constant state of heightened alert, the ward felt oddly serene and without stress. There were six beds in the unit, each occupied and under the constant supervision of two experienced nurses wearing gowns and face masks. The only sounds were of beeping monitors and the background hiss of humidified oxygen being delivered to patients through plastic face masks. Natalia's surgeon, Anand, had two patients on the ward that afternoon. He had finished checking on one when he turned and saw Natalia watching him from across the room.

He wandered to her bedside, picking up the chart from the end of the bed and checking the readings and statistics.

'Welcome back. How are you feeling?' he asked. 'Sore, I imagine.'

She nodded whilst he checked her pulse.

'You're doing well. Everything should be fine. The knife nicked a bit of your liver, which was not great, but I think we got to it in time. Everything should heal.' He smiled, glancing up at a machine to check her blood pressure at the same time.

'How long . . .' she said, but Anand held up his hand to stop her.

'You'll be here for at least three or four days, perhaps longer. We have to make sure you don't get an infection.'

'I must talk to . . . Calum,' she said, the sound hard to hear through her face mask.

'No visitors, I'm afraid, Natalia. Not while you're here. You might be able to speak on the phone in due course, but we need to keep you sterile for at least three days. Now, get some rest and I'll come and see you later.' He patted her hand and walked away.

'She seems to be doing okay,' he said to the senior nurse on duty. 'Blood pressure's a bit erratic, but that's to be expected. Pulse, body temperature and oxygen levels have all stabilised, which is good.'

'We're monitoring the drains. It's too early yet to know if she'll escape infection.'

'When's her next IV antibiotic?'

'She's due another two grams shortly.'

'Okay, good. Then there's not much else we can do for the moment except let nature take its course.'

'She's anxious,' the nurse said. 'Keeps asking after someone called Calum.'

'Yes, she mentioned his name to me.'

'With luck, he'll ring soon and then she'll be happy. If not, I might let the police know. They're the ones who've put the armed guards on the door.'

'I was going to ask about that.'

'She's the wife of a Russian diplomat, apparently.'

'Not someone called Calum, though?'

'It doesn't sound likely.'

'Okay, let me know if there's a crisis. Otherwise, I'll be back in two hours before I finish for the day.'

Chapter 55

London

The red police van spun around, tyres squealing, and accelerated away around the back of Kensington Palace, quickly hidden from the helicopter hovering overhead by a thick canopy of trees. Suddenly, the driver of the Mercedes jammed on the brakes, its rear door opening momentarily as Ross was dragged out the back and into another van parked immediately alongside. This second van was white and had a florist's name and livery stencilled on its side. The diplomatic protection vehicle, its rear door closed, immediately accelerated away with sirens blaring, the vehicle swap taking perhaps five seconds at most. The driver of the florist van, deliberately not in a hurry, took her time before starting the engine, setting off along Palace Drive at a much more sedate pace.

'Head down, say nothing until we get to where we're going,' the driver ordered from the front cabin. 'It won't take long.'

*

The NPAS helicopter followed the police Mercedes van as it navigated its way around Marble Arch and down Park Lane. In the

Command Centre, McIlvoy and Hutch watched its progression live on the screens in front of them, several of the Command Centre crew standing around enjoying a brief moment of success. One team member, still on the phone, came hurrying over as soon as her call was finished.

'I've just heard from the hospital. There was an attempted room entry, ten minutes ago. Nothing serious, a nurse whose name wasn't on the list. She didn't cause a fuss, simply turned around and went away again.'

'Description.'

'Hard to say, she was all gowned up. The interesting thing was, she had white hair, apparently.'

'See if you can get any CCTV images of her. Hutch, can we up the level of protection around the entire hospital?'

'That won't be easy but I'll see what we can do.'

'Did you see where North went?' McIlvoy asked.

'He simply disappeared,' one of Hutch's team said. 'Wandered out, didn't say a thing.'

McIlvoy shook her head, watching the screen as the van meandered its way back and forth around the congested streets towards Savile Row, in time pulling to a halt by the rear entrance to the police station on Old Burlington Street.

'I've had the chopper pilot asking if they can be released from our command,' Hutch said.

'Fine by me,' McIlvoy said. 'Now that Ross is back in custody, that part of the job is done.' The live camera footage disappeared from the large screens in front. 'Say thanks to the helicopter crew. Everyone did a fine job today.'

McIlvoy's mobile rang a short while later.

'Hello,' she said and stared at the floor, listening, her knuckles turning white as she gripped the handset.

'Shit!' she said angrily, eyes livid.

'What's up?'

'The bastard's only got away, that's what. The van is fucking empty!'

'What?' Hutch asked. 'We saw him arrested. He was in the van when it left Hyde Park. We all saw it.'

'Well, he's not there now. The two arresting officers have scarpered and there's no sign of Ross anywhere. We suddenly look like fucking idiots.'

'How could that have happened?'

McIlvoy's face was set firm, one name dominating her thoughts. Why did she have this nagging, sinking feeling that Brendan North was behind all of this?

Chapter 56

Washington

Herb Okumura could sense his boss's excitement as soon as he entered the DDO's office and closed the door.

'What's up, Nancy?' he said, slumping down in one of the visitor chairs and placing an open can of diet cola on the table beside him.

'There's been another meeting between Usmanov and the Russian President.'

'They only met last week, for God's sakes.'

'Apparently, Usmanov's wife has stolen secret papers. That's the crisis. They concern the love child.'

'Young Alexei, as we now know him.'

'Correct. Listen to the recording, then give me your reactions.'

They both sat in mesmerised silence as she played the recording.

'Fucking amazing!' Okumura said towards the end. 'This is like sitting in the President's fucking office. It's un-be-fucking-lievable. This time, we've gotta run voice analysis, just to be certain that they really are who we think they are.'

'It's been done. NSA have already confirmed this is the real deal.'

'I'm speechless. There's no way they might be yanking our chain, do you think?'

'You tell me.'

'I can't believe so. The tech guys tell me the Russians still don't have a clue about the compromised routers. I trust them. This is genuine. Why else does the man walk furtively through the underground Kremlin tunnels with no one knowing? I buy this, 100 per cent.'

'Run this by me one more time,' Turley said, sipping an iced tea as she spoke. 'I want to play devil's advocate for the moment. The Russian President has an illegitimate son that no one knows about. So what? He's the President. He can do what the fuck he likes. Look at our own President, for God's sake. If word leaked out that this kid was tucked away at some swanky Swiss school, sure there might be some mumblings about who's paying the fees, but what's the big deal?'

'The big deal, as you put it, Nancy, is that this is not only the President's son. It's also DESTINY's. So, the moment news gets out about the existence of young Alexei, everyone starts asking who the mother is. It risks exposing DESTINY.'

'Is that likely? All the traces will have been well-covered. The adoption papers will lead us nowhere. He'll simply be another child with no identifiable mother. If asked, they'll say she's dead or something.'

'Yes, but if the tables were reversed and we were running DESTINY, we'd be shit-scared about our asset if news about her love child was out there, however untraceable we believed the trail between mother and son was.'

'I guess. However, let's say we somehow managed to get hold of Usmanov's private papers, this notebook or whatever. What leverage does it actually give? Let's assume, as we heard on the tape, that anything written in it only concerns the boy. Say there's no mention of DESTINY. What's so precious about the damned notebook, then? No one will give a shit.'

'I don't buy that. The Brits have their own private operation against Usmanov. They call it Project WATCHKEEPER. Riordan didn't say as much to me when we met, but my hunch is they are hoping to turn Usmanov through some kind of entrapment. I'd wager that this notebook is part of what they believe will make Usmanov work for them.'

'Embarrass Usmanov? I don't get it.'

'Usmanov's wife falls for a Brit teacher who entices her to leave her husband and come and live in London with him. She fears for her life, so she steals some collateral from her husband, this notebook.'

'A document that proves the Russian President had a secret lovechild – big deal, so what?'

'Yes, but the "so what" is that maybe there's more in this notebook than Usmanov let on. Otherwise, why the sudden interest in getting it back? You heard them. "Almost zero – but not completely" was what he actually said when he was pushed about the chances that DESTINY was mentioned in the notebook. Usmanov's hiding something. Why else is he there, in person, in Moscow, fessing up? This notebook is red hot, you've got to believe it.'

'Is that fact or supposition?'

'As Rumsfeld might have said, it's an unknown unknown.'

'In my book that's a supposition.'

'Hang on. Usmanov doesn't drag himself voluntarily to Moscow to receive a bollocking and have his job put on the line from the Russian President, for God's sake, just because his wife has taken off with a notebook that has only mildly incriminating material in it. The stakes are much, much higher, we can both sense it. So, it would seem, can the Brits.'

'You think this teacher is working for them?'

'It has to be a possibility.'

'Then it's critical we get our hands on this goddamned notebook before either the Russians or the Brits.'

'What I don't get is why did Usmanov's wife sent the damned thing to Venice?'

'I can think of worse places.'

'I don't think she was planning a vacation, Nancy.'

'We should check out Usmanov's wife's friends. See if you can find anyone with links to Venice.'

'I'll get onto it. I'll also order a team to Venice right away. Sarah Warren's proven useful recently. I'll send her and Alex Brady.'

'Just find whatever's been stolen before Usmanov and the Russians steal it back.'

'Or the Brits.'

'Right. On this occasion, Herb, it's America first. If it comes to a head-to-head, we need that notebook heading to Langley. Do we understand each other?'

Chapter 57

Moscow

'What have you found?'

He was standing behind Irina's desk, peering over her shoulder. There were piles of paper scattered on the desk in front of her. Her body was so close that he could smell her perfume. It was an expensive brand and he instantly approved. He leaned forward further and felt his body press gently against hers.

'The cash drawdown records will be hard. Apparently, banking section keep separate ledgers for all Intelligence Services' activities. Unfortunately for us, most of the records are written up by hand. It has always been that way, a security issue apparently. We won't be able to access them without speaking to someone, which is what you asked me not to do.'

'What about Usmanov's diary?'

'That's been a lot easier. I spoke to his new secretary, Ludmilla. She, helpfully, has sent over screen shots of his diary for the last six months. I've printed them all off for you,' she said, gathering up several sheets of loose paper and passing them to Kuzlov. He pulled up a chair and set next to her as he scanned the documents, raising his glasses onto his head so he could read the detail in close up.

'So, immediately after he's drawn down the two hundred thousand, he travels across Turkey and into Syria for a few days. Then he returns to Istanbul, goes back and forth to the Balkans, makes one trip to Cyprus, then flies to London. Who is Alexander Timmerman, do we know?'

'A wealthy German businessman. One of the President's friends, so I understand.'

'Who Usmanov goes all the way to London to meet for dinner before heading straight back to Turkey?'

'So it would seem.'

'What about this trip to Geneva? What took him there, I wonder?'

'He made a similar trip a few months earlier.'

'There's no record here of who he was visiting, sadly.'

'To be honest, this feels like searching for a needle in a haystack.'

'Perhaps I ought to go to Istanbul myself. Have a nose around banking section, take a look at the ledgers, that sort of thing. I could exert a little pressure on Usmanov in person. See how he reacts. The man's guilty of something, I can feel it in my bones. Where is he at the moment?'

'Istanbul. When you asked me to call him earlier, he had just arrived at the office.'

'What are the flights from here like?'

'I've already looked for you. There's a direct Aeroflot flight that leaves Sheremetyevo later this evening.'

'Book me a seat. I won't need an embassy car, I'll grab a taxi at the airport. Then I can surprise Usmanov first thing in the morning. That will really make his day. Any news on how his wife is doing in London?'

'They have operated on her and she is stable.'

'Any word from Cristina Marinca?'

'I'll let you know the moment she calls.'

'Very good. I'm going to grab my overnight bag and head to the airport. It'll probably take me forever to get there.'

Chapter 58

London

They'd parked the florist's van in an underground garage and taken the lift to a fifth-floor apartment. The woman accompanying Ross was uncommunicative. He could sense she was a fellow-athlete simply from her physique. That, plus the way she carried herself: light on her feet and agile. She was younger than Ross, but that was fine. All he'd done was pull the emergency ripcord. Now it was time to go with the flow.

"Play along, but play hard to get. When a fish nibbles the bait, let the line out a bit and be prepared for a fight. A tussle or two is to be expected."

Well, he'd followed the game plan thus far.

The apartment came complete with babysitters. Muscle-bound former squaddies, by the look of things. Ross may no longer have been on the run, but he wasn't about to go anywhere either. The woman made a pot of tea and Ross took his mug and began thinking about Natalia.

Just keep the woman safe. Whatever you do, it's imperative that you don't screw that objective up.

Riordan arrived ten minutes later. She came with another man Ross hadn't met before.

'Calum,' she said, breezing in and taking a seat at the glass-topped table where Ross was nursing his mug of tea. 'I'm delighted you took us up on our offer. We'll sort everything out, I promise. Firstly, let me introduce Brendan. Brendan, Calum; Calum, Brendan.' The two shook hands and Riordan went straight down to business.

'First things first. Your Russian lady friend. She has a bad stab wound to the abdomen and was in surgery for almost two hours. The surgeon thinks she will be okay, but the big risk is infection. That and stray assassins.' She gave a weak smile. 'We believe the risk of the latter to be low.'

'When can I see her?'

'No one can, at present. Her ward at UCLH is in lockdown. Officially, for the moment, you remain high on the police's most-wanted list. I think we should rule out a visit for the time being. Brendan's little escape plan will have irritated one or two of our police brethren. They'll get over it. In the meantime, we'll try to organise a phone link, as soon as she's awake and able to talk.'

'How are you going to do that?' he asked testily.

'We're not completely without influence.'

The man named Brendan smiled but said nothing.

'I'm not sure I know what the fuck's going on any longer.' Ross glared at Riordan. 'Before I agree to anything, I'm going to ask one more time. Were you in any way responsible for all the shit and aggravation I've been through? Hacking my bank account and all that bollocks with the rucksacks.'

North chose that particular moment to head towards a table behind where Ross was sitting, taking his time as he poured himself a coffee.

'As I said before, Calum, and I'll repeat it again to avoid doubt. Neither myself, my team nor anyone working for the Security

Intelligence Service had any involvement with any of those things.'

The two stared at each other as Ross considered Riordan's words carefully. Across the room and out of Ross's sightline, North kept his back turned as he lifted a mug of coffee to his lips. It was a semantic lawyers' point, but one that Riordan had used cleverly. The Security Intelligence Service, more commonly known as MI6 – in North's own vernacular, the assassins – was a separate entity to the Security Service where North and his MI5 bloodhounds belonged.

'I'm not sure who to believe at the moment,' Ross said testily. 'Let's move on. What's the deal with me?'

'With you, Calum?' She studied her fingernails. 'As I mentioned, if you're willing to provide us with access to Usmanov and his secrets, then automatically you qualify to become a life member of our private members' club.'

'All past sins and alleged infractions forgiven?'

'Correct.'

'I'm damned if I know how you'll just wave a magic wand and deliver that.'

'I wouldn't worry. Brendan and his team are skilled at that sort of thing, isn't that right, Brendan?'

Ross turned to see North shrug a little sheepishly.

'It sounds like this Usmanov is quite the man.'

'He is, trust me.'

'I'll want immunity upfront. I don't need anything conditional on success.'

'Agreed.'

'Do I get that in writing?'

'I'm sure we can sort something.'

Which was refreshing, considering what he'd heard six months ago.

'Do I get that in writing?'

'Nope.'

'Then let's get that sorted right away. Now, if you don't mind, I need to use the bathroom.'

Chapter 59

London

Ross closed and locked the bathroom door, shut the lid on the toilet and sat down. He cast an eye around the small room. He had no idea if there were any hidden cameras or listening devices, but he doubted it. He touched the blue glass *nazar* that was still around his neck on its simple leather cord.

It keeps away the evil eye.

So far, the evil eye seemed more or less to be keeping its distance. He reached into his cardigan pocket and took out the chess set.

Keep it safe, Calum. It's special. One day I'll explain why.

Ross lifted the brass latch and opened the box. All the pieces were in their proper places. The box, when it was unfolded flat on the table, had holes in each of the sixty-four tiny squares, miniature plastic chess pieces in thirty-two of them. On one side of the box was the chessboard. On the opposite side under the lid was a thin layer of green felt.

Guard it with your life.

What had Natalia meant by that? He closed the lid and examined both the top and bottom. The box was made of plain wood, with a patterned motif on the lid. He looked for hidden panels, pieces of wood that might slide to one side to reveal a cavity. He couldn't find anything. Even along the sides, the box appeared to be just that: a simple wooden box.

Opening the lid once again, he peered at the chess set. He tried lifting the board from out of the box, but found that it was an integral part of the assembly and couldn't be removed.

What had Natalia meant?

Which was when he thought about the green felt. It fitted snugly into each corner of the lid. What if there was something underneath? He tried to hook a fingernail under one edge to peel the felt away, but he couldn't get a purchase on it, the corners and edges too tight. He glanced around the bathroom, looking for a small, sharp object that he could use as a tool, but nothing obvious came to mind. Then he saw the bathroom mirror and had an idea. The mirror was affixed to the wall with four screws, each screw head covered by a hemispherical, screw-in button which normally was removed by twisting it with a thumb to reveal the slot for a screwdriver underneath. Ross stood and tried removing one button, finding to his satisfaction that the head did indeed come undone without too much difficulty. The shape of the button wasn't perfect, but it had a rounded edge that looked sharp enough, or so he thought, to allow him to get a little purchase on the thin layer of felt. He tried it on one edge, putting the rounded edge as close to the sides of the box as he was able, seeing if he could scrape away a small piece of felt. His first attempt was unsuccessful, so he turned his attention to the long edge closest to the hinge.

To his surprise, when he applied a little pressure, the felt on that edge came away without too much difficulty. Now that he could grip it with his fingers, the felt peeled back easily. Underneath, written on the wood of the lid in black ink, was a simple message. There was a name: Claudia. Below it was a phone number and then one final word. A city.

Venezia.

Chapter 60

London

Riordan was finishing a phone call when Ross came back into the room.

'Ah, Calum. I've just been sorting the paperwork. It should be on its way shortly. Before we get carried away with ourselves, what exactly can you tell us about what Natalia has brought with her? In connection with her husband, that is. This has suddenly become everyone's top priority.'

Play hard to get.

'I'm not surprised. Until the ink is dry, what I am prepared to divulge is that whatever she's discovered is not here in London. She told me, this morning, she'd found treasure. She also told me where she'd hidden it – for safekeeping.'

'When did she tell you all this?'

'At the station this afternoon, moments before she was stabbed.' Ross felt the white lie come easily.

'So where is it?'

'Let's get the formalities completed, then I'll tell you. I will say one thing.'

'I'm listening.'

'Apparently, I'm required to collect whatever it is in person.' Another embellishment that Riordan would never know about.

'That depends on where.'

'It's outside the UK. Right now, I have no passport.'

'We should be able to fix something. Brendan?'

'I'll get on to it right away.'

'Good. You're not about to head back to Istanbul, by any chance, are you?'

'No such luck. It's not here, and it's not there either. For the moment, that's all I'm prepared to say. You're certain I can't see Natalia?'

'Positive.'

'Not even a phone call?'

'Sadly, at this stage, apparently not.'

Chapter 61

London

Lauren McIlvoy's day was about to get worse, if only she but knew it. Exasperated by her failure to catch Ross, she'd left Hutch and the team trying to find out what had happened to him, heading outside, meanwhile, to get some fresh air. She'd given up smoking several years ago but, right at that moment, she craved a cigarette. How had they missed him? Someone had to have helped Ross escape. Could it have been North? He'd been on his wretched phone the whole time Ross had been running around Hyde Park. Then he'd simply scarpered. Her phone rang. She looked at the number but didn't recognise it.

'McIlvoy,' she said, hitting the connect button.

'Lauren, it's Brendan.'

Deep breaths, count to five, stay calm and collected.

'Let's cut to the chase, Brendan. Were you responsible for this fuck-up with Ross this afternoon?'

'It's the reason I'm phoning.'

'That sounds like a yes.'

'It's complicated, I'm afraid.'

'Is that an admission of guilt?'

'In part, yes.'

'You utter bastard! You've been completely wasting my fucking time these last twenty-four hours all for what? Over one Russian who's been stabbed, one supposed killer who's got away while another thug's been killed. Meanwhile, hard-working police resources all over London have all been chasing their tails trying to find Ross for what reason? I suppose the rucksacks and everything were your idea, is that how it all happened?'

'It was a recruitment exercise that went off the rails. We're sorry, Lauren, me especially. Sometimes, we have to put people through the wringer to make everything seem authentic. It's been a hugely complicated little operation. Most of which, I'm not at liberty to discuss. With you or anybody. We never expected the Russian woman to get stabbed. If that hadn't happened, none of what happened subsequently would have been necessary.'

'You complete and utter bastard! I will be making a huge complaint about all of this. One fucking enormous complaint. And do you know what? I hate to admit this, but I'm going to enjoy seeing your career trashed over what you've put me and the team through today.'

'Lauren, darling, I know exactly how you must be feeling. Sure, lessons can always be learned, but it was a highly classified operation that we weren't able to warn you about.'

'I told you before. I'm not your darling and I do not want you *ever* calling me that, do you hear?'

'Look, Lauren, whatever makes you happiest. This has been complex. In support of our colleagues in the Security Intelligence Service, MI5 have been trying to run a highly sensitive recruitment involving Ross. That's all I'm permitted to say. The Director General is drafting a private and classified memo to the Metropolitan Police Commissioner as we speak, apologising for what has happened. I know it's not the result you wanted, but you did a great job as Gold Commander today. Hutch and the team were hugely impressed.'

'Don't you dare start patronising me. Am I supposed to be dropping all charges against Ross?'

'In a manner of speaking, yes. MI5 will 'fess up to the rucksacks and we're confident that everyone will realise that the man only died at the station today whilst Ross was acting in self-defence.'

'I don't know what to say. I feel completely and utterly humiliated.'

'Don't be. I know you don't want to hear this from me, but you did great today. Really, Lauren, you should be proud.'

'What do I say to Hutch and the team?'

'Tell them that MI5 have Ross and that the case is now closed.'

'And the media?'

'We'll say that Ross has been taken in for questioning and then it will fade away.'

'I hope you realise, Brendan, that I despise you for what you've put me through. You seem to take great pleasure in making my life a complete misery. You did all those years ago and you have, again, today. Don't deny it, I know it's true.'

'Quite the opposite. I wish we could make amends and be friends once more. I'd like that.'

'I'm not sure I could face seeing you again. Not now or ever, even.'

'Understood. But when and if you change your mind, please call me. I'd love to try to prove you wrong.'

Chapter 62

London and Venice

The flight to Venice left from London's City airport early the next morning, Ross grateful, for the moment at least, to have time to himself. Riordan's two babysitters had escorted him as far as the plane door before leaving him in the care of the cabin crew. No sooner had Ross begun to his settle in his seat than the aircraft door was closing and the engines could be heard starting up.

Riordan had delivered on her promise the previous evening. Both she and Ross signed multiple copies of a single-page document that seemed, to his layman's eyes, to exonerate him from all possible criminal charges. Ross had explained that the trail now led directly to Venice. North had delivered a passport, €1,000 in cash, a boarding pass, a debit card and a secure mobile phone. In exchange for the latter, he had handed over his old mobile phone and a burner, secretly retaining one of the burners he'd bought the previous afternoon.

The news from the hospital had been fair: Ross had been unable to talk to Natalia because she had been sleeping. Her condition was stable, about as good as expected, but still a long way from being out of the danger zone. Riordan had briefed him about his trip to Venice. On arrival, he would be met at the aircraft door by one of

MI6's contract staff in Italy, a Roberto Pesci. Pesci was going to accompany Ross throughout and would deliver him, and hopefully whatever package or information that had been sent to Venice by Natalia, back to Venice airport where a seat would be booked for him on the next available plane home. Riordan had been curt with Ross about one subject.

'Remember, Calum. Whilst you are swanning around Venice at the taxpayers' expense, your lady friend will be here, under our watchful supervision. Any funny business, or any attempt by you to run off on your own, the chances of you seeing your beloved on your return will be greatly diminished.'

Ross had lain in bed that night and sent a surreptitious text to a woman called Claudia using his burner phone. His message simply stated that he would be in Venice the next day. Not long afterwards, he received a single word in response: *perfetto*.

The flight was uneventful, the plane arriving on schedule at ten-thirty in the morning. As Ross emerged from the air jetty, a dark-haired man in a black leather jacket stepped forward to greet him.

'Calum? Roberto Pesci.' The two shook hands, and Pesci pointed towards the Arrivals area. 'We can take a shortcut if we head this way.' Ross moved to follow, accidentally colliding with a smartly-dressed woman with short brown hair pulling a roll-on suitcase. He apologised briefly, helping her to right her bag back onto its wheels before catching up with Pesci, unaware that the woman had deftly slipped something into his pocket.

'Transfer complete,' Sarah Warren whispered into a neck microphone, strolling with her bag in the opposite direction to where Pesci and Ross were now heading.

'Copy that. Target's lit up like a beacon.'

The two men walked out of the Arrivals area and followed the signs towards the lagoon.

'We'll take a water taxi,' Pesci said. 'It's quicker. Where do we need to go?'

'I don't know yet,' Ross replied truthfully. 'I need to make a call first.'

'Then I suggest that you do that as soon as we are on the water. In the meantime, we will head towards San Marco.'

They walked briskly along a raised covered walkway, a meandering passage that ended several hundred metres later with a final escalator down to the water's edge. Neither man spoke much, Pesci's eyes constantly checking in front and behind.

'You expecting trouble?' Ross asked at one stage.

'Aren't we always?' was all he received in return.

They walked with purpose towards a small group of boatmen who were loitering on the quayside. One man stepped forward, beckoning the pair over to his water taxi. Pesci spoke something rapidly in Italian, shrugging and debating with the driver briefly before Pesci seemed satisfied and indicated to Ross to follow. Both men clambered aboard the highly varnished, wooden boat, making their way to an open deck area at the stern after passing first through a narrow, interior cabin. The driver was already casting off and starting the engine, soon flicking the polished chrome gear lever into reverse, the boat responding by inching backwards. With a well-practised flick of the wrist that set the steering wheel spinning, the boat neatly pirouetted 180 degrees in the water until the bow was pointing out of the dock area. The boat began making its way sedately towards the marked open-water channel that stretched across the lagoon towards the island of Venice in the far distance. Ross and Pesci sat outside in the open air, the sun shining and the water on the lagoon a flat calm. Only once the boat had cleared the airport perimeter did the driver pushed the throttle lever all the way forward, the bow immediately lifting as the boat instantly picked up speed. The increased noise in the rear cockpit made conversation suddenly difficult.

'Are you going to make that call?'

'Hardly, with this racket going on,' Ross shouted above the engine roar. 'I'll do it once we get to San Marco.'

They had been going about five minutes when Ross noticed that the boat was being steered off to the left, away from the marked channel. It continued in this direction for several seconds before the throttle was killed and the engine died. Ross looked up and saw the boatman advancing through the interior cabin towards them at the stern. Something about the man's gait didn't seem right. He was fifteen feet away when a silenced handgun appeared in his right hand.

'Are you Ross?' he asked, waving the weapon directly towards Calum.

Before Ross had time to reply, Pesci began speaking in rapid Italian. The man with the gun simply swung his weapon in Pesci's direction and fired two shots in rapid succession, instantly killing the agent.

'Where's the notebook?' The man turned to Ross, speaking in heavily accented English. Ross's cardigan was flecked with Pesci's blood. He wiped his face with his hand and saw more traces of blood on his fingers.

'You just killed a man for no reason,' he said, looking at Pesci's slumped body on the decking.

'Shut the fuck up. I asked you a question. Where's the notebook?'

'San Marco,' Ross lied with an ease he didn't feel, the sound of another water taxi approaching suddenly audible. The noise caused the man to look up and curse in a language Ross didn't understand. He was too far away for Ross to charge at him. Instead, the boatman returned to the cockpit to restart the engine, but it wouldn't fire up. The man cursed again, trying several more times in vain, panic beginning to set in. Ross considered jumping out the back into the water. He changed his mind when he saw the second water taxi racing towards their stricken vessel from one side. As it drew close, several shots rang out, and Ross ducked down below the railing to keep out of the firing line. Next, there was a scream and the boatman, the man who had shot Pesci, suddenly fell into the water. Tentatively, Ross peered over the edge of the boat and looked at the other vessel now alongside. Which was when he saw a face he recognised. A fellow soldier. One whose soldiering career, much like Ross's, had been in units with the word 'Special' stamped everywhere.

'Are you going to stay there all day, matey, or can we kindly get a fucking move on? What we don't need, I would suggest, is the Italian police asking too many awkward questions.'

Chapter 63

London and Venice

It was a struggle for Lauren McIlvoy even to get out of bed the next morning, let alone contemplate heading into the office. She kept thinking about what Brendan North had said and done the previous day. It was troubling her. Expecting to be incensed, she found herself in a weird state: oddly calm and unstressed. Perhaps it had been because North had been so uncharacteristically honest – and indeed conciliatory. Or did she mean nice? She nearly tripped over the cat in her befuddled state as she made herself a cup of coffee and poured muesli into a bowl. She felt confused by her emotions. Scared, definitely. There was something else, though, something she wasn't ready to admit. Was it pity? Or was it different? Did a part of her still care about him? She shivered in her dressing gown at the thought, deciding there and then that she was going to need help from her therapist with all of this.

DC Frank D'Souza was at his desk when McIlvoy arrived at Savile Row police station a little later than normal.

'Back to the real world today, eh, Lauren?'

'Yes, down to earth with a bump, Frank.'

'What was it like, being Gold Commander for the day?'

'I had the Hutch looking after me. How could that have been anything other than exhilarating? It was great, actually. He's got a cracking team. I think they live off adrenaline. As you say, now back to the real world.'

'Calum Ross is a free man, I gather.'

'Correct,' she said, a look of resignation on her face.

'Which means you're no longer interested in knowing what he's up to, is that right?'

'I never said that,' she said, looking up at him, eyes instantly alert. 'What have you got?'

'Come and take a peep.' D'Souza swivelled a desk monitor so that McIlvoy could peer over his shoulder. 'This new facial recognition software we've been trialling. It's neat, especially with all the CCTV coverage everywhere. We've had Ross's face on alert since yesterday. Looked what popped up this morning at London City Airport.' His screen showed images from a camera positioned close to a British Airways jet parked on the apron, time-stamped at 7.27 that morning. The stairs were still in position and the aircraft door open. They watched as a car drew up and three men emerged, one of whom was Ross. The two other men walked with Ross up the steps of the aircraft before Ross was taken inside. His escorts then returned to their vehicle and waited for a dispatcher in her fluorescent vest to leave the aircraft and supervise the closing of the aircraft door. Then the two men drove away.

'Well, well, well. Where's the plane heading?'

'Venice. It should be on the ground at Marco Polo airport in about an hour.'

'Isn't Venice where Aldo Bernardi is based?' Bernardi was an officer in the Italian *Guardia di Finanza*, the specialist agency that investigated the illegal drug trade in Italy. McIlvoy had worked with Bernardi on a recent case, helping to apprehend, and then arrange the extradition of, two suspected masterminds behind a huge Italian drug ring.

'That's right.'

'I think I'll give Aldo a quiet call. It's not my responsibility any longer, but I am sure he might be interested in knowing about someone as interesting as Calum Ross about to arrive in his city.'

Chapter 64

Istanbul

Usmanov had been sitting at his desk, trying to place a call to the hospital where Natalia was recovering when the door to his office burst open and in barged Nicolai Kozlov. In his wake was his secretary, Ludmilla, apologising for her inability to keep the man from Moscow at bay.

'I'm sorry,' she spluttered in apology, but Usmanov waved her away as he got to his feet.

'Well, well, well. I supposed it was only a matter of time before you showed up here, Nicolai Anatolyvich.' Their handshake was perfunctory. 'You never mentioned you were coming here when we spoke yesterday.'

'It was a last-minute decision.'

'Why?'

'I would have thought that was obvious.'

The two men stared at each other, Usmanov eventually indicating to Kozlov that he should take a seat.

'How is your wife doing?'

'You tell me. You seemed to know so much about her when we spoke on the phone yesterday.'

'In what way?'

'You called her "my philandering wife", if I recall.'

'Director Borodin has been concerned for your welfare. No one at Yasenevo sits comfortably when an agent discovers his spouse is sleeping around.'

'Did Borodin ask you to take care of Natalia, is that it?'

'Of course not!'

'Then it wasn't you who engaged Cristina Marinca in a little private enterprise?'

The two men eyeballed each other impassively for several seconds, Usmanov's mentioning of Marinca's name registering momentarily in Kozlov's eyes. For a moment, the investigator's eyelids widened, just a fraction.

'Cristina who?' Kozlov said casually, few moments later.

'Someone once suggested to me that the difference between a seasoned field agent and a simple investigator was a matter of basic intelligence.' Usmanov took some satisfaction in seeing Kozlov's cheeks redden. 'If, by the way, I do discover that someone in Moscow commissioned Marinca to kill my wife, just for the record, I will not be letting the matter rest there. I presume we both understand each other?'

'Frankly, I don't know what you're talking about.'

'Very good. Tell me, what is so important that you travel all the way here from Moscow overnight and barge into my office unannounced? I have other things I am meant to be doing.'

'I'm afraid I am here with the Director's specific authority. Either you provide a full and appropriate explanation about what happened to the missing two hundred thousand dollars we discussed yesterday. Or else I will instruct the Consulate's security detail to arrest you. If that happens, you will be immediately suspended from all duties and flown directly back to Moscow pending a formal investigation. The matter is entirely in your hands.'

'Is that all?' At which point, to Kozlov's consternation, Usmanov began to laugh out loud. 'You come all the way here, wasting scarce Russian cash resources on flights and hotels, just to ask me this! Nicolai Anatolyvich, you're an imbecile!'

'How dare you call me that!' the Muscovite raged, once more on his feet. 'I should have you arrested right now for your insolence. Admit it, you stole that money. I'm willing to bet it's sitting in some grubby little secret bank account somewhere. I know all about your regular trips to Switzerland, visiting your own private banker, no doubt. You think you're so clever, able to swan around here, there and everywhere with no accountability to anyone. Well, this time, Oleg Ivanovich,' he said, spitting out the patronymic, 'you failed to factor in me. I'm going to prove your guilt. You, my friend, are about to spend the rest of your meagre little life in the gulag, assuming you survive the interrogation.'

He pulled out his mobile phone and scrolled through to a number and hit dial.

'Who are you calling?' Usmanov asked, the grin on his face as wide as ever.

'Consulate security.'

'I suggest you put the phone down before you make a complete fool of yourself.' He watched as Kozlov hesitated. 'You want to know what happened to the money. So, I will show you.' He got up from his desk and went to open the door for Kozlov, grabbing his jacket along the way. Kozlov heard his call being answered, thought twice about speaking, then on a whim ended the call and followed Usmanov out of the office.

'Where are we going?'

'You'll see,' Usmanov said, pressing the nearby elevator button and waiting.

Two floors down, they meandered through various corridors, Usmanov leading the way until they came to the Consul's private suite of offices. Usmanov approached the Consul's secretary, who recognised her visitor and immediately stood up as he approached.

'Good morning, Vladlena. I have with me a special visitor from Moscow. He is keen to see what I have in the Consul's safe. Would you be so kind as to open the safe and let me have the large attaché case I left with you a few months ago?'

'Of course,' she said. 'Please wait here a moment and I will fetch it for you.'

A few minutes passed and then she was back, holding a large, brown leather case which she passed to Usmanov.

'Is there a private room I could use for a few minutes?'

'Why, you can use the Consul's office if you like? He's away all day in Ankara.' She led the way into a grand room, indicating a large meeting table in one corner where the two men could sit in privacy. Once they were alone, Usmanov placed the attaché case on the table and looked at Kozlov.

'I've had a sensitive operation running for some time. It concerns an Iranian nuclear scientist who has been an invaluable source of high-grade intelligence. His daughter was kidnapped by rebels who demanded two hundred thousand dollars as ransom. I met certain intermediaries in Syria, took the money with me in order to show our willingness to help secure her release, in good faith. In the end, the money wasn't needed. The Americans bombed the compound where the rebels were holding the daughter and she died. I returned with the money and decided, given all the financial cuts we are all struggling to live with, not to return it to banking section, but lodge it in the Consul's safe. It's all here. Open the case and count it all if you like.'

Kozlov stared at the case, a grim expression on his face. Eventually he undid each of the clasps on either side of the handle and flipped open the lid. Inside, in bundles of one hundred-dollar bills, were twenty piles of cash, exactly as Usmanov had said.

'You broke procedure by not returning this to banking section. I will be making my report,' was all Kozlov could say defiantly. His body language, however, told a different story. He had lost this particular battle and it showed.

'You do that, Nicolai. However, before you step on another plane wasting scarce Roubles, just remember one thing. I will find out who commissioned Cristina Marinca to kill my wife. When I do, that person is going to regret it for a very long time.'

Chapter 65

Venice, Italy

They crossed the lagoon towards the island of Venice at full throttle, only reducing speed to a crawl to conform to the speed limits strictly enforced by the Venetian police, electing to head in a clockwise direction around the island toward San Marco.

'Who was that other boatman?' Ross was standing in the cockpit alongside the other man.

'A Russian.' Cigarette smoke was once again filling the small space. A different brand that Ross didn't recognise, but still the same old cheap lighter.

'Are you sure?'

'I'd been following him since before your plane touched down.'

'He killed my contact. Two bullets, bam, bam, no questions asked. It was brutal.'

'Here.' The man rummaged inside a small locker beside him and eventually found a small rag. 'Take this. There's a bottle of water inside the cabin. Better get rid of the blood on your face and hands.'

'Any better?' Ross asked a while later.

'I guess. You're not actually my type.' He grinned at his weak joke, but Ross didn't rise to it.

'He asked me about a notebook.'

'Who did?'

'The Russian.'

'And?'

'I know nothing about a notebook. Well, I don't yet.'

'Too bad. For him, I mean. Water under the bridge now. Perhaps literally.'

'Thanks for watching my back, back there. I thought he was going to kill me.'

'He would have done. Shame about your friend. Who was he?'

'Someone called Roberto Pesci.'

'Never heard of him. MI6?'

'I guess.'

'Bloody amateurs. I told you. No wonder they set up our lot.'

'Did your parents ever give you a name?'

'Probably.'

'Are you and I now working together?'

'We've always been working together, you stupid fuck.'

'So, what can I call you?'

'Bruce.'

'Seriously?'

'Pick a name.'

'Okay then. How about Flynn?'

'Why Flynn?'

'Why not?'

'Sounds good to me. Flynn it is. Let's find a coffee and we can plan what we do next.'

The man now called Flynn tied the taxi to a wooden pillar on one of the side canals just beyond the eastern tip of the island. Together they strolled a short distance to a small pavement café.

'What's your plan, soldier?' Flynn asked, double espressos on the table in front of them both. Flynn flicked a sachet of sugar against the side of the table, tore the top off and poured the contents into his cup.

'Natalia gave me the name and contact number of someone to call, here in Venice. A woman called Claudia.'

'Have you called her yet?'

'Texted, yes. Called, no.'

'Then I suggest now might be the time to make the call.'

Ross dug in his pocket for his burner phone. As he pulled it out, a small, coin-shaped object fell to the floor.

'Hello!' Flynn said, stooping to pick it up, a cloud of cigarette smoke engulfing him. 'What do we have here?'

They looked at the object, similar in size and shape to a flat battery, a bit thicker than a few coins stuck together.

'That, my friend, is a tracking device. Who would have given you that, do you think?'

Ross thought about this for a while in silence.

'At the airport,' he said after a pause. 'I bumped into a woman. Or, rather, she into me. Tripped over her case. I stopped to help her pick it up. She thanked me and moved on.'

'Gallant. English or Italian?'

'English. No, wait, American. I remember her accent. Short dark hair. Kind of cute-looking.'

'Americans,' the man called Flynn said, lighting another cigarette. 'The C – I – fucking – A!' They both sat in silence, contemplating the tiny electronic device on the table in front of them. 'So, here's what we're going to do. The Russian said he was looking for a notebook, you say?'

'Correct.'

'So, the Americans will be looking for a notebook too, don't you think?'

'Possibly. I don't know what the fuck is going on any longer.'

'Don't be a dickhead. Call the woman, tell her you want to meet later in the day, say in the middle of the afternoon; meanwhile, you're simply calling to check she's got Natalia's package. Ask her how big it is, what it feels like inside. I've an idea up my sleeve. As soon as you've made the call, place the tracking device back in your pocket and we'll jump in the taxi once more.'

*

Besides Sarah Warren and Alex Brady, Herb Okumura had drawn on four other Italian-based assets to support the rapidly unfolding operation in Venice. Meanwhile, an overnight search of Natalia Borisenko's known friends and contacts had identified one person who looked promising. Her name was Claudia Cuccinelli, and she was believed to be based in Milan, almost 300 kilometres away. Then, a few hours earlier, the breakthrough they were looking for. One of the Langley-based researchers had discovered that Cuccinelli was no longer in Milan: a few years ago, she had, it seemed, left her husband and moved to Venice. She was known to be living somewhere on the island of Giudecca but no one had located a physical address. The only photograph they'd unearthed was an old stock photo used by the Corriere Della Sera newspaper when Cuccinelli had worked there several years earlier.

Okumura directed Warren, Brady and one other, Malone, to focus on Ross, and sent the other three to scour the streets and alleyways of Giudecca hoping to find the woman. Malone was the technical guy on the team. He was enthusiastically tracking Ross's physical location on a small tablet he carried with him. He lived in

Venice, which meant he knew the island and its waterways in great detail.

'Great job on planting that device, by the way, Sarah,' Brady had said as they waited to leave the airport complex. They had been delayed in their pursuit of Ross by a blocked fuel line on the boat that Malone had commandeered for them earlier in the day.

'Glad to know I haven't lost the knack.'

'Any idea where he's heading?'

'Your guess is as good as mine.'

It had taken a frustrating twenty minutes to clear the blockage, but Warren and Brady were relieved to see that the tracking device appeared operational and still tantalisingly close. As they finally began making their way across the lagoon, they could see on Malone's screen that Ross's water taxi was rounding the eastern corner of the island close to a small park where the Biennale arts festival was held.

Whilst Malone navigated the boat through the water channel, Warren and Brady stared at the pulsing red circle on the tablet computer.

'He's stopping,' Brady said to no one in particular, the red circle now stationary by a small canal on the map.

'Here, let me see,' Malone said, reaching for the tablet and examining it carefully. 'Okay, I get it, they're near Arsenale.'

'How long before we can get there?'

'If I keep to the speed limit and don't attract attention from the *polizia*? About fifteen minutes, perhaps a bit more.'

'And if you break a few rules?'

'Less than ten.'

'Well, what are you waiting for?'

They were doing well until they reached the northern coast of the island, close to the heliport on the roof of the *Ospedale*. Four powerful police motorboats appeared from out of the Santa

Giustina canal, two setting off at speed, sirens blazing, toward Marco Polo airport and two heading in the same clockwise direction as their vessel. For a while, all three boats were travelling side by side, Malone having little option but to keep to the speed limit.

'Are we being checked out?' Malone shouted from the cockpit.

'I don't think so, no.'

'Sorry about this, folks. If we keep at this speed, it'll add about five minutes.'

'Too bad. Ross is back on the move again,' Warren sighed.

'Shit!' Malone shouted. 'Where's he heading now?'

'Appears to be towards the island of Giudecca.'

'Sounds like he's set up a rendezvous with this Cuccinelli woman,' Brady said. 'I'll alert the others.'

*

The man Ross knew only as Flynn expertly steered the water taxi directly towards the floating pontoons of the *vaporetto* stop at Redentore, the location he'd carefully chosen on the island of Giudecca. Somewhat ironically, it was only one stop away from where Claudia Cuccinelli had caught the ferry the previous day at Palanca, but only Flynn was aware of that particular fact.

During the short crossing to Giudecca, Ross had taken control of the boat while Flynn went to the back to make some calls in private. As they rounded the magnificent church and campanile of San Giorgio Maggiore with its colonnaded front that directly faced the Campanile San Marco across the lagoon, the bell tower in the middle of St Mark's square, Flynn reappeared. He had yet another cigarette in his mouth.

'All set my friend, exactly as we discussed. Take a table at the Al Redentor restaurant just along from the *vaporetto* stop. You can't miss it, it has big red umbrellas over the tables. She'll be along in less than an hour. Try a pizza while you're waiting, they're meant to be excellent.'

'And after that?'

'Assuming everything goes to plan, make your way back to the place I'm about to drop you off at. Your very own taxi will be waiting.'

'You think this will work?'

'Trust me, this is going to work. The only problem's going to be if works out a bit too well.'

'What do you mean by that?'

'You'll see.'

Chapter 66

Venice, Italy

Ross felt confused. If this was what being a spy was like, he was enjoying some bits, but not necessarily all of them. He'd seen his fair share of dead bodies in the forces, even killed a few, though he'd taken no pleasure in seeing Pesci being shot dead so unnecessarily. For no good reason and with no means to defend himself, either. The killer had been a cold, ruthless bastard. Where had he sprung from? One of Usmanov's men, according to Flynn.

He took a seat at a square table set for four with great views across the grey-blue waters of the lagoon, checking to make sure that the small homing device was still in his pocket. This was the other Venice, the part that tourists didn't visit. It was unspoilt, pretty and remarkably quiet. He would bring Natalia here one day, he vowed. He was only doing this for her. That, and out of some perverse loyalty to the man he now knew as Flynn, although whichever part of Land of Hope and Glory he actually hailed from still far from clear. At that particular moment, however, the sun was hot, there was a gentle breeze, and for entertainment he had passing ferries, *vaporettos* and pretty Italian women in short skirts to keep him occupied. What was not to like?

The restaurant was set some distance back from the water's edge, the small courtyard directly in front of where he was sitting creating a feeling of open space bathed in natural sunlight. Since it was lunchtime, Ross ordered a glass of prosecco and a *pizze frutti di mare*. All on expenses, North's €1,000 feeling a welcome weight in his pocket. This part of being a spy suited him well.

He had been sitting alone for thirty minutes, one glass of fairly decent prosecco and half a pizza down, when he realised he was being watched. There were at least three of them, including to his surprise, the cute-looking, dark-haired woman he had bumped into earlier. She had taken a table behind him, even though there were plenty of empty seats with better views of the water right next to his. The other two were muscular guys, sitting at a separate table at the far side of the restaurant, each drinking a beer. Both were in his line of sight, both trying desperately not to look directly at him, both behaving in ways that twitched Ross's radar. There might have been others walking around, or loitering nearby, he couldn't say. He checked his watch. The time was nearly one o'clock. Nearly showtime.

She didn't actually appear until fifteen minutes after the hour.

Ross had ordered an espresso when, out of the corner of one eye, he saw the woman approaching. It wasn't a grand entrance, more the nonchalant, relaxed gait of someone at ease with herself. With blonde hair, slightly curly, sunglasses perched on top, she wore almost no make-up. The most striking feature was her vivid red 'Biennale' t-shirt, worn under a leather jacket and denim skirt. Over one shoulder was a cloth bag with La Biennale de Venezia stencilled on the side. The bag was moderately full.

'Calum?' she said, coming directly to his table, one arm extended in greeting.

'Claudia?' he said, standing, taking her hand in his and greeting her in the way only English people do so well.

She took a seat immediately next to him, her back to the pair of watchers across the restaurant, thus able to look sideways and see the American with the short, dark hair if she was so minded.

'Would you like a glass of wine, a coffee? Perhaps even a slice of pizza?'

'No, thank you.' Her accent was unusual. It didn't sound Italian. To Ross's unsophisticated ear, it had more of an Eastern European resonance than anything. 'I won't stay long. I bring, as you know, a gift from Natalia. She asks that you keep it safe.' Which was the moment she passed across the shoulder bag, Ross taking it with both hands. He peered inside, a rectangular, padded UPS packet the only contents. He felt the weight of the parcel in his hands before placing the bag on the floor so that it leant against a table leg.

'I shall leave now. Say hello, please, to Natalia for me. She is safe and well?'

'Not too bad,' Ross lied, not wanting to prolong her departure. He stood and they shook hands again briefly, then she disappeared back the way she had come. Ross sat down. After indicating to the waiter for the bill, he picked up the bag and looked once more at the padded envelope. It was unopened, Ross feeling the outline of something solid like a book or a desk diary. Perhaps even a notebook.

The waiter reappeared with the bill. Ross counted out two €20 notes from his wallet and handed them to the waiter with a wave of the hand, the amount he'd given more than enough to provide a reasonable tip. He was replacing his wallet in his trouser pocket when he looked up to find the cute-looking American woman pulling out the same chair that his last visitor had vacated.

'Hello,' Ross said, surprised. 'I think we may have bumped into each other somewhere before.' He felt awkwardly aware that he sounded more like a corny James Bond actor than the serious spy he was trying his best to be. At which point, the two muscle-bound guys from across the room walked across the terrace and sat down at the remaining two vacant seats at his table.

'We can do this nicely, with no fuss, just between friends,' the woman said in a soft American accent. 'Or you can cause a scene. Which would be unpleasant. Lots of plates would be broken, glasses smashed, bodies severely beaten up. You can imagine the kind of thing.' She smiled as she said this. Ross smiled back at her.

'Are you trying to proposition me?'

'Don't be so fucking patronising,' she hissed, all hint of her earlier charm vaporised. 'Hand over the goddamned parcel the woman gave you, and we'll be gone.'

Ross didn't flinch. To his credit, nothing moved at all. He was like a rock, staring directly at her, the cold hard stare that comes from hours spent training in units that have the words 'Special' stamped everywhere. Which was when the muscle-bound goon sitting next to him leant across and picked up the shoulder bag. Ross continued to stare at the woman. Not even his eyes had moved.

'If that leaves this table, one or more of you will regret it,' he said, barely moving his lips.

All three Americans stood, the woman smiling thinly.

'I very much doubt that. I think, Calum Ross, you'll find you're completely outnumbered. Good day to you.' They walked away without looking back. Ross, still unmoving, watched them leave in fascination.

Chapter 67

Venice, Italy

To be fair, the Americans managed to walk almost thirty metres from Ross's table before the first thug emerged through a side door of the adjacent building, his huge presence blocking the woman's path. Almost simultaneously, two more heavily-built thugs materialised from out of nowhere to take up positions to the rear of the two muscle-bound American goons, one of whom was still carrying the shoulder bag. Ross could see the glint of steel blades reflecting in the noonday sun. A fourth – it became clear that he was in charge – emerged from around the corner of the small piazza by the water's edge and addressed the woman directly. Ross felt like he was in a theatre, watching the drama unfold on the stage directly in front of him.

'You have something that was stolen from us.' Russians. Why was Ross not surprised?

Without waiting for pleasantries, one of the Russians at the rear slashed at the bag's shoulder strap. The American who'd been carrying the UPS packet was instantly relieved of his precious cargo. In the process, this man suffered a bad gash to the shoulder. The other American next to him attempted, unwisely, to stop this assault. For his efforts, he received a deep slashing wound to his wrist and forearm from the second Russian. The American woman, meanwhile, was by now fumbling for something in her handbag. The first Russian simply picked her up in his huge, muscular arms, carried her to the water's edge and dropped her over the side. She screamed as she hit the water. Then, as quickly as it had all kicked off, the four Russians disappeared, the UPS parcel departing with them.

It took less than a minute from start to finish, Ross watching the unfolding scene with some amusement. As waiters and patrons from the restaurant rushed forward to help, it was time for Ross to leave. He slipped out the side, making his way towards the *vaporetto* pontoon at Redentore a short distance away. There, waiting as promised, was a water taxi. Behind the wheel, cigarette well underway, watching all the action, was Flynn.

'Quite a scene, huh?' Flynn said, once Ross was on board.

'They fell for the dummy parcel trick.'

'Knew they would.'

'It was amusing to watch.' Flynn cast off from the pontoon, heading back toward San Marco once more.

'You still got that tracking bug on you?'

Ross dug in his pocket and pulled it out.

'Time to feed the fishes, don't you think?'

'Too right,' Ross said, flinging the small device into the water as far as he could. 'Must be time for me to call the real Claudia.'

'I agree. Where do you want to make the drop?'

'Any suggestions?'

'Ever been to the Gritti Palace?'

'No.'

'Swanky hotel. They have this great terrace bar, right by the water.'

'Is that important?'

'Being by the water? Sure. When the Russians find out they've been duped, they will not be taking it lying down now, will they?'

'So, I meet the girl, get the parcel, leap into a passing taxi, is that it?'

'Ian Fleming would be proud of you.'

'How much fuel is there in the tank?'

Flynn consulted the gauges.

'Plenty. Why?'

'Just hatching an escape plan. Let's find somewhere to grab another coffee. I need to make a couple of calls.'

'This woman, right?'

'Correct. Plus, my escape plan.'

'I'm your escape plan, remember?'

'Maybe. But you're forgetting. In theory, you don't exist. It's time I spoke to some real people back in London if I'm to stand any chance of getting out of here alive.'

Chapter 68

Venice, Italy

Aldo Bernardi didn't quite know what to make of his conversation with Lauren McIlvoy until two things happened later that same day. The first was the sighting of a dead body floating in the Venice lagoon, not far from Marco Polo airport. When the airport *polizia* were sent to investigate, they found the man to have been shot twice before ending up in the water. Bernardi was immediately informed since the police officer on duty thought it could have been a drug-related killing. Shortly before midday, they identified the man as one Roberto Pesci, a known contractor for the British Security Intelligence Services. Alarm bells started to ring in Bernardi's head.

The second incident was a reported stabbing of two Americans on the island of Giudecca, about an hour later. Again, the matter was referred to Bernardi since this, too, had the hallmarks of a drug-related revenge attack. Until they discovered that one of the injured parties was a known operative of America's CIA.

Putting two and two together to make a much larger number, Bernardi immediately reflected on the conversation he'd had with McIlvoy that morning, wondering whether these two incidents might be connected and involve the British operative, Calum Ross. McIlvoy had emailed through police photographs of Ross. Now, armed with this extra information, at shortly after 1.30 in the afternoon Bernardi made an urgent phone call to a senior contact of his in the Venetian branch of the *carabinieri*.

When it wants to be, the various branches of the Italian police system – whether the national police, the *carabinieri* (which deals mainly with military and defensive matters) or the *Guardia di Finanza* – can all be highly efficient. Within one hour of Bernardi's call, the *carabinieri* had emailed Ross's picture around various key locations in Venice: not only to the airport and railway station but also to museums, popular restaurants and, most important of all, to the concierge desks at the majority of hotels in and around Venice. Ross was a person of extreme interest to the authorities. A small, but non-trivial, reward of €5,000 was offered to anyone who gave information that led to his apprehension.

As often happened in Italy, most recipients of these emails either ignored them, or programmed their email servers automatically to junk them whenever received. The one group that rarely did this was the network of hotel concierges. A much-underestimated group of highly knowledgeable and influential people, the concierges were a formidable resource available to a wide number of different groups – and that included the police authorities. They knew from experience that when it came to vigilance and knowledge, hotel concierges often knew more secrets than many. Especially concerning the whereabouts of certain visitors on the island.

*

They had set the meeting for 3pm. By 2.25 in the afternoon, Cuccinelli was ready to leave her apartment, her head covered in a silk scarf. Perched on her nose was a pair of large, dark sunglasses covering a considerable portion of her face. The package from Natalia had been placed in a paper carrier bag, itself tucked deep within a capacious handbag that she cradled close to her body as she made her way to Palanca. When she boarded the *vaporetto*, she opted this time to sit inside, in a position that gave a clear view of all passengers around her. There was no sign of the man with the missing index fingertip this time, nor anyone else she thought might be watching, although she couldn't be certain. At San Marco, she walked the short distance to the Gritti Palace, hurrying through the narrow streets, constantly checking over her shoulder. Again, she couldn't see anyone or anything unusual. However, there was this lingering, nagging doubt in her mind that someone was following her, that she was about to let her friend down.

By the time she reached the side entrance of the hotel, her anxiety had only increased. What if this man was late? What if others showed up and tried to wrestle the package from her? She could feel her stomach muscles tighten, feeling compelled to take deep breaths as she struggled to stay calm. The time was two minutes to three o'clock. Taking a final, deep breath, she entered the hotel displaying more confidence and fortitude than she felt, making her way directly to the Riva Lounge bar directly overlooking the Grand Canal.

'Claudia?'

Cuccinelli's journalistic eye gazed up at the trim, athletic-looking man with approval, his dark, scraggy hair swept to one side: long at the back, unruly at the sides. He was wearing an odd item of clothing for Venice in May, she thought – a cardigan, with three buttons undone. Otherwise, she could understand why her friend might have fancied this man. She lifted her sunglasses up onto her head, stood briefly, and shook his hand.

'Calum, it's nice to meet you.'

She had removed her scarf whilst waiting for Ross to arrive. Momentarily, in the warm May sunshine, sitting on the terrace of the Riva Bar, Ross thought she looked like a model: neat, black hair swept behind her head and tied at the back, and with sparkling blue eyes and a pretty smile. Then, their greeting over, she let the dark sunglasses slide back into place, the brief flash of beauty he'd been allowed to see once more hidden from view.

A waiter came and hovered. They both ordered tea.

'I'm afraid Natalia told me nothing about you,' he said. 'Only to come and see you, I'm sorry.'

'That's okay. I know perhaps only a little bit more about you, not a lot. I think it's better this way. How is she?'

Ross gave a potted version of what had happened in London.

'Oh, my God! Is she going to be okay?'

'She's had surgery and is now recovering. They wouldn't let me see her yesterday. There's a risk of infection.'

'I can imagine. But who did this to her? This is terrible.'

'That's anyone's guess. Quite likely, it was Russians.'

'Oh my God!'

*

Giuseppe Lacastro had been head concierge at the Gritti Palace for several years, taking over the reins from his father who had also held the same position for years before him. That particular day, Lacastro had come on duty at two o'clock in the afternoon. After familiarising himself with that day's guest arrivals and departures, he had just finished scanning the email from the *carabinieri* about Ross when he noticed a man of Ross's description entering the hotel lobby and making his way directly to the Riva Bar. This was not a hotel guest, of that Lacastro was certain. He decided to keep an eye on him, walking to the entrance of the hotel's terrace lounges and observing the man greeting a pretty woman who looked as if she'd been waiting for him. It was the same man, Lacastro was sure. He returned to his desk and lifted a telephone to his ear, dialling the number mentioned in the email. An extra €5,000 would indeed be most welcome.

*

'Natalia mentioned something about having given you two gifts, Calum. Do you know what she meant?'

Ross laughed, swallowing a mouthful of tea before answering.

'Sure. First there was this,' he said, showing her the blue glass *nazar* on its leather chain around his neck.

'That's cute,' she said. 'I have an almost identical one that she gave me. What else?'

'The second was this.' He dug in his cardigan pocket and removed the chess set, opening the brass latch. 'Your name and phone number were written on the lid, underneath the felt. Here, let me show you.'

She peered in fascination, finally satisfied that Ross was who he claimed to be.

'Very good. Then I must give you the parcel she sent to me,' she said, opening her handbag and removing the brown paper bag she had wrapped the package in. Ross took it and peered inside. The envelope looked virtually identical to the one he'd been given by the woman on Giudecca only a couple of hours earlier.

'Have you looked inside?' he asked, hearing the distant sound of a police siren for the first time.

'You mean did I open the parcel? No, of course not.'

'Good. Thank you. What you've done is kind. It will be a big help to Natalia.'

He cocked his head and listened. There were now at least two police sirens sounding very close.

'I think it is time for me to get going,' he said, standing. He reached into his pocket for some money, but she put her hand on his.

'I'll take care of the bill. Just keep safe and send my love to Natalia.'

Two police launches were converging on the hotel's landing jetty, one uniformed policeman leaping onto the pontoon just as another other policeman came in through the main entrance accompanied by the head concierge.

'Signor Ross?'

'Yes.'

'Please come with us. We have a few questions we need to ask.'

Ross, gently but firmly, was then led by the arm towards the pontoon and bustled aboard the police launch. He looked back at Claudia and saw alarm written all over her face. He shrugged at her and smiled as the boat cast off from the mooring.

Chapter 69

Istanbul

Usmanov was back at his desk, Kozlov thankfully long gone and that morning's painful episode for the moment behind him. He had been lucky. Lucky to have made a two hundred-thousand-dollar profit on the chess piece that Timmerman had purchased. A profit that had allowed him to travel to Zurich on his way back from his last trip to Villars, withdraw this profit in cash, leaving another two hundred thousand remaining in the secret Swiss account. Lucky, in turn, to be able to return the original two hundred thousand dollars back to the Consulate. Not to banking section but, even better, to the Consul's safe. That had been a nice touch.

The Bakelite phone on his desk suddenly interrupted his thoughts.

'*Da*,' he answered, tersely.

'You have a secure call from Venice,' Ludmilla said.

Usmanov stabbed the button on the top of his phone and the light came on. The call was now secure.

'What news?'

He listened, stony-faced, his fingers still drumming the table.

'We still have influence with the *carabinieri,* though, don't we?'

He swivelled his chair around and got to his feet, pacing back and forth as the other party spoke.

'Then now's the time to call in favours. You absolutely cannot lose this damned notebook!' His voice was loud and angry. 'I hear you, but you will simply have to try harder. I will not accept failure!' he shouted furiously and slammed the phone back into its cradle. A few seconds later, there was a gentle knock and Ludmilla put her head timidly around the door.

'Is there anything I can do?'

'Leave me alone!' Usmanov shouted and slumped down in his chair, his head in his hands.

'God help us all if this goes wrong now,' he muttered to himself as the door was gingerly closed once more.

Chapter 70

Venice, Italy

The policeman in command of the first launch had a decision to make. The headquarters of the *carabinieri* in Venice was at the Piazzale Roma, at the northern end of the island, close to where cars coming to the island were forced to park and abandon their vehicles. The easiest and quickest route was to head northwards from the Gritti Palace up the *Canal Grande*. This was likely to be congested, but it was more direct. Alternatively, he could take a longer, sweeping loop to the south, past the island of Giudecca and around the island of Venice clockwise. Being a confident Italian, with a loud police siren at his disposal, he chose the direct route – possibly, in hindsight, not the best decision he was to make that day.

Ross sat at the stern, the policeman who had escorted him from the hotel close by. Sirens blaring, the launch headed confidently into the heart of the wide canal, clusters of diagonally striped poles marking the edges, some red and white, others blue and white. Past the distinctive white building that housed the Penny Guggenheim collection; under the hemispherical pedestrian footbridge by Academia where crowds of people stared down at them; and around a sweeping corner to the right, the ancient buildings on either side casting long shadows on the water. Up ahead, near to

Rialto, *vaporetti* were bunching in a group and starting to block the canal, waiting for pontoons to be vacated before they could move on. Weaving in amongst them were several *gondolieri*, their distinctive black boats full of tourists, some with accordions playing, others with people singing, the boatmen dressed in their characteristic hooped vests and straw hats. Plus, naturally, a few water taxis adding to the congestion. One, in particular, had caught Ross's eye. A boat that was fast approaching from the rear. Nonchalantly, he turned his head a fraction to take a closer look. All he could see in the boat's cockpit was cigarette smoke.

The congestion by now had forced both police launches to reduce their speed to a crawl, a fact that gave Flynn a narrow window of opportunity to squeeze his boat closer. Ross braced himself, trying to judge when Flynn's taxi would be alongside. Without warning, Ross leapt to his feet, shouting at the policeman next to him, pointing with his hand at something he'd spotted on the far bank. Human instinct made the policeman turn to look, which was when Ross seized the moment, spun on his heel and leapt over the launch's railing and onto the stern deck of the water taxi now alongside. He landed heavily on his bad knee, made worse because Flynn hit the throttle as soon as he saw Ross in mid-air, making for a gap he'd seen open up between two gondolas. In his haste, he inadvertently clipped the golden tail of one as he sped away.

'You okay there, matey?' Flynn shouted from the cockpit.

'Sort of. Might have buggered the knee a bit, but too bad.'

'You got the package?'

Ross raised the brown paper bag in his hand as Flynn turned around briefly to look.

'Then all we've got to do is escape from a few angry Italian policemen.'

'I've an idea.'

'We might need it. Hold on, we're in for a bit of cat and mouse. You were a specialist boatman once, weren't you?'

'Sure,' said Ross, remembering only too well his amphibious vehicle training.

'Then come up here and lend a hand.'

*

Ross took over the controls with the two police launches about twenty metres in his wake. In open water, the authorities were likely to outsmart this single-engine boat, but Ross was nonetheless impressed by the taxi's acceleration and manoeuvrability, quickly concluding that he might, after all, be able to give his pursuers a run for their money.

'Can you read a map?' he shouted at Flynn.

'Does a bear shit in the woods?'

'So, let's take to the side canals and see if we can shake them.'

Ross spun the wheel to starboard and hit the throttle, the sound reverberating off the walls that closed in on all sides as they raced through the narrow canal. A lone gondola scurried to one side as first Ross sped past, followed swiftly by the two *polizia* launches. They passed under several low pedestrian bridges, both men instinctively ducking as they tore through the narrow aperture with inches to spare. The houses viewed from the water were nothing like so grand as when viewed from the front: building after building of crumbling red-bricked and concrete facades, the noise of the police sirens resonating everywhere.

'Take a left here,' Flynn yelled and Ross executed a clever banking turn, dropping the boat's speed just enough to round the sharp corner but accelerating into the final part of the turn, narrowly missing the edge of the building on the corner by a hair's breadth and gaining valuable distance on their pursuers.

'You've done this before.'

'Kind of.' Up ahead, there was a long barge heading in their direction. It forced Ross to reduce his speed sharply to squeeze past. The police launch in their wake came within seconds of ramming the taxi's engine from the rear, about to bring them to a grinding halt when Ross, at the very last second, found himself in clear water once more and hit the throttle. The taxi surged, Ross executing another sharp turn at speed, this time to the right, clearing the corner easily and gaining even more distance on their pursuers. The taxi powered onwards in a wide, looping turn, narrowly avoiding two gondolas laden with tourists before it suddenly burst out into open water, back into the Grand Canal once more, having woven a curious, U-shaped path through the various side canals. Ross spun the wheel hard left, the boat banking and creating a powerful wave of water that drenched several Asian tourists being sung to by their *gondoliere* in the middle of the open channel. Behind them, several metres in their wake, the two police launches were still in pursuit, sirens blaring.

'We need a Plan B,' Ross yelled to Flynn. 'If we stay on the main canal, the police will catch us. I'm going to take the next left and cut through the back waterways once more.'

He spun the wheel again, the taxi this time darting down a very narrow canal, the roar of the engine loud and rasping as the sound echoed off the walls, a powerful eddy formed by the high-speed manoeuvre sufficient to cause a group of gondolas, moored to one side, to bob around furiously in their wake. To their rear, the sound of the police sirens was getting louder once again.

'We've a problem,' Flynn shouted some time later. They were in a stretch of water that twisted and turned sharply, left and right, temporarily having lost sight of their pursuers.

'Out of cigarettes?'

'Worse. This is a dead end. You need to chuck a U-ey.'

'Oh, shit!' Ross said before spotting his opportunity around the next corner: a small boat hideaway tucked off to the left. He slammed the throttle into reverse and deftly spun the wheel.

'Hang on tight, we might scrape the woodwork a bit here,' he shouted, looking over his shoulder and reversing erratically into the small, enclosed space. There was a sharp splintering sound as the boat's rear fender hit the sidewall, Ross reversing the throttle again just in time to save crashing the engine into the wall at the rear. Only just making it, too, since no sooner they had come to rest than the two police boats came careering past. The driver of the lead boat spotted where the taxi was hiding and shut off the power, but the boat in his wake didn't react fast enough. It ploughed straight into the back of the boat in front as it slowed.

'That's a waste of two good boats,' Ross said, slipping out of the hideaway and accelerating away towards where they had just come from. 'Can you get me back to the main lagoon?'

'Sure. Take a right, then immediately left at the next corner.'

'No more dead ends this time.'

Ross manoeuvred the boat with ease, increasing the power through the turns before reaching another T-junction.

'Finally, a right here and that should do it.'

Sure enough, in the distance, they could see an expanse of daylight, suggesting the end of the canal.

'We can stop up here on the left,' Ross said. It was a small landing stage used by one of the hotels.

'Because?'

'This taxi is on the wanted list,' he said, bringing the boat to a halt right by the hotel entrance.

Flynn leapt onto the small platform and tied the boat to a wooden pillar.

'Don't forget your brown paper bag,' he called out.

'Checking in, sir?' a uniformed porter said, coming to greet them both.

'No, sorry, we've come to meet a friend. Can you keep an eye on the boat for me?' Flynn said. 'I won't be long.' He looked at Ross and winked.

'You look as if you're hobbling a bit, matey.'

'Bloody knee,' said Ross. They emerged through the front of the hotel. Off to their right, they could see throngs of tourists walking along the lagoon waterfront. 'What are your plans?'

'Making sure you get back in one piece. The question is, how do we get you off this police-infested place.'

'Me? I've got a plane to catch.'

'Not out of Marco Polo you haven't. They'll have the place in lockdown.'

'I've a better option.'

'Oh yeah?'

They walked to the *vaporetto* stop at the water's edge by San Zaccaria and Ross bought two tickets.

'Are you coming?'

'Where to?'

'The Lido, of course.'

'We haven't got time to top up the tan and watch the birds.'

'Humour me.'

They boarded the number 17 *vaporetto,* sitting outside in the open air as the vessel chugged its way towards San Nicolo on Venice's Lido. It was well after four in the afternoon, the sun already starting to lose its heat.

'Bet you're glad you wore the cardy now, matey,' Flynn said as they disembarked, immediately lighting another cigarette and looking around to get his bearings. 'Oh, I see where we're going. You clever sod.'

'We could have taken the taxi. On the open water, however, my guess was a police launch would have whipped us.'

'You're a resourceful bugger when you put your mind to it.' He laughed. 'Now I understand why you had to call London.'

The Aeroporto Nicelli turned out to be a small grass strip used principally by the local flying club and the occasional charter.

When they entered the main building, Ross found his pilot already waiting.

'I'm pleased to see you, sir,' the pilot said. 'I was a bit worried. They close the airport here at five. Are you ready to go?'

'Give me two minutes,' Ross said, and turned and walked back to where Flynn was standing.

'I just wanted to say . . . thanks,' he said hesitantly. 'Not sure exactly what for, but there we go. In a funny way, I enjoyed myself.' He grinned and Flynn simply shrugged. 'I still don't know who you are. We did okay, I think. When will I . . .?' He hesitated, not quite knowing how to ask the question he knew was not going to be answered.

'Maybe sometime, who knows? Meanwhile, go and visit that Swiss bank and enjoy the money. You've earned it. I'll see you around. You did well, today. Your boat-handling was something else. Oh, one other thing.'

'Yes?'

'When you get debriefed in London, remember: I never existed. This all happened without me. You must concoct some story. Just don't start inventing a bloke called Flynn. They wouldn't believe you, anyway.'

'That might be hard.'

'Too bad. Those are the rules.'

'I'll think of something.'

'I knew you would. Now, be gone.'

They bumped fists and with that, Ross turned and followed the pilot out to the Cessna 172 sitting on the grass, its doors open.

'Where's the first stop?' Ross asked, climbing into the front passenger seat.

'Ljubljana in Slovenia. It's about a hundred miles from here. There's an EasyJet connection to London that, at a pinch, you should be able to make if we hurry.'

Chapter 71

London

Somewhat to Ross's surprise, he found Frances Riordan waiting for him at the end of the air bridge at Stansted Airport. She gave him a scant welcome, flashing her MI6 card at a security scanner that released a door allowing them both to descend to apron level. Her car and driver were waiting at the bottom of the stairs, her large frame finding stairs an awkward encumbrance. By the time they were sitting side by side in the rear of the car, she had regained some of her composure. To Ross's unfamiliar eye, she was dressed in the same outfit she had been wearing the previous day – which, he realised, was an accusation that could also be levelled at himself. Welcome to the world of spies, he concluded.

'You had an eventful trip, by all accounts, Calum?' At this late hour, her voice sounded deeper and more masculine than he remembered.

'I found what we wanted,' he said, patting the paper bag that he'd been clutching the whole trip home. 'Though not, as you suggest, without incident.'

'What's the story on Pesci? Two bullets to the head is what we heard. Did you do that?'

Ross outlined briefly what had happened, about the Russian shooting Pesci in his zeal to acquire the notebook.

'He specifically asked about a notebook? That's very interesting,' she mused, lost in her own private thoughts.

Ross, remembering Flynn's words, now began weaving a little fabrication. In particular, how Pesci had been standing at the stern of the taxi when he'd been shot, his body disappearing over the back of the boat. How Ross had overpowered the Russian and thrown him off the boat too before continuing on towards Venice.

'Convenient to have lost the Russian, Calum. Was he dead when he hit the water? It's just that no body's been found.'

'I've no idea. I hit him a few times, but I doubt he was dead when he went over the side.'

She suddenly seemed weary of the conversation, more eager to see what Ross had brought back with him.

'May I?' she asked, her arm outstretched.

Ross handed over the package and watched as Riordan opened the UPS packet carefully. Inside was a small, black leather notebook. Riordan put on a pair of reading glasses and began flicking through the pages.

'Oh my,' she muttered to herself, sometime later, noticing a couple of loose-leaf pieces of paper and examining them. 'What a cunning bastard.' Ross could see that she was holding what looked like bank statements.

'What do they say?' Ross asked, but received no reply. Instead, he was left alone to stare out the window as the car sped down the motorway towards London.

'Can you read Russian?' she asked sometime later.

'No.'

'Then this will mean nothing to you.' She laughed at him, which Ross, for some reason, found hurtful. 'You should get that new Russian girlfriend of yours to teach you. All spies need to learn Russian.'

'How is she?'

'The Russian woman?' She glanced across at Ross, momentarily removing her reading glasses. 'About the same. She's still not allowed visitors, though you might be able to speak to her on the phone, so I'm told.'

'What happens next?' he asked. 'About me, I mean.'

'You and the woman go and live happily ever after. Assuming she makes it,' she said matter-of-factly as she put her glasses back on.

'Great.' He stared out the window again at the empty nothingness. 'I meant as far as the service goes. One short, sharp assignment and we're done. Is that how it works?'

'What more do you want, Calum?'

'You tell me. I'm only here because you asked me to help.'

'For which we're very grateful. Especially for this,' she said, holding up the notebook. 'This is dynamite.'

'So, what about it? Do I get paid? At least for what I've done?'

She looked across at him, over the top of the glasses this time, and frowned.

'One step at a time. We have a set daily rate for our consulting staff. This' – she lifted the notebook once more – 'constitutes a very good day's work. Thank you.'

A short time later, the car pulled up at the end of Ross's street, a short distance away from Archway station. Riordan leant forward to talk to the driver.

'Gerald, do you have that package?'

The driver reached beneath the passenger seat and pulled out a manila envelope. Riordan handed it to Ross.

'Your keys to your flat, your mobile phone plus one burner phone. You can keep the phone and the money we gave you yesterday and hand them back as and when. Please report to reception at Vauxhall Cross at nine tomorrow morning. We'd like to start your debriefing session promptly.'

'All in a good day's work,' Ross said, feeling instantly deflated.

'I think you'll find your apartment's been given a thorough spring clean in your absence. Brendan tells me he sent his housekeeping team around earlier. Plus, more good news: your bank seems to have found the money that it misplaced from your account. They assured Brendan that they'd hand-delivered a new debit card to your home address earlier today.'

'I supposed I should be grateful,' Ross said, climbing out and smiling sarcastically at Riordan. 'Thank you, Gerald, for the lift.' He shut the door firmly and set off down the road to his apartment. Riordan buzzed her window down.

'See you in the morning, Calum. Nine o'clock sharp. Please don't be late.'

Chapter 72

London

Riordan had been as good as her word. North's housekeepers had gone over the apartment so thoroughly that it looked as good as new. All his clothes were neatly folded or on hangers. Even the kitchen had been thoroughly cleaned. He checked the cupboard off the hallway. There were no rucksacks, no strange objects, his cleaning equipment neatly in one corner. Finally, he looked at the secret hideaway in the skirting board. The board was neatly back in place, but if he'd been expecting to find his missing laptop, money and passport, he was mistaken. The space was empty. On the floor by the letterbox was an envelope from his bank. It contained a new debit card, a letter of apology and an offer to waive the £500 of emergency funds the bank had lent him to compensate him for the trouble they had caused him.

He checked his watch. Remarkably for such a long and eventful day, it was only 9.30 in the evening. Riordan had told him yesterday that Natalia was at UCLH – University College London Hospital. It wasn't that late: perhaps he might be able to talk to her? He located the switchboard number using his mobile phone and hit dial. This proved to be the start of a long and arduous journey but, miraculously, about fifteen minutes later, after a lot of waiting for unanswered phones to be picked up, he eventually connected with someone who promised to get the phone to Natalia.

'Hello,' a voice said croakily in his ear some while later. It sounded weak and tremulous, but unmistakably hers.

'It's me.'

'Calum, my God! Where are you?' Calum smiled. She had unwittingly broken her own, unbreakable, rule.

'Back in London. How are you?'

'Improving, I think. Bored. Missing you.'

'Are you comfortable?'

'No. They say I will be here for days. When are you coming?'

'As soon as they let me. I went to Venice today. I met your friend. All went well. She gave me a present.'

'My God, Calum, you are amazing. That is wonderful. I am now so happy.'

'I love you. Get some rest and mend quickly.'

'I love you, too. Come quickly. On this matter, I absolutely insist.'

Chapter 73

London

'Opinions, anybody?' Sir Anthony Defries asked once the three of them were settled and the green light over the door was lit. Maximum-security precautions in the ultra-secure conference suite in the depth of MI6's building were now operational.

'Something of a revelation,' Jennifer Harper said, flicking a strand of silvery-grey hair behind an ear and fiddling with a pencil that had been resting beside her papers. Harper, a fluent Russian speaker and one-time Russian case officer during the Cold War era, was MI6's Head of Specialist Operations and Frances Riordan's de facto boss.

'Frances?'

'There is a certain irony about it all,' she said eventually. 'The Russian President, the homophobic male pin-up, produces an illegitimate son who turns out to be homosexual.'

'I agree,' chipped in Harper. 'So much of a revelation, not even Usmanov felt able to tell his friend!' She had dazzling blue eyes that, when needed, could be used either to bestow blessings of charm or to kill a conversation dead. She gave Riordan a rare, dazzling smile. 'This information,' she said, her hands on the photocopy in front of her, 'is unprecedented. You are to be congratulated, Frances.'

'Yes,' Defries said. 'I admit, I had urged Frances to stop wasting time pursuing what seemed to me to be such a flaky operation. Now I have been proven wrong, and I apologise.'

'In fairness,' said Harper, 'Frances and I also discussed this. At length,' she added, looking deliberately at Sir Anthony as if to make her point. 'I was only prepared to let Frances have so much wiggle room before we re-evaluated where we had reached. Anyway, all's well that ends well, isn't that right, Frances?' The eyes had switched to an icy blueness.

'I think what we need to be discussing today is what we do with all of this,' Riordan said, her gravelly voice resonating in the enclosed room. 'Apart from the fact that ORION appears to have been pilfering funds. That fact alone should make him willing to work for us. It's a complicated picture that goes something like this.

'The man who is the Russian President and this person, DESTINY, have an illegitimate son which nobody knows about. They both agree to put the boy out to adoption, DESTINY foregoing the pleasures of motherhood in favour of returning to work and becoming a well-placed Russian spy. ORION, meanwhile, agrees to keep a godfatherly eye on this young lad, acting as his friend the President's conduit to ensure the child is educated at the best schools and well looked after. DESTINY, meanwhile, becomes an increasingly important Russian asset, one that only the President, ORION, and DESTINY's agent handler – incidentally, this is not ORION, so we understand – know about. ORION goes to the boy's school every six months, on his friend's behalf and as a favour to his friend, and discovers, to his horror, that the boy is homosexual. ORION now faces a dilemma. Does he tell his friend, knowing that he is more than likely to go apoplectic? The ignominy of having a son who was gay would crush the Russian President. If it were public, he would be ridiculed, especially after all the homophobic rantings he's recently made. No, ORION knows that, in his rage, his friend's most likely reaction would be to have the boy killed, regardless of the consequences. If that happened, ORION also knows that DESTINY's fate would be jeopardised, if not compromised.' She looked up to see if the others were still with her.

'So, what does ORION do? He keeps the news about the boy's sexuality secret from his friend. We have seen ORION's contemporaneous notes at his most recent meeting with the school's headmistress. "MUST," he wrote, double-underlined and in capitals, "find out more about relationship with Didier P. How long and WHO KNOWS?" again, these last words in capitals. "Can it be suppressed? Besides MS, WHO ELSE KNOWS?!!" More block capitals. Then, moving forward to the transcript of the second meeting in the Four Seasons hotel which you've both seen, there's no mention of this subject.'

'So, we might have ORION compromised, is that what you think, Frances?' Defries asked.

'On its own, maybe. Or maybe not. However, when you consider we now have evidence of ORION dipping his hand in the till and creating a little nest egg for himself. We've seen the bank statements. They're the real smoking gun.'

'Are we confident that this is genuine misbehaviour and not some little slush fund his friend the President might have decided to give him?'

'It would appear so. ORION was being investigated by one of Borodin's investigators for apparent misuse of state funds.'

'Was being?'

'They apparently couldn't find the smoking gun and the investigation has gone cold. We must see what ORION says about it all when we talk to him.'

'Thoughts, Jenn?'

'It's a tantalising opportunity. Think about what it would do to our credibility with the Americans.'

'And others, too,' Riordan chipped in.

'I hear the Americans nearly beat us to the prize. How come?'

Harper looked at Riordan and nodded, as if permitting Riordan to disclose some operational details.

'They tried to steal the notebook from us. We had a small operation underway. In Venice, with the British teacher I told you about.'

'Ah, yes. We lost a man, I hear. An Italian contractor. Pesci, I think his name was?'

'That's correct. According to Ross, the Russians were trying to get the notebook back and shot Pesci.'

'We at least now know why the Russians were so keen to get their hands on it,' said Harper.

'This chap, Ross. He seemed to do rather well, didn't he? I mean, he was only a schoolteacher, isn't that right, Frances?'

'Correct. Although, he was a soldier once.'

'Yes, you told me. Special Forces. I'd keep an eye on him, if I were you. He might be useful to us. How's ORION's wife doing?'

'Touch and go. Looking slightly more, rather than less, positive.'

'So, I have a suggestion to make,' Defries said, both women knowing that this was a decision now coming their way. 'Find a way to contact ORION and suggest that it would be appropriate for him to come and visit his sick wife here in London. Leave him in no doubt that it is essential that he comes. Get the Ambassador involved if it makes it easier. We need to find a safe house. Who's going to run him?'

'I suggest Frances,' said Harper, her eyes steely blue. 'Unless anyone has any better plans?'

'Very good, Frances it is. Who else is WATCHKEEPER-cleared, apart from us three?'

'At the moment, nobody,' Riordan said. 'Except, I did mention it briefly to Okumura, but only in scant detail.'

'Then let's keep it that way unless or until, shall we?'

317

'What more should we say to the Americans?' Riordan pressed.

'Absolutely nothing.'

'They're going to be pissed.'

'Let them be. They shouldn't have been so keen to steal from us in the first place, should they?'

Chapter 74

London

Ross's debriefing was long and arduous and took place in a windowless room below ground. There were two of them, both nameless: a man, younger than himself, with a trimmed beard and zero sense of humour; and an unsmiling woman of indeterminate age who wore thick glasses and kept shaking her head, as if disapproving. They both took notes and alternated between roles: one playing good cop, the other bad. As suggested by Flynn, Ross had to embellish certain bits of his story, some parts not without difficulty.

'How did you know it was a tracking device?' the woman asked him at one stage.

'I'd seen them before in the military,' he lied.

'Where, precisely?'

'I'm afraid I am not at liberty to disclose that information.'

'What made you think of using the island of Giudecca?' the man asked.

'I'd been to Venice several times in the past.'

'When was the last time you were there?'

'Four years ago.'

'Where did you stay?' And so it continued. Question after question. At one stage, Ross was almost tempted to walk out, but his desire to outsmart them made him want to stay the course.

'Where did you find the woman who posed as Claudia in front of the Americans?'

'She was a friend of Claudia's. When I rang Claudia, she agreed to ask her friend to help.'

'What was her name?'

'I never asked.'

'Did you pay her?'

'No.'

'What made you think the Americans would come and find you?'

'Because of the tracking device.'

'How did you know it was a tracking device?'

'As I said, I'd seen one before.'

'How do you know it was the woman who bumped into you at the airport who put it in your pocket?'

They finished one complete run-through, and then went back to the beginning and started all over again, with only a short break for lunch. Ross thought he might just have performed well enough since, by around five in the afternoon, his two inquisitors closed their notebooks in unison and escorted Ross back to the front reception desk.

'We'll be in touch in a few days,' the bearded man said to him. 'In the meantime, enjoy some time off.' He smiled and Ross, once more feeling oddly deflated, was dismissed.

The news from the hospital was mixed. Natalia was still allowed no visitors. Her temperature was higher than the nurses were happy with, and her surgeon decided that she was to be kept in isolation until it was back to normal. Otherwise, she was feeling much more herself. She and Ross spoke several times a day. Meanwhile, Ross joined a gym to strengthen his damaged knee. He even ended up going to the sports shop south of the river to buy the support strap he had been about to get when all the fun and games with the rucksacks had kicked off a few days earlier.

It was on the evening of the fourth day, when he'd all but given up any thoughts of working with Riordan or her colleagues ever again, that he received the call.

*

'Calum, hello,' Riordan greeted him as he was shown into yet another windowless meeting room by a flunky. There was no handshake, simply an indication, given by a nod of her head, that he was to take a seat at the other side of the table. 'Help yourself to a tea or coffee,' she said, pointing to a tray. 'We're just waiting for someone.'

In time, the door opened, and in walked a woman slightly older than Riordan. She had silvery-grey hair and the most penetrating blue eyes that Ross could recall seeing.

'Calum?' the woman asked, closing the door and coming forward to shake his hand. 'Jenn Harper. Good to meet you.'

She was carrying a bundle of papers and placed them on the table beside her.

'Calum, we've got ourselves a small crisis and we'd very much like your help. How would you like to come and work for us?' She gazed at him with a smile, the warmth of her eyes catching Ross off guard.

He swept a stray lock of unruly hair to one side as he thought about what to say.

'You mean, I did okay in Venice?'

'We're not very good in the service at giving compliments,' Riordan chipped in. 'If you hadn't done well, we wouldn't be talking to you once again.'

'Let me put it a different way,' Harper said, again all smiles. 'Just to be clear. We think you did a fabulous job in Venice.' She gave Riordan an icy stare. 'So much so, we want to offer you a position. Right here, right now. We have something we want to discuss with you. We need, however, to cover a few formalities before we go any further.'

'What's the position?'

'We can come to that later.'

'How much are you going to pay me?'

'A basic salary of £70,000.'

Ross considered this for a while.

'Where do I sign?'

Ten minutes later, Harper put down her pen, placed the forms Ross had signed back in her pile of papers, glanced briefly at Riordan, then began speaking.

'We are now able to brief you about an operation that we only ever refer to in the service by the codename WATCHKEEPER. There are only four people who are WATCHKEEPER-cleared: the Chief of the Service; Frances and myself; plus now yourself. You are never to discuss WATCHKEEPER with anyone other than the three of us, is that clear?'

'Perfectly. What is WATCHKEEPER?'

'WATCHKEEPER has been the operation that you've already been part of. Attempting to recruit Oleg Usmanov as an agent working, in secret, for the British.'

'Dear God Almighty!' Ross said, conscious that all eyes were on him. 'Now you tell me!' He ran a hand through his hair. 'I take it that that notebook played a key part in all this?'

'Correct. Let me lift the veil a little so you can understand what this has been all about,' Harper said. She then proceeded to relate a story about a Russian President and his one-time lover, an illegitimate son called Alexei and the role that a spy called Oleg Usmanov had been playing both in dipping his hand in the till and in helping to protect his friend, the Russian President.

It was only later, Ross having lost track of time, when Harper finished and turned to Riordan.

'What have I missed, Frances?'

'I think you've covered the bases.'

'You mentioned that you've met with Usmanov?'

'Correct, although we only ever refer to him by his official codename, ORION. We suggested ORION come to London, on the pretext that his wife was critically ill and he ought to be here.'

'And you put it to him that you knew about the stolen monies and about Alexei being homosexual?'

'We did.'

'And that you knew he deliberately had withheld that information from his friend, the President? What was his reaction?'

'Anger. Incredulity that we'd known. Sheer terror when we mentioned the agent DESTINY by name. I still don't think he yet knows how we know, but he was in shock, wouldn't you agree, Frances?'

'He was a broken man, Calum. Suddenly, after all the planning, we found ourselves pushing against an open door.'

'So ORION's agreed? Agreed to become a British spy?' Ross pressed.

'In these sorts of coercive situations, one can never be totally sure what is agreed and what isn't. I think ORION is resigned to the fact that he's he will have to start co-operating with us.'

'So where do I fit in?'

Riordan shuffled uncomfortably in her seat, glanced at Harper, then continued.

'He's a clever man, is ORION. He knows exactly how far he can push, and when he's at the limit. He understands that we have him entrapped; perhaps he's even grudgingly respectful of our efforts. It had been our intention to let me become his agent handler.'

'I can sense a "but" somewhere.'

'Well, yes, as you rightly surmise, Calum. There is a "but". The "but" is that when we put that to him, he flatly rejected the idea.'

'Is he in a position to?' Ross asked.

'What he said,' Harper interrupted, ignoring Ross's question, 'was that he'd only consider being co-operative if you became his agent handler and not Frances.'

'Me?'

'Precisely,' said Riordan.

'Is he in a position to make demands like that?'

'That's a moot point.'

'What the fuck do I know about running a Russian spy?'

'It's a stretch, we admit, but with a lot of support, we think you'd cope.'

'This man has been doing it for years. I'm a complete novice. Why did he want me, for God's sake?'

'You earned his respect. For what you did in Venice and, I quote, "because I hear he's a good chess player". He seems determined that it is you.'

'I'm not so sure. Shit, I've been screwing his wife, for fuck's sake.'

'He tells us that won't be a problem.'

'And you're cool with the idea?'

'If you are, then so are we. Our considered view is that you might even be good in the role.' It was Harper speaking, this time her blue eyes giving Ross their warmest smile.

'Well, this is all a massive shock.'

'But you might be prepared to give it a go?'

'You really think it's a flyer?'

'We wouldn't be talking to you otherwise,' Harper went on. She let her words hang in the air, a stony-faced silence descending on the room for a while.

'Well, in that case,' Ross said eventually, 'I suppose I have little option but to try.'

'Excellent. Which places the burden on us to ensure that you'll be well-equipped and supported for the role.'

Chapter 75

London

At ten in the morning, Ross was sitting on the third bench from the left, just below Kenwood House, looking directly out over Hampstead Heath. The view, down a slight incline, was of gentle, lush green parkland: of trees in fresh leaf; and a verdant lawn that was freshly mown. Given everything at stake, Ross was understandably apprehensive about his forthcoming meeting. The message from ORION to any bloodhounds or assassins from the Security Services who might have been tempted to shadow Ross had been clear: no surveillance, or else the meet wouldn't happen. Ross was thus on his own, feeling more than a little exposed.

Checking his watch, at exactly ten minutes after the hour he left the bench and walked along the gravel path as he'd been instructed, keeping to the tarmac and then forking right, down a dirt track amongst the trees. He ambled along gently, his weakened knee feeling strong once more, the route deserted save for a lone jogger who quickly disappeared from view.

'English woodlands at their very best,' a Russian voice behind him said, the man deftly emerging through a gap in the bushes. He was taller than Ross had imagined and wore a flat cap on his head. It didn't hide the salt-and-pepper tufts of grey hair at the side, colours that matched the short, goatee-like beard beneath his chin.

'So, I finally get to meet the English teacher who's been screwing my wife!'

Ross looked startled.

'Don't look so worried. I wish you and Natalia only happiness.' He smiled and then extended his hand as they ambled along. 'We can be friends, surely?'

Ross hesitated, then shook the offered hand. They continued walking.

'It was over a long time ago. Our marriage, I mean. In this job, families do not even merit a second place. Are you enjoying being back in England?'

'A bit mixed, to tell the truth. It's been rather too busy. Hardly a dull moment, in fact.'

'Viktor tells me he misses chess club with you.' Usmanov smiled. 'His game seems to have improved.'

'Yes, I think he has talent.'

'So do you. I was impressed by what happened in Venice.'

'News travels fast.'

'Are you surprised?'

'Not particularly.'

'I liked the trick you pulled on the Americans, incidentally. That made me smile.'

They walked in silence for a while, both considering what to say.

'It seems I have little option but to give the British a helping hand. It was my mistake; loyalties can be so fickle in the spy business. Anyway, thanks in part to you, I now have new masters to serve. I couldn't face dealing with Riordan – is she man or woman, I couldn't tell? So, I asked for you. I thought we might get on well. Now that I've met you, I can see that my assessment was right.' He looked at Ross and smiled.

'I'll do my best.'

'You'll do your best! Ha, the British bulldog spirit, I think you call it. You and I can meet and play chess. I would like that. In fact, I have a proposition that I want to discuss.'

Ross said nothing, his mind troubled by a sense that they were being followed. He checked his rear but saw no one.

'I think we're safe,' Usmanov said, also looking. 'So, my proposition. Why don't you come back and live in Istanbul? Natalia can live with you. There would be no hard feelings on my account. As I told you, our marriage is over. I am not a proud person. You could teach at the school. I'm certain the headmaster, Granger, would be amenable. I could exert, perhaps, a little leverage. Natalia could keep her job; you and she wouldn't need those clandestine meetings at the Swiss Hotel anymore either.' He chuckled. 'Come, Calum, I work in the spy business. Now, so do you. We make it our business to know what is going on. Plus, you could teach Viktor more chess. What do you say?'

'To Istanbul? Did you mention it to Riordan?'

'Sure. The official MI6 position was that, if you are content, they thought it might be possible.'

'I would need to check with Natalia.'

'She will like it. I plan to see her this afternoon. I will put it to her.' He turned and looked at Ross's face. 'Don't be surprised! I am a Russian diplomat and her husband. Naturally, the hospital lets me see my wife. Do not be afraid, no harm will come to her, I promise.'

'How's your chess game?'

'Better than yours, I hope.'

'We might need to put that to the test. In principle, my response is that if Natalia says yes, and assuming Riordan is content, then I, too, would be happy.'

'That is good. I could show you my collection of rare chess pieces. I would like that.'

They had arrived at a small clearing, the path forking in several directions. Ross felt increasingly uneasy for some unshakeable reason. Usmanov could sense it. They stood still, contemplating which path to take.

'I think we are alike, you and I, Calum. In time, I think you will make a good agent and we will make a strong team. You have a good nose for trouble.'

'Why do you say that?'

'You sense that someone is following us, don't you?'

'It's only a suspicion. They promised me we would be left alone.'

'Always trust your instincts, Calum. You and I are now on the same side, playing a dangerous game. We need always to be watching each other's backs.'

'Very good,' Ross said, his voice still apprehensive.

'We share similar tastes. Chess, women – and now spies. We even share a good friend, someone who speaks highly of you. As a matter of fact . . .' Usmanov chose that particular moment to turn around. Ross followed suit and quickly realised that his instincts had been right all along. They had been followed.

Sauntering towards them, looking calm and relaxed, was a familiar face. A man who grinned as he approached the clearing, a cloud of cigarette smoke swirling on all sides. No one spoke a word, the man winking at both of them as he silently passed by, an index finger, its tip missing, raised to his lips.

'Welcome to the world of spies, Calum,' Usmanov whispered to his new MI6 agent handler.

Epilogue

Eight months ago, The Russian President's private dacha

'Your move, Oleg Ivanovich.'

'I'm thinking!'

'We are playing chess, not solving the world's problems.'

'I'm not so sure. I've been doing a lot of thinking recently. In fact, I have a proposition to test on you.'

'In that case, we need vodka!' the President said, and located a special bottle of Stolichnaya Elit from a freezer in his substantial kitchen. 'Try this, it is excellent.' He unscrewed the cap and poured two ice-cold shots into thick toasting glasses. 'A toast. *Druzhbe!* To friendship!'

'*Druzhbe!*' They both drained their glasses in one hit and smiled at each other.

'Not bad, eh? Those stupid fuckers keep giving me bottles. Now, let me hear your proposition.'

'I was playing chess with my son Viktor recently, teaching him some moves. In particular, the power of sacrifice.'

'I like sacrifice.'

'It got me thinking. Perhaps, with the West in turmoil and their beloved democratic processes failing, this might be the moment for someone like myself to become a double agent. A human sacrifice.'

'Have you gone crazy? You, my friend, need more vodka. Your brain is not thinking straight.' The President poured a further two shots, both chinking their glasses and draining the ice-cold liquid once more in one gulp.

'Let me finish. There's this little *maskirovka* I've been thinking about. This masquerade involves making the West believe there is another highly-prized Russian spy at large. Someone so senior, so important, a spy on track for *the* highest office. This information, assuming it could be delivered credibly and believed universally, would set hares running. Who is this mole, they would ask? How do we find him or her? Which country is he or she in? All the while, everybody is running around in circles, totally distracted.'

'You're a cunning bastard, do you know that? I like this. This Russian mole doesn't exist, we simply pretend he or she does. As Trump would say, "Fake News!" We need another toast.' He poured two more shots. 'To Fake News!'

'Fake News!' Usmanov again swallowed his shot in one, once more feeling the icy drink hit the pit of his stomach.

'So, why not pretend that this fictitious Russian mole is a woman? We can call her DESTINY. The *maskirovka* is that DESTINY and yourself, once-upon-a-time, have a romance.' He saw the look on his friend's face and continued quickly. 'Remember, this is fiction. DESTINY, in this fiction, bears the Russian President a son, in secret. Neither wants the child discovered, so the boy is adopted. DESTINY becomes a more and more successful spy. You become one of the most powerful men in the world.'

The Russian President now gave Usmanov a fixed stare.

'The boy's mother is dead. She is an irrelevance,' he said tersely.

'I know that, and you know that, but no one else would ever know. Instead, we pretend otherwise and weave our fiction. The boy exists, so let's pretend the boy is DESTINY's son, as well as yours. This is our *maskirovka*, a fiction we let the West learn in a totally credible way.'

'How?' The President's voice sounded sceptical, his brow furrowed.

'Since one half of the fiction is true – you do have a son, something that has been kept secret from the world, you and I being the only two people alive who currently know this – we use this fact to make the fiction more credible. I visit your son's school twice a year on your behalf and report back on progress, is that not correct?'

'*Da.*'

'So, next time I report back from a visit, let's meet in the old Moskva hotel. Why? Because we know the CIA bug the rooms. However, they think we don't know about their snooping. So, they will believe that we are meeting away from the Kremlin so we can discuss highly secret matters, in a place where no one would ever be listening. Secret matters such as a verbal progress report from me on the love child that you and DESTINY are proud parents of.'

'Devious. Very cunning. We make use of those eavesdropping wireless routers that those idiots in the CIA are convinced we know shit about. And we talk about DESTINY.'

'Correct.'

'I love it.'

'There's more. The sacrifice. As part of the *maskirovka*, we let the West come to believe that I might be susceptible to blackmail, someone who could be turned to working for the West.'

'How do you convince them of that?'

'Because I intend to steal some SVR operational funds and secrete them in a Swiss bank account of my own. Let the West discover the bank statements, learn of my treachery, allow them to blackmail me. Let them also learn that I am aware of DESTINY and that I also know the identity of your secret child. I would be a highly-prized double agent if they could turn me.'

'What benefit would Russia gain by this sacrifice?'

'Immense. It would be part of a disinformation strategy designed to tear the West apart. DESTINY is one example. They would think that by turning me, because of our friendship and because of DESTINY, they could influence you through me. We could set the British against the Americans, the Americans against the French and so on. In the long term, only Russia wins.'

'You're a sly, devious bastard, Oleg!' He slowly poured two more shots as he considered the proposition once more. 'Are you planning on telling Borodin?'

'I plan to tell no one, apart from yourself.'

'What if someone discovers that you've been putting your fingers in the till and stealing money from Mother Russia? It's a risky strategy, my friend. I may not always be around to help you.'

'I know that. However, there are too many leaks in the system. I can't afford to tell anyone. Least of all Borodin.'

'That may be risky, even if it is wise. Very good, if that is your decision. Here's to your *maskirovka*!'

They clinked glasses and drank, the Russian President suddenly serious.

'Would you really need to steal the money? I could arrange for a Swiss bank account to be set up in your name. Perhaps with a million or two US dollars in it. Wouldn't that be enough?'

'No. I need to be seen to be stealing it. Only then will the blackmail work against me.'

'You would need to be very careful. Pretending to be a double agent, pretending to steal Russian money whilst feeding the West a load of horseshit, I mean.'

'I know. I've been thinking about that. I have a plan forming. It involves my unfaithful wife and a clever honey trap using some gullible young fool. An unsuspecting man, British, most likely – in revenge for the humiliation the British bestowed on my father. Someone naïve enough to lead me, unwittingly, into the West's open arms with no one questioning how I came to be there. If I could pull that off, it could prove to be the start of something truly incredible.'

----- The End -----

Acknowledgements

I need to put on record my huge thanks to my wife, Ginny, for putting up with a husband who plots at strange times of the day and night – and for the time she spends tirelessly reading and re-reading different versions of this manuscript, telling me what works and what doesn't. A special thank you also to Nick and his brother Sam, both busy young men but always keen to give different – but helpful – perspectives on their father's attempts at writing!

I am grateful to everyone who continues to support my new career by buying my books and spreading the word about my writing to their friends, families, book groups and colleagues. I am especially grateful to those who take time to post me reviews and give feedback.

To my creative writing cohort from the summer of 2019, another 'thank you'. We had a lot of fun, we gave each other much support but we also provided much-needed constructive feedback along the way. Good luck to you all in your endeavours.

Finally, there are one or two who have not been acknowledged, deliberately, but to whom I remain indebted. Sometimes it is better - and safer - that way.

Thrillers by the same author

The Morpheus Network
The Dossier
The Gambit
The Markov Encryption
The Reluctant Trader
Powder Day

If you've enjoyed this thriller, why not head to www.davidnrobinson.com and sign up to David's exclusive mailing list.

This is how you get to hear about:

* Exclusive bonus content

* Pre-release announcements

* Free book extracts

* Exclusive competitions and giveaways.

For information on all of David's other books, visit www.davidnrobinson.com.

THE STAND-IN

About the Author

David Robinson was a partner and chief operating officer in an international accounting firm, and latterly held the same role in an international law firm. It took him 36 years and several million air miles to do, arguably, what he should have done several years earlier: give up the day job and focus on a lifelong ambition to write thrillers. Page-turners. Action and adventure stories with twists and turns right to the very last page.

With few parts of the world that David has not seen first-hand, he uses his personal knowledge, connections and a professional interest in technology to craft fast-paced thrillers that are very much set in the real world. Locations that he knows personally. Present-day plotlines that try to be as credible and true to life as possible. Fictional backstories to events currently in the public eye.

David lives with his wife close to the city of Cambridge, England. Together they support several local charities, including the world-renowned Cambridge Union debating society where David is a trustee.

Visit www.davidnrobinson.com to learn more about David and his writing.

Printed in Great Britain
by Amazon